In honor of
Florence Mummey
1999 Eckerd 100 Honoree
"Eckerd Salute to Women Volunteer's Program"

Double Dealer

A Bert and Nan Tatum Mystery

Double Dealer

Barbara Taylor McCafferty
and Beverly Taylor Herald

Kensington Books
http://www.kensingtonbooks.com

KENSINGTON BOOKS are published by

Kensington Publishing Corp.
850 Third Avenue
New York, NY 10022

Library of Congress Card Catalog Number: 99-65261
ISBN 1-57566-507-7

First Printing: February, 2000
10 9 8 7 6 5 4 3 2 1

Printed in the United States of America

To our daughters,
Elizabeth Anne Young
and Rachael Emily Taylor—
who resemble Bert's daughter, Ellie,
only in how very much they are loved
by their mother and aunt

Chapter 1

●

Nan

I wasn't looking for trouble.

Contrary to what that very large man yelled at me.

And I most certainly wasn't looking to get my twin sister and me tangled up in another murder.

Contrary to what some people have said. On talk shows. On competing radio stations, oddly enough.

I'm Nan Tatum, the midday jock on WCKI-FM, one of Louisville, Kentucky's country-music stations. While I'll admit that my ratings have once again been boosted by all the media coverage about this latest unfortunate incident, it was certainly not something I planned. Hell, it's not even something I understand. I mean, I wish I could say my ratings have climbed because people like the sound of my voice, or they're entranced by my wit and wisdom, or even that I've got great taste in music. Unfortunately, it's pretty obvious that ain't exactly it.

Apparently, there are actual, live people out there in Radio Land who prefer to chitchat on the air with someone who, along with her twin sister, has had the misfortune of being involved in a murder case or two. Or three. Or four, even. I don't get it. The way I see it, it's sort of like wanting to talk to someone who's survived an appearance on one of those television docudramas that have names like *When Farm Animals Attack*.

I can't imagine why anybody would want to spend time getting up close and personal to anything as gruesome as murder. In fact, before this last mess, Bert and I had pretty much made up our identical minds that we'd spent all the time dealing with murder that we ever wanted to. From now on, when it came to murder investigations, we were going to do like all those antidrug commercials say you should do: Just say no.

We'd been involved in enough homicides, thank you. If we got involved in any more, people were going to start avoiding us. Hell, we were going to start avoiding *each other*.

We wanted to call a halt to all this sordidness before people started using our names as a synonym for murder, much like people started using Monica Lewinsky's name as a synonym for—to put it delicately—presidential activity. Bert and I were beginning to fear that one day soon we'd turn on the television news and hear some policeman say, *Yes, we suspect foul play; it looks like it could be a Nan-and-Bert.*

I'm sure whoever wrote all those Bobbsey Twins books would love that. Probably about as much as Bert and I love being named after the older set of Bobbseys. This last, of course, was our mother's cute idea. She'd made up her mind to name us after the Bobbseys when she was expecting us, and even though we'd turned out to be identical twin girls instead of boy-and-girl fraternal twins like the Bobbseys, Mom had not let a little thing like that stop her. She'd just lengthened Bert's name to Bertrice for the birth certificate and then immediately started calling her Bert for short.

Bert and I have not quite forgiven Mom for the whole Bobb-sey thing, and it's almost forty years later.

Which brings us to what I really was looking for on that hot day in August—a birthday present. That's all. I was just trying to find a birthday present for Bert that she wouldn't be able to guess for once.

Surprise gifts are hard to come by when you have a twin sister. Since Bert and I have genetically identical brain cells, we often find these cells—though few in number—running in the same direction. We've even bought Mom the exact same gift for Mother's Day, right down to the same cloyingly sentimental, flower-bedecked card. (Mom loves it when you gush.) At Christmastime, Bert and I have to go out of our way not to even think of our gifts for each other in each other's presence; or the other one will guess it for sure.

This time, though, I'd hit on what I'd thought was a sure winner. Bert and I were coming up on our mutual birthday—actually more like hurtling toward it—the big day, August 22, being only a scant two weeks away. We were turning forty, the Big-Four-Oh, the Pinnacle, the Mountain Peak, after which everything else seems to go downhill. Like, for example, one's muscle tone. And one's buttocks. And one's self-esteem.

If it sounds as if I was feeling a tad depressed about the impending big event, good, I'm making myself clear. Bert, on the other hand, was not even the slightest bit anxious at bidding her thirties a fond farewell. This may have been partly due to the fact that whereas I was in a nonboyfriend interlude, she had not one but *two* guys vying for her affection.

Bert was currently dating Hank Goetzmann, a homicide detective whom I myself had formerly dated. Not that I'd want the man back. No, the short time we'd dated was far too long. I'd found out pretty quickly that Goetzmann was one of those men who, if you asked if his glass was half-full or half-empty, would get out a ruler and measure. Anal retentive is definitely not my type.

Also sniffing around Bert's back porch—to use a quaint phrase our mother used to use all the time—was her ex-husband, Jake Powell. Jake, Lord love him, had done Bert the colossal favor of running off with his secretary a few years back. As in that old Christmas classic, *It's a Wonderful Life*, Jake had given Bert a look at what life would be like without him; and, son of a gun, she'd actually preferred it.

Still, I'd noticed she hadn't exactly told Jake an absolute "forget it" when he came sniffing around, his hat in his hands and that dumb poor-me look on his face—but that was probably because of Ellie and Brian, Bert and Jake's two kids. Both were almost out of college now, but, Bert being Bert, she probably felt a little guilty about giving Jake the old heave-ho. Even if he'd heave-hoed her first.

Like Goetzmann, Jake was not my type, either. Unless, of course, I had a thing for vain, selfish, egotistical jerks with the morals of a rabbit. Still, regardless of Goetzmann's and Jake's imperfections, Bert had two reasonably good-looking guys foaming at the mouth over her. I, on the other hand, just had the foam on that single glass of Stroh's I found myself drinking every Saturday night. Dateless. Manless. Prospectless. Watching must-see TV.

Given my current state of mind, it seemed to me that our fortieth birthday was the perfect time to look backward, rather than forward. I planned to go way back, too, for Bert's birthday present, recalling bygone times when the world was our plaything.

And when playthings were our world.

I was planning to find some toy or doll that we'd played with as children and wow Bert with nostalgia. Bert is an absolute sucker for that kind of thing, too, always oohing and aahing over some old song we'd embarrassed ourselves singing too loud in high school, or some old board game we'd come to blows over, or some old doll we'd dismembered as kids.

Of course, Bert doesn't exactly remember those times that way. Bert recalls our childhood as idyllic. Two chestnut-haired moppets running barefoot through sunlit fields of— I suppose—amber waves of grain. All I remember is that if we did any running barefoot, we sure as hell stepped on a bee.

Bert, of course, is very aware that there is a slight difference in the way she and I recall the past. That's why Bert would not in a million years guess that I'd get her anything to remind her of those days. That's also why this idea was perfect.

In fact, up until the extremely large man began screaming at me, things had been going pretty well. I'd managed to get away from the radio station right after my midday air shift without Charlie Belcher, the program director, grabbing me before I could get out the front door.

Charlie is the reason that too often my job does not end the second I turn off my mike. It's Charlie's job to drum up publicity for the radio station, and my goodness, how the man loves his job. With appalling regularity, Charlie has extracurricular activities planned for me—delivering dinner to some contest winner, or standing in the rain giving out bumper stickers at the latest country-music show, or promoting some sale at a local mall.

Luckily for me, Charlie was nowhere in sight as I hurried out of the production studio and all but ran for the front door of the radio station. I hurried down the River City Mall toward the lot where I'd parked my Neon. I gunned the motor and resolutely headed for the Gigantic Flea Market.

Have I mentioned I hate to shop?

I know it's contrary to popular belief that a woman might actually dislike wandering around, looking for something to throw her money away on, but as far as I'm concerned, that popular belief isn't so popular.

As far as Bert is concerned, it's not a popular belief—it's gospel. For her, shopping is pretty much like breathing. For me, it's more like trying not to suffocate. This is especially true on those rare occasions when I've tagged along with Bert to the Gigantic Flea Market, held in the Left Wing at the Kentucky State Fairgrounds, located just off the Watterson Expressway on the way to the heart of downtown Louisville. The Fairgrounds are located next to the airport, which is itself located next to the theme park, Six Flags Over Kentucky Kingdom.

The way I see it, Louisville's city planners must've wanted to give a visitor to the city the unique opportunity to take an airplane trip, ride a roller coaster, and eat an overpriced, undercooked hot dog at a basketball game all within a five-mile radius. In other words, Louisville could offer the world-weary traveler three places in close proximity where he could potentially throw up. Strangely enough, this added attraction is not mentioned in any of the city's travel brochures.

Because of the central location and the fact that it's held only once a month—the second Friday, Saturday, and Sunday of each and every month—the Gigantic Flea Market is indeed gigantic. It draws more people, I do believe, than a Garth Brooks concert. Apparently, tons of Louisville citizens actually want to get trapped inside a huge building with a mob of strangers, most of them pushing baby strollers or pulling shopping carts—or, worse, riding in those little motorized carts—directly in front of you. All to buy a T-shirt that reads: *Beam me up, Scotty—there's no intelligent life here.* Or to buy fudge so hard it's probably left over from the last flea market. Or to acquire the most recently discontinued Beanie Baby at only twice the original cost.

I mean, what can I say? It doesn't get any better than this.

Gritting my teeth, I turned into Gate 1 at the Fairgrounds. Although the flea market is advertised as a free event, it costs three dollars to park your car. The only way you could get in free is if you had somebody drop you off, and even then, you'd probably have to be dropped from an airplane flying overhead. That's because the people at the admission gates—which incidentally are located more than a mile from the front entrance—are not going to let you set foot into the Fairgrounds without forking over three bucks.

For my three dollars, I enjoyed the privilege of parking in a grassy area that was so far from the Left Wing of the Fairgrounds, I was pretty sure it had another zip code. Fortunately, the long walk winded me a little, so it took a moment after I finally staggered into the huge room housing the flea market for the sickly sweet smells of cotton candy, caramel corn, and stale perfume to register. Those smells, combined with the constant hubbub of indiscernible conversation, hurried me through the milling crowd to a smaller room toward the back.

In this back room, there's a special antique section that

is far less crowded than the other areas. Once inside the open doors to that area, the noise level subsided to a genteel roar, and no one sold anything remotely resembling food. The only odors were of mildew and furniture polish, a decided improvement.

I glanced around—and found myself staring at a young Dean Stockwell, himself only about six years old, who was staring at Randolph Scott, who was staring at a scowling man in a fedora. The group was part of a movie poster advertising a 1940s flick called *Home Sweet Homicide*, one of my favorites. I found myself smiling. OK, I might actually end up enjoying this shopping trip after all.

I began leisurely walking up the aisles crisscrossing the room—aisles lined on both sides with booths crammed with collectibles dating back to the turn of the century.

From what Bert has told me, the flea market sells booths to each dealer. A "booth" consists of three tables arranged liked an upside-down U. On the tables are smaller plastic tables and shelves that the dealers themselves bring in. It's on these shelves and small tables that the dealers display their goods, precariously stair-stepping their shelves on top of each other to add inches of display space. The object is to display everything so that a visitor to the booth can see all items for sale with a single glance.

From what I could tell, there appeared to be a kind of contest going on between the dealers to see how many items could actually be displayed on just three tables. I personally would've given extra credit to those dealers who, in a rush of ingenuity, had used the floor space under the tables, too—spreading tablecloths out and displaying items even in areas no one could see unless they crawled on their hands and knees. Which I noticed some people really were doing. These people looked so gleeful at the riches they were finding under there, I might've been tempted to do the same except that I also noticed that the view people get when you're crawling under a table would not be one of my best.

I must've wandered around aimlessly for about an hour. What I hadn't counted on, when I first thought up getting Bert this surprise gift, was the fact that I was going to have such an extensive choice. I couldn't believe how many of the things that Bert and I had played with just yesterday, it seemed, were now designated antiques. Our Shirley Temple doll, our ranch-style tin dollhouse, and our Jon Gnagy art kit were displayed right alongside china dolls in lace-trimmed, ankle-length dresses from the turn of the century. I don't want to sound supersensitive—but my bad mood was taking a nosedive. You could actually get the idea that the children who'd played with these antique items were now antiques themselves. I stared at Captain Kangaroo lunch boxes, Deputy Dawg comic books, and flower-covered toy Volkswagen Bugs. Good Lord. I was beginning to feel like Methuselah.

I'd finally made up my mind to just grab something and get the hell out of there—before I bought a genuine Zorro sword and cut my throat with it—when a Barbie doll on a shelf caught my eye. I went over and picked her up.

You really have to hand it to the woman who created Barbie. Long before Betty Friedan started writing about women's liberation and Gloria Steinem started trying to convince us how great we looked without makeup, Barbie's inventor gave us a doll who showed the world what women really wanted: beautiful clothes that came off easily, a big, flashy convertible that needed no maintenance, and a boyfriend who couldn't say a word. Back then life had been so simple.

The Barbie I picked up had real eyelashes, long, straight blond hair pulled up in a bow at the top of her head, and a figure I believe I read somewhere was supposed to be 38-24-32. Obviously, the poor thing was deformed. She was dressed in a one-piece jumpsuit covered with flowers, complete with bell-bottoms and hot pink pilgrim shoes. Her tiny waist was jointed so that she could easily turn from side to side, looking, no doubt, for even more clothes. And, perhaps, considering how tiny she was, a sandwich.

I turned the doll over in my hand, thinking that she looked a lot like a Barbie I'd beheaded when I was nine. Of course, the guillotining of my doll had taken place after I'd given it a haircut that presaged Michael Jordan's. As I recall, as my Barbie met its untimely end, Bert had been carefully washing and play-ironing her own Barbie doll's little dresses and setting its hair in tiny plastic curlers. I remember thinking, even back then, that keeping Barbie looking like Barbie was way too much work.

I glanced over at the guy who apparently owned this booth—an obese, bearded man who was at that moment talking to another customer. This guy looked to me as if he'd gone out of his way to enhance a faint resemblance to Orson Welles. Not the urbane Orson Welles of *Citizen Kane* fame either, but the overweight Orson of "We sell no wine before its time" fame. This guy even had an ascot and brass-tipped walking cane. Orson didn't even glance my way, so intent was he on putting the hard sell on a teenager in baggy jeans and a St. Xavier school jacket. The kid was interested in a replica of the Star Wars battleship—complete with flashing lights that simulated blowing some hapless planet to kingdom come. Orson was telling him that it was "an educational toy."

I turned Barbie over again, noting the tiny plastic bag dangling from her right arm. Inside the little bag was an orange vinyl two-piece swimsuit with some kind of white net cover-up. This was another thing, I now recalled, that I'd always disliked about old Barbie. She dressed better than I did, and back then—before Mattel decided to make her a doctor or a teacher—she didn't even have a job, for God's sake.

Behind the Barbie's little plastic bag was a price tag, dangling from the same wrist. I flipped it over and almost had a heart attack. One hundred and seventy-five dollars and no cents! As far as I was concerned, the tag should've read *no sense*, because you certainly couldn't have any if you paid that much for an old doll.

"That's a first issue 1967 T-N-T—Twist & Turn Barbie," Orson said. The teenager was nowhere in sight now. Orson's little pig eyes were on the doll as if Barbie were made of gold. Of course, at these prices, maybe she was.

"With"—he paused for effect—"her original swimsuit and cover-up." Orson made it sound as if this was about as grand as, say, having her earrings made of real diamonds. "Not only that," he went on, "but this T-N-T is wearing 'Pajama Pow.' Made only in 1967 and 1968. Very rare, very fine."

"No kidding," I said, putting the doll back on the shelf.

Evidently, this was not the breathless response he'd been expecting. Orson tore his eyes away from the doll and glanced at me. Then he sort of morphed into a different guy right in front of my eyes. He looked as if he were being strangled, his round cheeks puffing out like one of those poisonous adders you see in *National Geographic* magazine.

His face flushed a deep red, and he began to shriek. "YOU! YOU!" he sputtered. "YOU! Yoooouu!"

I glanced around, then pointed at my chest. "Me?"

Orson was advancing on me now. "Whom else could I be talking to?" he asked loftily. "How dare you! You have got some nerve showing your face around here!"

"Excuse me?" I looked around again. Was this guy serious? There were a couple of other people in his booth, and several people standing in nearby booths. Their heads swiveled in our direction.

"Are you looking for trouble? Is that why you're here?"

"Trouble? No, I—"

"Did you think I would forget you, you—you bitch!" Orson yelled at the top of his rather sizable lungs. "That I would ever forget your ugly face?"

OK, that did it. Now I was mad. I could stand being called a bitch—there have been times when I considered that a compliment—but *ugly?* While I will admit that Bert and I are not anywhere close to beautiful—our hair is blah brown, our eyes are blah brown, and while we're both slender, we might also be described as bony—I don't think we're ugly either. This guy was making it sound as if small children ran at the sight of me.

"Now just a minute, Buster. Who do you think you're calling—"

The jerk didn't let me finish. "How dare you come back here? HOW—DARE—YOU!" He gasped for breath, waving me away. "Get out! Get out of my booth! YOU! You, you—"

"Look, Jerko, I have no idea what you're talking—"

Once again he didn't let me finish. "Don't give me that!"

he yelled. "How dare you! How dare you!" Orson was actually shaking his cane at me.

The man was clearly deranged. Before his keepers
showed up to take him back to the home, I thought I'd bid
him a not-at-all-fond farewell. I started to back up, but people from the other booth had come over by then, standing
behind me, no doubt to watch the show. Whether they meant
to or not, these people were effectively blocking my way,
preventing me from leaving.

I turned back to Orson. "Look, I have never met you before
in my life," I said flatly, crossing my arms. "I don't know what
you've been smoking, Ape, but I'm telling you—"

"Did you hear that?" he shrieked to the crowd. "You
heard her! You're all witnesses! She's maligned me again!"
He shook his cane at me again. "I'm going to sue you—you
hear me?"

"Look, how can I malign you? I don't even know you!
Don't you understand English?"

From behind me, I heard someone ask, "Isn't that the
deejay from WCKI?" Inside, I cringed. Oh, perfect. Another
great public-relations moment.

Orson was still yelling. "I'll show you what I understand.
I understand my rights! You can't just call me a thief! I'll
sue you! You and that damn daughter of yours! You two
will wish you'd never heard of Franklin Haggerty!"

"Hey, I'm already there," I said. Then I realized what
he'd just said. My *daughter?* All at once, I knew exactly
what had happened. I don't know why I hadn't thought of
it before.

It had to be Bert.

Bert must've come here, too, only with her daughter
Ellie. Hell, maybe she'd even come up with the same idea

for a surprise gift for me. Whatever the reason they'd been here, somehow, Bert and Ellie had gotten into a fight with this clown.

Haggerty was raving even worse now, something about me and my daughter having called him a charlatan.

I just stared at him. *Charlatan* wasn't a word that Bert would use, but Ellie might. In fact, now that I thought about it, Ellie did take after her father in one respect—they both had hair-trigger tempers. I could picture Ellie getting into a screamer with this yo-yo, and Bert leaping in to defend her daughter.

I started smiling and shaking my head at the guy, my hands out in a gesture of appeasement. After all, the guy had simply made a mistake. "I've got it figured out," I began. "It—"

"You'd better be figuring out which attorney to call!" Haggerty shouted, nodding to his audience.

OK, he could be annoying—that was clear. I tried again. "Sir, you've got me mixed up with my twin sister," I said. "It was her, not me, that you had your argument with. You've made a mistake."

This announcement certainly gave him pause. He paused long enough to suck in more air, and then yelled, "You're the one who's made a mistake! Pretending you're a twin so I won't sue you! Well, I'll sue you, all right. You just see if I don't!" Haggerty punctuated his sentence by poking his cane in the air at me for emphasis. "You just wait!"

He sounded like some bully on the school playground. A bully that was really getting on my nerves.

"I told you," I said. "It wasn't me."

Someone in the crowd offered, "She really is a twin, Frank. My wife and I listen to her all the time on the radio—"

Ah, a fan.

Haggerty took the new information well. "Oh yeah? Well, just because you're this big-shot radio star doesn't mean you can walk all over the little people!" he yelled.

Little people? Apparently, he hadn't looked in the mirror.

This conversation seemed to be going nowhere. I turned to leave. If I had to push the people in front of me aside, I was getting out of there. I looked over my shoulder at him. "It really wasn't me. I really am a twin, OK?"

"And I'm the Easter Bunny!" Haggerty bellowed.

More like the Mad Hatter. Fortunately, the crowd finally parted before me like the Red Sea.

"Don't worry about it, Miss Tatum. The old coot does this kinda thing all the time," a low voice murmured as I brushed by. "Haggerty's a real hothead." I looked in the direction of the voice. The guy was tall with exceedingly broad shoulders, shoulder-length blond hair, and eyes so green, it made you wonder, does he or doesn't he? Wear contacts, of course.

Green Eyes immediately smiled at me. Wearing faded blue jeans, a blue chambray shirt with the sleeves rolled up, and brown leather moccasins, he had a zippered hip purse hanging on his belt, the telltale mark of a dealer who had to make change.

I returned his smile. He was kind of cute.

"You just be sure to mention our little ol' flea market on your radio show, okey-doke?" he said.

My smile froze. I didn't trust myself to respond.

Chapter 2

●

Bert

Nan looked like she was having a cow. Come to think of it, Nan looked like she was having a whole herd as she barreled past me into my apartment.

My apartment is one half of a duplex that Nan and I share in the Highlands area of Louisville. Technically, I suppose, the word *share* is not exactly accurate. What I should've said is that I rent one side of a duplex that Nan owns.

Lest anybody get the idea that I'm the underachieving Tatum twin, I want to make it clear that I, too, once owned real estate. However, shortly after discovering my husband Jake was playing house with his twentysomething secretary, I went out of the house business altogether and got a divorce instead. Jake had to pay me alimony for a while, but even with that, it was obvious right from the start that I wasn't going to be able to afford the house I'd lived in ever since my two children were born.

It used to bother me that my landlord is a woman ten minutes younger than I am, but these days I'm mostly just glad I've got a roof over my head. I'm usually very glad that this same roof is over Nan's head, too. It's great having her right next door.

Occasions such as this one, however, are notable exceptions.

In fact, if I'd known she was going to act like this, I'd never have answered the doorbell. I don't want to sound snippy, but I've got enough on my mind these days without having to put up with Nan's moods.

Nan headed straight past me into the living room, flopped down on my sofa next to my daughter Ellie, and then just sat there, saying nothing, with a big frown on her face.

I hate this game.

It's a game I played far too often with Jake during the twenty-plus years that he and I were married: *Guess What The Problem Is. Guess* is sort of like *Twenty Questions* in that you keep asking questions, trying to guess what is making the other player look so miserable. Unlike *Twenty Questions*, though, if you haven't guessed the answer after asking twenty questions, you don't get to give up. You're still supposed to keep guessing. It is for this reason that this game could also be called *Twenty Billion Questions*. Also unlike *Twenty Questions*, there are no winners. Everybody loses—you lose time, you lose patience, and if the game keeps going on and on, you lose your temper.

I followed Nan into my living room, and sat down in the Queen Anne chair flanking my couch. I have mentioned to Nan several times exactly how much I loathe playing *Guess*, and how much I prefer people—when they're upset about something—to just spit it out. Having made myself abundantly clear, I would not have asked Nan what the problem was if she'd held a gun to my head.

My daughter, Emily Eleanor, on the other hand, at the ripe old age of twenty, apparently has not played *Guess* anywhere near as often as I have. Or it could be that my daughter just likes games better than I do. After all, Ellie had been totally absorbed in playing the computer game *Myst* on her Apple laptop when Nan came in. I'd actually tried a couple of times to start up a conversation with Ellie, but each time she'd answered me with monosyllables and turned back to her game. It was only when Nan sat down next to her, frowning, that Ellie finally stopped playing and turned to stare at her aunt.

After a minute or so, Ellie was still staring.

Nan was still frowning.

And I was wondering if I should start a load of laundry.

Ellie was spending the summer sharing her time between me and her dad, before returning to the University of Kentucky in the fall. She'd just spent a week with Jake, staying in his guest bedroom, and had arrived on my doorstep only a couple of days ago. She'd arrived—no surprise—with several bags of laundry, and had immediately laid claim to my washing machine.

That is one nice thing about college—if your children don't learn anything else, they do learn to appreciate appliances. Ellie had been appreciating my washer almost nonstop ever since she walked in my front door. So much so that I had not had a chance to run even a small load of my own things.

I'd just about made up my mind that I might as well use this spare time to get a wash load out of the way when Ellie finally said, "OK, Aunt Nan, who died?"

Ellie actually asked that, right out loud and everything, and I didn't have even the slightest hint of a premonition. Which, I do believe, pretty much blows the theory that twins have more ESP than other people.

"Who died?" Nan was asking. "What do you mean, *who died?*" She continued to frown.

I almost smiled. You have to admire a really skilled *Guess* player. Answering a question with a question was a time-honored ploy.

Ellie ran her hand through her bangs. Up until this summer, she'd had gorgeous, wavy, long blond hair. I used to brush it for her, one hundred strokes every night, when she'd been in elementary school. A few weeks ago, though, Ellie had declared, "The only woman in Kentucky who still wears her hair long is Loretta Lynn, so unless I want to take up the guitar, I think I need a haircut."

Ellie's hair was now a very short bob, straight as a poker, with bangs to her eyebrows in the front and tapered into a sort of wedge in the back. Ellie insisted that it was the very latest look, and I'd had to bite my tongue to keep from telling her that it bore a remarkable resemblance to the haircut Dorothy Hamill had made famous during the 1976 Winter Olympics.

"What I mean is," Ellie was now saying to Nan, in a tone of infinite patience, "what's the matter?"

Nan's answer was quick, if not informative. "What makes you think there's anything the matter?"

I got to my feet. *Twenty Billion Questions* could take some time.

Seeing that I was about to walk out in the middle of her game, Nan hurried to add, "We're just going to have to reinstate Twinstant Replay, that's all."

That stopped me in my tracks. "Twinstant Replay" was what Nan and I had at one time called our getting together at the end of each and every day and replaying everything we'd done during the day. Nan and I hadn't done Twinstant

Replays since college. Back then we'd spent almost an hour every evening going over everything significant that had happened when we weren't together. *Everything significant that had happened* back in college, of course, had mainly translated to: *any guys we'd met.*

Nan had come up with Twinstant Replay after I'd snubbed some guy she'd been cultivating for months. It had not been my fault. To me, the guy had not been the least bit attractive. Far from it, to be blunt. During our freshman year, Nan had gone for artistic types, with long hair, dirty jeans, and moody stares. Me, I'd preferred men who, on occasion, bathed.

"Twinstant Replay?" Ellie echoed, looking first at Nan and then over at me. "What in the world is that?"

As she explained it all to Ellie, Nan started frowning all over again. "It seems to me that we're going to have to start doing Twinstant Replays again," she finished, "particularly if *some people*"—here Nan put an extra emphasis on those last two words and glanced over at me; the woman was as subtle as a train wreck—"are going to run around, calling other people names, and getting me in a lot of trouble. I mean," Nan went on, sounding injured, "if there's even the slightest chance I might run into people who are going to jump all over me, in public, where other people can hear, I think I deserve to be warned that these people should be avoided."

I took a deep breath and sat down again. Ellie seemed to be having trouble figuring out who all these people were that Nan was mentioning. Ellie's big blue eyes definitely looked confused. It no doubt helped to be working with the same brain as Nan. I knew exactly who Nan was talking about. Actually, it wasn't all that hard to figure out. How many people had I called names recently? Let me see, adding them all up, counting every single person, the sum total would be: one. I took a deep breath. "How was I supposed to know that you were going to the flea market?" I said. "You never go to flea markets!"

Nan glared at me. "I certainly won't be going back to this one. Not if that guy is going to yell at me again!" she said. "In public! Right in front of everybody!" She went on, giving us a play-by-play account of her encounter with that awful man at the Gigantic Flea Market.

Halfway through Nan's story, Ellie was not looking confused anymore. She was looking angry.

When Ellie gets angry, she always reminds me of her father. Just like Jake, her blue eyes always go a shade darker, and her face goes several shades of pink. Ellie is like Jake in another way, too. She can lose her temper in a split second—one minute she's honey-sweet, the next minute she's ready to go for somebody's throat.

She seemed to be leaning toward this last now. "I can't believe that jerk was yelling at you! He's got some nerve," Ellie said. "Franklin Haggerty is the one who should be yelled at! He's nothing but a crook!"

Nan shrugged. "I don't know about the guy being a crook, but he sure is a first-class jerk—"

Ellie interrupted. "Oh, he's a crook, all right. He's a fucking swindler—that's what he is!"

Ellie's eyes had darted quickly toward me right after she said the F-word. I kept my face perfectly still, registering no reaction at all. Ellie knows how I feel about her using language like this. It just sounds so vulgar—certainly not the way a young lady should talk. The last time I said something about it, though, Ellie had seemed delighted to tell me at length how she was all grown up now, and how these days she could decide for herself what was right for her. She certainly didn't need her "Mommy" telling her how to talk.

Oh brother.

As a mother, you expect that one day your child will be cutting the old apron strings. I'd just never realized that she'd be saying a few four-letter words when she did it.

Here lately, I've also begun to suspect that Ellie is talking like this just to watch the blood drain from my face. The language she'd used to that awful man—even if he had deserved it—had been enough to scorch your ears. I was pretty sure that Ellie would not have used those particular words if I had not been there. I really think that here lately she's been deliberately trying to shock me. That, of course, was why I didn't react this time.

I refused to be shocked.

Nan—whose own language every once in a while is only slightly saltier than a sailor's—didn't even seem to notice what Ellie had just said. "Swindler?" Nan repeated. "You mean, like he's pulling some sort of scam?" Her tone was skeptical.

"Aunt Nan, he's selling vintage Barbie dolls in new boxes!" Ellie said this the way anybody else might say, *He's been robbing banks!*

Nan looked disappointed. "New doll boxes?" She glanced over at me and then back at Ellie. "And the problem with selling new stuff would be . . . ?"

Ellie rolled her eyes. "They're the boxes that came with the 1994 Thirty-fifth Anniversary reproductions of Barbie! They look just like the original boxed dolls. Haggerty is claiming that his dolls are totally original, box included, and he's asking hundreds, even thousands for some of his so-called vintage Barbies. According to my friend Chris, Number One Barbies can bring up to ten thousand dollars in the original box."

Ellie said it like everyone in the world knew that. Apparently, Nan didn't. She gaped. "Ten THOUSAND bucks? For a *doll?*"

I'd heard all this before, when we were standing in front of Haggerty and Ellie was—to use one of Ellie's own phrases—reaming him out. "Some rare dolls are even more expensive than that," I put in.

Nan shook her head. "I cannot believe it. All that money for a Barbie—"

Ellie nodded. "Mom didn't believe it either. In fact, she took up for the asshole at first, until I showed her that one line on every single box had been smudged so that you couldn't read it. It just happened to be the line that said that the boxes were reproductions. The fat turd had scratched over it to make it illegible. What a shithead!"

OK, I couldn't stand it. Maybe I could put up with *fat turd*, but *shithead* was too much. "The guy's name is Haggerty, I believe. Franklin Haggerty," I said.

Ellie just looked at me. Her eyes clearly said, *And your point?*

I ignored her. "And I wasn't defending Mr. Haggerty back at the flea market. I just like to give people the benefit of the doubt, that's all. He could've just made an honest mistake, and not even known that the boxes he was selling were new." Of course, once I saw the way he'd deliberately doctored the boxes, and heard the way he yelled when somebody pointed it out, I realized that Ellie had been right on the money. The guy was a crook, all right. A crook with a mouth almost as foul as my daughter's.

Ellie turned back to Nan. "Haggerty didn't just sell fake vintage doll boxes, either. Chris said that Haggerty put a Twist & Turn Barbie head on a Talking Barbie's body, redid her hair, and called it 'all original' on the tag. Haggerty labeled a Casey doll a Twiggy, and it's not. And he painted over the green ears on a Bubblecut Barbie, which you could only tell if you held it in the light just right. *And* he put a really cheesy wig on a fifties' Toni doll and said it was all original. The man is nothing but a criminal!"

Nan first nodded, and then looked puzzled. "Since when did you become a doll collector, Ellie? Next, you'll be standing in line to buy the latest Beanie Babies."

Ellie crossed her arms over her chest. "Chris says Beanie Babies are probably just a fad. Remember Cabbage Patch dolls? Remember Tickle Me Elmo?"

Nan was still looking at her blankly.

"OK, remember Pet Rocks?"

Nan momentarily brightened.

"Well, Chris says people were buying all those things like crazy and now, where are they?" Ellie went on. *"Never buy anything that someone manufactures as a collectible.* That's what Chris says."

"Who *is* this Chris?" Nan asked.

Ellie looked down at her laptop, turning the thing off. "Chris Mulholland. He's a dealer at the flea market, selling old toys and collectibles. I met him at UK. He was in one of my classes."

Nan looked as if she was about to say something more, but Ellie didn't give her the chance. She hurried on. "Poor Chris has had a pretty hard time, but you'd never know it to talk to him. Just a few months ago, both his parents were killed in a car accident—and then, after the estate was settled, he was left with nothing." Ellie's voice was filled with sympathy. "But Chris is determined to finish college. Being a dealer at the flea market is how he's earning money for tuition and books. Chris really liked the business. Until he noticed that some of the dealers were selling bogus items and undercutting his business. He's even complained to the people running the flea market, but they won't do anything. Chris says that most dealers are honest, but some are simply scam artists. The bad thing is, nobody seems to care, as long as they're making a buck. The crooked dealers just stick out signs that say, 'Items sold as is' and *'Caveat emptor.'* "

Ellie was winding up now. "It's honest people like Chris who pay the price for the crooked dealers because Chris can't match the cheaper deals."

"Well, well, well," Nan said. "Chris Mulholland." Her frown had totally vanished. "So, Ellie, tell me, is this Mr. Right? Or Mr. Right Now?"

I shifted position in my Queen Anne chair. Nan makes me so mad sometimes. She actually seems to think that a woman can't just be friends with a guy—that there is always something else going on. It was the dawn of the new millennium for God's sake, as Ellie was always reminding me. Men and women could just be pals, couldn't they?

Not to mention, I'd asked Ellie a similar question, and her answer had been a little indignant. "Mom," she'd said, "Chris and I are just buds." I remembered her response quite clearly, because it had taken me a moment to realize that *buds* was short for *buddies.*

Ellie did not look indignant, however, at Nan's question. Instead, she smiled. "Chris and I are friends. That's all."

Nan returned Ellie's smile. "Yeah, right, you two are just friends. And Bert and I are just sisters. So what happened to Ted?"

Ted? I blinked and turned to look at Ellie. Who was Ted? I hadn't heard anything about a Ted.

Ellie shrugged. "Turned out Ted was just making me the lucky-duck offer."

"Oh," Nan said, sympathetically.

OK, now I was totally confused. I must've looked it, because Nan turned to me. "You know, it's the offer most guys make: *You lucky duck, I'm willing to sleep with you tonight.*"

I blinked, and turned to look at Ellie. *What?* Some guy was trying to get *my baby* to go to bed with him?

What I was thinking must've shown in my face because both Ellie and Nan started talking at once. "Don't worry, Mom," Ellie put in. "I'm not an idiot."

"Don't worry, Bert. I told Ellie that she should wait for a guy who makes her a better offer than the lucky-duck one," Nan said. "An offer that at least involves the use of the word *love.* And other words like, oh, say, *not dating anybody else.* You know, words like that."

I tried to smile, but let's face it, my head was spinning. I couldn't decide which was the most upsetting—my baby being propositioned, or my baby obviously confiding in Nan more than she did me. I'd known, of course, that Ellie thought that Nan was cool—and that Ellie thought I was, well, her mother. A thing which, I believe, is inherently un-cool. It had never occurred to me, though, that Ellie would be telling Nan things she didn't tell me.

"Boy, Aunt Nan," Ellie said, "you should've seen Mom

go after Franklin Haggerty. She practically leapt down his throat after he started yelling at me!"

What Ellie was doing was so transparent, I would've had to be comatose not to pick up on it. Obviously, Ellie wanted to change the subject bad. And she wanted to make me feel better, so I'd stop looking as if I'd been poleaxed.

"She was just great!" Ellie went on. "Mom actually told the guy to drop dead. Right in front of everybody!"

"Wow," Nan said. "You told him to drop dead, huh?"

I gave them both a faint smile. Oh, yeah, I'm hell, all right. God's gift to assertiveness training.

The two of them continued to smile at me for the rest of the evening. Nan stayed for dinner, Ellie insisted on cleaning up afterward, and throughout it all, they kept smiling at me and telling me how great it was that I'd told somebody I'd just met that I wanted his life to end immediately.

Of course, the next morning they had a slightly different opinion.

Chapter 3

●

Nan

I suppose when most people see a cop at their front door, they feel a little apprehensive. Visions of unpaid parking tickets dance in their heads. Or they instantly recall how they cut that guy off in traffic the other day without using an appropriate hand signal. Or worse, they recall that they had indeed used a hand signal—one that had been all too appropriate—and that was the problem.

When I answered Bert's doorbell and found Detective Hank Goetzmann standing on her porch on Sunday morning, I didn't feel the least bit apprehensive. Not even a twinge. Of course, when your twin sister is dating a cop, it's not exactly a big deal to have him show up once in a while.

The only other thing that could possibly make me uneasy about running into this particular cop is the fact that I, too, had once dated him. If I thought about it, I suppose I might feel a bit self-conscious, remembering some of the things we did to and with each other. That's pretty much why I make it a point not to think about it. When a forest fire has finally burned itself out, you don't think about the trees when you're looking at the ashes. Goetzmann, as far as I was concerned, had certainly made an ash of himself.

He and I had fallen into true lust shortly after we met.

Nowadays I can't believe it, but back then I'd thought, with his marine haircut, stocky build, and square jaw, Goetzmann was a dead ringer for the actor Brian Dennehy: a big, sexy hunk. These days I think Goetzmann looks a lot more like Ed Asner with hair. Or maybe Captain Kangaroo without his coat. Not to mention, what I think he's a big hunk of, I'd never say out loud in front of Bert.

Looking back on it now, I would say that Goetzmann and my relationship had chilled in about ten minutes, but in reality I suppose it had taken a little longer than that.

Twenty minutes tops.

Actually, I'd cooled off about the time I'd discovered that Goetzmann really was the power-mad control freak I'd first thought he was, and he'd cooled off about the time he'd realized that he liked my package but not what it wrapped. Luckily, he had a choice of the same wrapping on an entirely different set of goods. That pretty much explained Hank's subsequent switch to Bert and my subsequent sigh of relief.

I barely gave Hank a glance as I left Bert's front door open and hurried back to her blue chintz sofa and *Cathy* in the Sunday comics. "Bert's in the kitchen," I threw over my shoulder at him. I sat down, retrieved my glass of Coke from the end table where I'd left it, took a sip, and turned the page to *Rex Morgan, MD.*

"Bert is *baking,*" I added, without looking up. I couldn't help the note of amazement that crept into my voice. Bert's domestic leanings have always been a mystery to me. I don't know where she gets it. As I mentioned earlier, Bert and I are supposed to be working with the same brain cells, and yet, believe me, my brain cells do not make any sense out of baking. I mean, sure, if you're on a covered wagon, headed west, maybe you might feel a little inclined to whip something up. Particularly if you're one of the Donner party. Barring that, however, it seems like a colossal waste of time. Not to mention, you can work all day, and the only thing you'll have to show for your efforts is a mountain of dirty dishes. If you're really good, you'll have the privilege of living with a lot of overweight people. Nope, the way I see it, if there's anything even remotely like a Winn Dixie or a Kroger or a Super Wal-Mart within an hour's drive—or even a day's drive if you're on the aforementioned covered wagon—all I can say is, "Better Betty Crocker than me."

Cleaning, I do believe, is an even bigger waste of time than baking. It's one of the few jobs that, no matter how well you do it, you're just going to have to do it again. Of course, that explains why I often spend Sunday mornings over at Bert's side of our duplex. In her pristine apartment I can actually find the Sunday *Courier-Journal.*

I was on the last frame of *Rex Morgan* when I realized that Goetzmann had made no move whatsoever to go into the kitchen. I glanced over at him again.

And saw something I didn't recognize in his expression. What was this? Embarrassment? Discomfort? I was surprised to see something else, too.

Make that someone else.

A man was standing right behind Goetzmann. A Mount Rushmore of a guy, Goetzmann could easily eclipse the sun, so my not having spotted the other guy who'd come in right behind him was not exactly a surprise. What was surprising was that the other guy was Goetzmann's partner, Barry Krahzinsky.

At six inches shorter than Hank's six-three and about one-sixty to Hank's two-thirty, Barry always looks to me like a teenager pretending to be a cop. Traces of acne on his cheeks, his flattop haircut and his baggy clothes add to the illusion. I'd been shocked when Hank told me that Barry was almost thirty-five.

What I gathered in an instant from the presence of Barry, though, was that this was no social call. The last time I'd seen Barry, there'd been a corpse on the premises. That could lead a person to believe that he and Goetzmann had to be on Police Business. Capital P, capital B.

Uh-oh.

About the time that little revelation hit me, Bert wandered out of the kitchen, wearing an oven mitt on her left hand, and holding a pan of steaming cinnamon raisin muffins. A rich aroma of cinnamon and vanilla came in with her. "Why, Hank!" she said, smiling. "I didn't hear you come in. What a nice surprise!" She headed straight for him, her mouth already puckering up for a little welcoming smooch.

Goetzmann, naturally, began to back away. He could not have looked more horrified if Bert's smile had revealed newly sprouted fangs. I remembered then that the guy had this dumb rule. What was it he'd called it? NPD. Oh my yes, how could I ever forget NPD? You'd lean toward him to give him a kiss in a movie theater, and he'd murmur, "NPD." No Public Displays of affection.

The first time he'd said it, I'd thought he'd was referring to the New York Police Department, and I'd briefly wondered if New York had some kind of ordinance against kissing. And, even if they did, what did that have to do with us? My reaction, of course, after Hank had quickly explained what NPD really meant, had been to inquire how he felt about PDA—Public Displays of Anger. As I recall, he had not been amused. The man has no sense of humor whatsoever.

Bert now looked neither angry nor amused. She looked puzzled, until Goetzmann did this little sidestep so that Bert could see Barry. Bert took one look and froze for a moment. It was kind of funny. I sat there on the couch and watched Bert run through the same deductions that I had just made in exactly the same amount of time. She glanced uneasily at me, and then back at Goetzmann. "Why, what's wrong?"

Barry stepped forward. "Nice to see you again, ladies. We're just here on a routine inquiry. Just routine."

"Routine," Bert repeated after him, her voice distracted.

"So, Bert," Barry asked, "do you happen to know a Franklin Haggerty?"

I shifted uneasily on the couch. It wasn't the question that concerned me. It was the questioner. Goetzmann, the Senior Control Freak of North America, was letting Barry conduct the interrogation? Goetzmann had once started telling me how to drive, and we were still parked, for God's sake. What on earth was going on?

Bert noticed who was taking the lead, too. She raised her eyebrows at Goetzmann. He just looked at her, his face betraying nothing, until Bert turned back to Barry. "Well, sure," she said. "Franklin Haggerty is that horrible, horrible man at the flea market."

"Nan?" Barry turned to me. "Do you know him?"

"Yeah. He's that horrible, horrible man at the flea market," I said. "What's this about?"

"How well do you two know him?" Barry asked.

"Not very well," Bert answered, gesturing toward the two blue chintz wing chairs flanking her sofa. "Would you two like to sit down?"

After both men took their seats, looking uncomfortable, and Bert sat down next to me on the couch, Barry cleared his throat. Not a pretty sound. One, in fact, that made you very glad there wasn't a spittoon anywhere handy. "So you two both knew Haggerty pretty well?" he said.

Bert and I both began shaking our heads in unison. "Oh no," Bert said. "My goodness, we didn't know him well. Oh my no. Not at all." Her tone implied that if either of us had known him well, we should be ashamed.

"We pretty much had a screaming relationship with him," I said. "What's this about?"

Bert must've thought I was being too blunt. She frowned, and then asked, "Can I get you gentlemen any coffee?" Turning to me, she added, "More Coke, Nan?" As she said this last, Bert evidently noticed that she was still holding the muffin pan. She held it out toward the men. "Muffins?"

I just looked at her. Bert and Martha Stewart could be best friends. Apparently, we were the target of some kind of police investigation, and Bert's chief concern appeared to be that she might not be considered a good hostess. I could just see her and Martha putting their heads together. Now what would be the perfect thing to serve during an interrogation? Something light, not too spicy, and definitely not too filling, in case one of us ends up taking a trip downtown in the back of a police car.

Bert noticed my look and glared back at me. Unfortunately, as her twin, I know her so well I could practically hear what she was thinking. *Look, Nan, just because we're the object of a dragnet is no reason we have to be rude.*

I swear, if Bert didn't look exactly like me, I'd be certain she was switched at birth.

After everyone had declined Bert's offer of baked goods and beverages, I tried again. "So what's this about?"

"When did you see Franklin Haggerty last, Bert?" Barry asked, ignoring me.

Bert obligingly filled him in on the yelling match she and Ellie had enjoyed with Haggerty the day before. "He was terribly rude," she added. "He used the F-word, the S-word, the B-word—"

Oh God. If Bert was going to go through every word Haggerty had said, we'd be here all night. "He used pretty much the entire Curse Alphabet," I put in.

"You were there?" Barry turned to me.

"Not with Bert. I was there a little later, when Haggerty mistook me for Bert. So I got a rerun of what he'd said to her. What's this about?" I asked again.

Barry ignored me again. "When did you see Haggerty last, Nan?"

I was getting a little tired of having my questions ignored, but what the hell? I told them as fast as I could what had been said. There was only one bad moment, when I told them that Haggerty had called me a few choice names. Unlike Bert, I decided it would be faster just to say it out loud. "He called me a bitch, right out loud, in front of everybody. Can you believe it?"

I made the mistake of looking over at Goetzmann just as I said that last. If I hadn't known better, I would've sworn the man was faintly nodding his head. It was only then that I recalled, in the last days of our relationship, Goetzmann had actually used that word to describe me himself.

I stared straight at him. "Can you imagine what kind of a low-life jerk would call a woman such an ugly name?"

Hank shrugged, meeting my look head-on. "I can't imagine," he said.

It was the first thing he'd said since we sat down. There

was a moment of silence; then Barry cleared his throat again. I really wished he'd stop doing that. Hell, Bert ought to forget about the muffins, and get that man a lozenge.

Turning back to Bert, Barry said, "Tell me, Bert. Was it your daughter Ellie or you who told Haggerty to—and I quote—drop dead?"

Uh-oh. I glanced over at Goetzmann. I didn't really need to ask what was going on anymore. I was pretty sure I knew.

Bert was looking uncomfortable. Apparently, good hostesses do not tell people to drop dead. "Well, yes, I did say that," she said, looking down at the muffins she was still holding. "But Mr. Haggerty was very rude first. Why, some of the things he said were—" She broke off as something occurred to her. "Did he file a complaint or something? Because he really has some nerve, what with the yelling and screaming he did. He was awful!" She turned to Goetzmann. "Hank, you should've been there—you would've wanted to hit him. He said the most vile things just because Ellie pointed out the scam he was pulling!" Bert was now gesturing with the muffin pan, punctuating her every word. "That horrible, horrible man really has some nerve to file—"

Bert was really getting agitated. I reached over and touched her on the arm. "Bert," I interrupted. "Haggerty hasn't filed a complaint—"

She stopped her harangue and looked at me. "How do you know?"

I shrugged. "Hank and Barry are homicide cops." I looked over at the two of them. "So this has got to be a homicide we're talking about. Someone's killed the S.O.B., right?"

For only the second time since he sat down, Goetzmann

spoke. "Early this morning, as Haggerty was arriving at the Fairgrounds for the last day of the flea market, some person or persons unknown met him in the parking lot. When Haggerty was finally missed at his booth, some of the flea-market directors went looking for him. They found him right next to his van, with a single bullet wound to the chest."

Barry continued, "Unfortunately, that one bullet severed the guy's aorta. He was probably dead before he hit the ground. We think the murder weapon was the handgun found next to his body. Haggerty's own .38, missing one round."

Goetzmann went on. "We think the individual or individuals who killed him probably didn't go there to murder him. But the argument escalated—and probably Haggerty pulled his gun. The individual got it away from him and shot him. Now we really need to find that individual."

I just looked at him. "Do you really think that individual was Bert or me? Are you kidding?"

Goetzmann sighed. "We're talking to everyone who had a recent argument with the guy. Your names came up."

"It's just routine," Barry added, smiling. I hated to break it to him, but hearing that wasn't exactly a comfort. A few thousand volts in an electric chair are just routine.

"Believe me, there's a long list of people this guy had fights with," Goetzmann went on. "It seems this Haggerty fellow made a practice of loud and protracted arguments. It was how the guy seemed to handle any complaints. Your names were at the head of the list, though, because you'd fought with him just yesterday."

Was I wrong, or was there the faintest reproach in his voice? I glanced over at Bert, but she didn't seem to have noticed. "We'll certainly try not to argue with any more future murder victims," I said.

Bert blinked at me, going on smoothly. "And if there's anything we can do to help, Hank," she said, "just let us know."

Goetzmann, instead of answering her, looked at his shoes. Uh-oh.

"Well, there *is* something," Barry said.

Bert looked at him expectantly. "Yes?"

"Can you tell us where we might find your daughter?"

Seated next to her, I could feel Bert suddenly tense. I looked over at her and saw the line of her jaw harden. Gripping the muffin pan tighter, she leaned forward and spoke only one word.

"Ellie?"

Oh yeah. I could swear there was smoke coming out of her ears.

Chapter 4

●

Bert

There was no smoke coming out of my ears. Not even a wisp.

I was just concerned, that's all. I realize, of course, that most mothers are all too eager to have their children questioned by the police. They just can't *wait* to have their offspring dragged downtown and grilled, and they can only hope that one day their very own flesh and blood will appear in a police lineup.

Me, I'm funny that way. I just wasn't all that thrilled at the prospect of Ellie having to go through some stupid interrogation. I would've thought that Nan, of all people, would sympathize. She and I had certainly endured far more than our share of lovely little chats with men wearing badges.

I was not angry, though. If I'd been angry, would I have told Hank and Barry where to find Ellie? I don't think so. And yet, with almost no hesitation at all, I said, "Ellie isn't here right now. She went to help her friend, Chris Mulholland, at his booth at the flea market."

I would've thought that anybody would've been able to commit that little bit of information to memory, but Barry apparently wasn't anybody. He nodded solemnly, pulled out a small spiral notebook from his back pocket, and flipped it open with the same kind of studied nonchalance with which Captain Kirk activates his communicator. Barry then took a ballpoint pen out of his shirt pocket, turned back to me, and asked, his voice as emotionless as Spock himself, "The flea market?"

"The Gigantic Flea Market," I said. "Chris has a booth in the antiques section, too. Just like Mr. Haggerty did."

Barry nodded as if he knew exactly what I was talking about, but I had my doubts. Particularly since I watched as he wrote it down, and I could see that Barry had spelled "flea" with two *e*'s. Hank noticed it, too. He glanced toward me, and then immediately looked away, a tiny smile pulling at the corners of his mouth.

It took real concentration not to smile myself. It didn't make it any easier to know that Hank refers to Barry as *Bare* when we're alone. I hadn't even met Barry when Hank first started talking about him, so I'd thought at first that Hank was just shortening Barry's name a little and calling him *Bare* as a nickname. Hank, however, explained that he was simply referring to just how full of smarts his partner's head was.

Hank has such a great sense of humor. One of the things I love about being with him is how much he makes me laugh.

He might also be the sweetest man I've ever met. When Bare was finally finished asking his questions and had turned to leave, Hank took me aside, and whispered, "Don't worry about us talking to Ellie, OK? It really is just routine." He then leaned a little closer and added, his voice barely audible, "Consider yourself kissed."

I was smiling when he and Barry went out the door. I really was. I still wasn't crazy about Ellie getting asked a lot of silly questions, but knowing that Hank would be there made me feel a lot more at ease.

Nan and I spent Sunday afternoon like we often do: working. I know. I know. You can't grow up in Louisville, Kentucky, and not be well aware that if you work on Sunday, you're breaking one of the Ten Commandments. We are right in the middle of an area of the country that a lot of Kentuckians refer to as the Bible Belt. If this is the Bible Belt, Louisville is the Buckle.

When I was a kid attending Sunday school here, I'd thought that avoiding work on Sunday made a lot of sense. Of course, back then I'd thought that avoiding work any other day of the week made a lot of sense, too. Once I grew up, though, I changed my mind. Nowadays I'm pretty sure that if Moses had been a woman, he'd have suggested to God that maybe He ought to reconsider that goofing-off-on-the-Sabbath commandment. What with Nan and me both working on Saturdays quite a bit, Sunday is often the only day we have to get household chores done. Sunday, more likely than not, is the day Nan and I clean our apartments. Mine is simple dusting and vacuuming; Nan's is more like reclaiming a toxic-waste dump. Once we finish our cleaning and reclaiming, we're generally on a roll, so Nan and I top it all off with a week's worth of laundry.

Nan and I almost always end up doing these mundane chores together. Before anybody starts thinking that Nan and I are joined at the hip—that perhaps we have ourselves confused with twins of the Siamese persuasion, and we should race each other to the nearest mental-health clinic— I'd like to add that Nan and I do these jobs together because we both hate them. Doing them together makes cleaning and laundering seem more like visiting.

It also makes the day go by a lot faster. Before we knew it, Nan and I were folding shirts and underwear and assorted pieces of clothing still warm from the dryer. We'd settled ourselves and our laundry down in front of the TV to watch Scully and Mulder once again fight aliens on the *X-Files*. Here in Louisville on Sunday, reruns of old *X-Files* are shown on one station about three hours before another station shows the current show. I've always figured the station showing the current show doesn't mind another station showing the syndicated reruns because it's pretty much like priming the pump for their viewers.

Unfortunately, on tonight's pump-priming episode, Scully had no sooner told Mulder that she most certainly did not believe that the woman they'd just met was an alien from outer space—even though the woman's eyes glowed a bright orange about every ten seconds—when my telephone rang.

The phone is on an end table right next to my sofa, but usually when I'm watching television, I let my answering machine get it. Mainly because here lately it seems as if every single time the phone rings, I'm subjected to a sales pitch. I really hate to interrupt a favorite television show to listen to some idiot ask to speak to "Bert Totem" regarding the special deal now being offered exclusively in my area on aluminum siding.

Tonight, though, I was distracted. By Nan, wouldn't you know it? When the phone first rang, Nan was saying, "You know, I cannot believe, after all these years on the air, that Scully is still wondering whether or not there are aliens out there. Is she kidding? Hasn't she been watching her own show? Is she a dim bulb or what?"

I just stared at Nan for a moment. If anything, Scully is one of my role models. Cool and calm under fire, and yet, not a strand of her hair is ever out of place. Whatta woman. "Nan," I said, "Scully is in the FBI. She cannot possibly be stupid."

The phone rang again.

Nan shrugged again and finished folding a T-shirt. "I want to see Scully's SAT scores."

"Nan," I repeated, "the woman is an FBI—" The phone rang yet again, and without thinking, I reached over and picked it up.

Nan kept right on talking, cutting me off. "In fact, I'd like to get a look at any test our Miss Scully had to take to get into the FBI, too." She glanced at the phone in my hand. "Are you going to answer that?"

"Hello?" I said into the receiver.

Not surprisingly, it was one of those computer-generated voices. Usually, this is the part where I hang up, but this time the first five words got my attention. "This is a collect call—"

The rest of it made my stomach hurt.

"—from an inmate at a state correctional facility—"

I must've looked startled, because Nan stopped folding and just looked at me. "What is it? What's wrong?"

I would've answered her, but I was afraid I'd miss something the electronic voice said. Not to mention, I wasn't sure yet how to answer her, anyway. In the past year or so, Nan and I had been instrumental in sending several people to prison. In my humble opinion, they had richly deserved going to prison. At the time, in fact, prison had seemed like the best place for them. If for no other reason than that it was a place where they could mingle with their own kind. Now I wondered. Could this caller be one of those people? In which case, there was probably very little chance that this was going to be a thank-you call.

"The caller is . . ." Here the recorded voice paused for the live person to say their name. My heart actually speeded up.

"Emily Eleanor Powell." My daughter's voice was clear, if a little shaky.

"Will you accept the charges?" The recorded voice went on.

"Yes," I said. "Yes, I will." Even to my own ears, I sounded pretty stunned, but I had a good excuse. I *was* stunned. Good Lord. What was Ellie doing in a—how had that stupid voice put it?—*correctional facility?* I hated to say it, but if one of my children were going to end up in jail, I would never have guessed in a million years that it would be Ellie. Brian, maybe. He's been caught speeding a few times, and he hung out for a while with a pretty wild crowd in high school. But Ellie? Ellie had quietly graduated fifth in her class.

So, could this be a joke? This *was* Ellie, after all. The girl who'd woke me up on April 1 one year, yelling that someone was outside, breaking into my car. I'd jumped out of bed, grabbed a broom of all things, and clad only in shorty pajamas, I'd raced outside. I'd circled the car three times, brandishing that stupid broom before Ellie had appeared, laughing her head off. "April Fool's Day, Mom!"

If she was joking this time, I might be the one who ended up in a correctional facility. For daughter abuse.

I was going over all this in my mind as the electronic voice was instructing me to press one on my telephone to accept the charges. I did as I was told. Ellie must've known what I might be thinking, because the first thing she said when we were connected was, "Mom, this isn't a joke."

My stomach felt as if a giant hand had squeezed it. "Ellie, good Lord, what—"

Ellie interrupted me. "Now, Mom, don't get all excited. I'm just under arrest, that's all. No biggie."

No biggie? Was she kidding? If getting arrested wasn't a biggie, then what was? Being detained by the Gestapo? Ellie has always been rather blasé about things, but I couldn't believe I'd need to explain to her why ending up in jail is not exactly inconsequential. This, however, didn't seem to be a good time to go into it.

"Ellie, what on earth did you do to get arrested?" I said.

Across from me, Nan's eyebrows went up.

"I mean," Ellie was going on as if I hadn't said anything, "getting arrested might've been serious when you were my age, but these days, people get arrested all the time."

If I hadn't heard the tremor in Ellie's voice that told me just how scared she really was, I might've answered her with the first thing that came into my mind. Which was: *That's right. When I was little, it was a terrible thing to get arrested. Mainly because that meant there would be one less person to fight off Indian attacks after we pulled our covered wagons into a circle.* Knowing that what I was hearing was just bravado, though, made it easy for me to let that one go. "Ellie, hon, what happened?"

Ellie either didn't get what I was asking, or chose to ignore my question. "Well, they gave us each one phone call right after they brought us here, and I tried to call Dad, but all I got was his answering machine. So they let me call you." She took a deep breath. "Mom, do you think you could come downtown to the jail?"

"I'll be there as soon as I can," I said. "What do you mean, after they brought *us* here. Who's *us?*"

"Me and Chris."

"You and Chris?" I said. My head was spinning. "Both of you got arrested? What for? Did Hank take you in?"

Inside, I was already starting to seethe. Could the man have told me not to worry, and then turned around and arrested Ellie? If that was so, I believe I might make use of a quote often attributed to Queen Victoria: *We are not amused.*

"We didn't do anything. Not really. And Hank didn't arrest us. It was the other guy."

Bare? That idiot had arrested my daughter?

Ellie was hurrying on. "Look, Mom, I'll explain every-thing when you get here, OK? They're telling me to speed it up, so I've got to go. See you soon?" Her voice sounded a little tremulous now that she was getting off the phone.

"Sure thing, sweetheart," I said. "I'll be right there."

After I hung up, my mouth was so dry, I could hardly talk. While I tried to explain to Nan that Ellie and her friend, Chris, had apparently been arrested for not doing anything, I got the phone book out. I'd just told Ellie I'd come down-town to the jail, and I had no idea where it was. I'd been to the police station before, but I wasn't sure the Jefferson County Jail was even in the same building.

I flipped to the blue section of the phone book, to the part headed *Louisville Government,* feeling woefully inadequate. Somehow, I was pretty sure that Ma Barker had probably never had to look up the address of the jail in the phone book after one of her kids got arrested.

"What am I supposed to do now?" I asked Nan. "Am I

supposed to bail Ellie out? Will we need to make bail? Should I call an attorney? Where the hell is the jail?"

Nan put her hand on my shoulder. "Before you start calling in Perry Mason, let's find out what's going on, OK? We don't even know what she's been charged with."

I found *Jail—Jefferson County* between *International Offices* and *Jefferson County Memorial Forest.* The address was 600 W. Jefferson Street. Not really terribly close to the Police Department.

Thank God, Nan did the driving. Otherwise, there'd have been several pedestrians bouncing off our fender. About halfway down I-65, I thought of something. "Do you think this could be about that Haggerty guy's death?"

Nan glanced over at me, giving me a look that said she'd thought of that roughly two seconds after Ellie had called.

"Oh dear," I said. "Oh dear, oh dear, oh dear."

Nan raised a hand. "Quit with the *oh dears*, OK? You're making it sound as if Ellie is being held in a Turkish prison. She's in the Jefferson County Jail, for God's sake. We'll get her out tonight, by posting bail or whatever, and it will all be behind us. No biggie."

I stared at Nan. *No biggie?* Could it be that my daughter had more in common with my twin sister than she did with me? Genetically, Nan and I were supposed to be exactly the same, so technically, Nan really could be as much Ellie's mom as I was.

I took a deep breath, trying to calm down. I think I did pretty well, too. I was hardly shaking at all anymore as we pulled up in front of the large, asymmetrical, gray stone building at Sixth and Jefferson.

It being Sunday, there were several empty parking spaces across from the building, and Nan pulled into one.

For a moment, we just sat there, looking at the building across the way.

The downtown Louisville jail is most definitely not a Turkish prison.

Unfortunately, that's about the only positive thing you can say about it. It is housed in a truly ugly building that takes up the entire block between Jefferson and Liberty Streets. That's right. Some of the windows in the jail actually look out on Liberty Street. And they say that people in law enforcement don't have a sense of humor.

It was almost six by the time we arrived. The dimly lit first floor looked forbidding. Nan and I decided to head for the place with the brightest lighting and what seemed like the most people milling around—the basement.

Going through the glass double doors at the bottom of the steps was a lot like entering a bus terminal. There were rows and rows of scarred, black plastic chairs anchored to the floor. Lining the walls was a variety of vending machines offering such treats as cans of Coke and Diet Pepsi for a dollar, miniature bags of potato chips for seventy-five cents, and ice-cream bars for a dollar and a half. I suppose the thinking here was: People hanging around the jail probably are accustomed to extortion anyway.

Some of the people sitting in the chairs looked as if maybe they'd been delivered with the chairs. One old guy had fallen asleep with his head thrown back and his mouth open. It was my guess that, in and around Open Mouth and a couple of the others, cobwebs were starting to form.

Nan and I would probably have ended up sitting on the scarred black chairs, next to the others, except that the bald cop behind the desk on our left recognized us as soon as we walked in. "Well, hi!" he said. "Hank told me to watch for you. You remember me, don't you? I remember you from the picnic."

He was looking straight at me, but I don't think that was because he could tell me from Nan. I think he was looking at me because I just happened to be the one who'd come in the door first. I smiled at Baldy, just like I recognized him, but I was pretty sure I'd never seen him before in my life. I also knew, from looking at the glazed expression on her face, that Nan didn't remember him any more than I did. I'd been to a couple of picnic-type functions with Hank, but this guy sure didn't ring a bell. Fat, bald, with startlingly piercing blue eyes. I wanted to ask him how long ago that picnic had been—to gauge whether it might've been Nan who'd been dating Hank back then, or if it really had been me and my memory was shot—but the guy hurried on. "Hank's tied up, but he told me to send Bert back when you two got here." His glance had wandered to Nan when he said this last. After that, his eyes started doing the twin-bounce, going from one of us to the other and back again. "Boy. You two really do look alike."

I stepped forward. "I'm Bert," I said. "Can Nan come back with me, too?"

Baldy was already shaking his head before I'd even finished. "Nope, just the mom."

Nan did not look delighted.

Baldy picked up a phone, mumbled a few words, then directed me to a narrow hallway on my left, indicating a room all the way down at the end. Walking down there without Nan at my side was not something I particularly relished, but I knew that Nan was watching me as I walked off. Sometimes, I really would like her to think that I have some guts.

Even if she's mistaken.

As I walked down the corridor toward the room where I was to meet Ellie, a tall policeman with a prisoner in tow passed me. Without even thinking, I averted my eyes, as if actually seeing somebody under arrest would be like seeing somebody in a state of undress. An invasion of privacy.

"Aren't you Ellie's mom?"

I jumped at the sound, and looked over, half-expecting the speaker to be the policeman. It wasn't.

It was the *prisoner*. The tall cop with him had stopped to talk in low tones with a female cop. The two policemen seemed not at all concerned that the prisoner was talking to me, but I had the feeling that both of them were listening to every word, even as they spoke to each other.

"I'm Eleanor Tatum's mother," I said.

"Hi, I'm Chris Mulholland." He extended a hand to me, but his handcuffs kept him from reaching very far. He gave me a sheepish grin, and shrugged, as if only slightly embarrassed by his predicament. "I've been hoping we'd finally meet"—he began, and then shrugged again—"not like this, of course—"

I didn't know what to say. *Nice to meet you* seemed a little too enthusiastic under the circumstances. Unable to think of something more appropriate, however, I found myself just staring at Chris in silence. No wonder Ellie was smitten. He really was quite good-looking: tall, over six feet, with an athletic build and guileless, clear blue eyes. As he spoke, a shock of sun-streaked blond hair fell into his eyes. He tried to brush it away and was again hampered by the cuffs.

"Look, is Ellie okay?" Chris asked. "I'm really sorry I got her into all this—"

"We need to move along." The tall policeman had finished his conversation and was now tugging on Chris's arm.

"Tell Ellie it'll be all right," Chris said, as he moved past me. "Tell her there's nothing to worry about, OK?" he called to me over his shoulder.

It took me a little while to pass on the message. In fact, I must've sat in the little room I'd been directed to, at a battered oak table, staring at the dirty walls painted institutional green, for a good fifteen minutes before the door finally opened. I'd thought Hank was going to be meeting me, but it was Ellie who walked in. I almost cried when I saw her, but a female cop with a meaty jaw, who looked as if she'd probably had a couple of women my size for supper and was perhaps now in the mood for a snack—followed Ellie in, positioning herself next to the door. If I'd discovered that this woman's name was something like Gorilla, I wouldn't have been surprised. Crying suddenly didn't seem like all that good an idea. I was pretty sure I'd read somewhere that it was better not to show any sign of weakness in the presence of wild animals.

Giving Ellie a big hug apparently wasn't a good idea, either. I started toward Ellie, but Gorilla shook her massive head and waved me back toward the chair I'd been sitting in.

It was kind of irritating. Did Louisville's Finest actually think that I might slip Ellie a metal file or something so that she could go to town on the bars of her cell? Did they believe that I was going to sneak her in some drugs? I mean, good Lord, look at me. As a criminal, I was pathetic.

No matter what the police thought, I ended up just patting Ellie on the shoulder as we both sat down at the table. The woman cop glowered.

"Boy, Mom, am I glad to see you!" Ellie said. For a brief moment, I thought I saw tears shining in her eyes. She glanced toward Gorilla, however, and blinked them away.

"Oh, sweetheart," was all I could say for a minute, as I continued to weakly pat Ellie's shoulder. Clearing my throat, I said, "OK, now, tell me what happened." I leaned toward Ellie as she began to talk.

"Oh, Mom, it's just so unfair!" Ellie said. "They've arrested Chris—just because he talked with that Haggerty guy!"

I frowned. So far she herself had been arrested for doing nothing. And Chris was in jail for talking. If I didn't know better, I'd think the Louisville police had some kind of quota to meet.

"Yes, I just saw—" I started to say.

"I mean," Ellie went on, cutting me off, "just because a few people saw Chris talking to Haggerty early this morning and then—out of the blue—this jerk shows up dead, they think Chris killed him. It's just ridiculous!"

It *was* hard to believe that the guy I'd just met could've committed murder. I needed, however, for Ellie to cut to the chase. "Ellie, why are *you* here?" I asked.

Ellie was shaking her head. "Those stupid cops came to Chris's booth, and, sure, he's going to be nervous. So what if he denies talking to Haggerty—and then some people say they saw them together. It doesn't mean he killed him! It just means he was nervous, and—"

"He denied talking to Haggerty, huh?"

Ellie ran her hand through her blond bangs. "Well, yeah, and there was some screaming and yelling between them, too—but it was all Haggerty, being a jackass—"

I couldn't help interrupting. "Sweetheart, calling a dead man a jackass is probably not good."

Ellie rolled her eyes. "Anyway, once he started getting yelled at, of *course* Chris pushed the guy. Anybody would. You know how mad Haggerty can make you. Shaking his cane at you and screaming bloody murder."

I stared at her pointedly, but Ellie didn't see the connection.

She went blithely on. "But for the police to actually think Chris shot that fat old jerk. Why, it's just so stupid!"

I lifted a forefinger. "Referring to a murder victim as a *fat old jerk* is probably not good, either," I said.

Ellie rolled her eyes again. "Mom," she said, "I have enough to worry about without having to make sure I'm being polite!"

I took a deep breath. My daughter can be so exasperating sometimes. "Ellie, I wasn't worried about your being polite. I was worried about your saying such things in jail. Where people can hear you." I glanced pointedly over at Gorilla by the door. Her eyes were closed, but I had a feeling she was memorizing every word.

Ellie followed my gaze. "Oh," she said. "Yeah."

"So why are you here?" I asked yet again.

"Well, if everybody had just kept their stupid mouths shut, the cops wouldn't have thought a thing about it. But the people at the flea market made it sound as if Chris could've actually done it! We've got to help him, Mom—we really do—"

"Ellie, why are *you* here?" I didn't want to sound unsympathetic with regard to Chris and his plight, but the truth was, I was a bit more concerned with Ellie's plight at the moment.

"Poor Chris," Ellie went on, "he's got nobody to look out for him. His parents are dead, and his sister hates his guts—she'll just sit still and let Chris go to prison for the rest of—"

"ELLIE!"

Ellie blinked and looked at me. "What?"

"Why are *you* here?"

She looked at me as if I'd just asked the most nonsensical question. "Mom, I got arrested."

Apparently, I needed to spell it out for her. "What is the charge?"

Ellie shrugged again, but I noticed her gaze dropped to the scarred wood of the oak tabletop as she replied. "Well, I think it's assault."

I gasped. *"Assault?* You assaulted someone?"

"Well, they were being so rough with Chris, treating him like a common criminal. And, Mom, he hadn't done anything to deserve it. They shouldn't even have taken him in for questioning. It's just really so incredibly stupid!"

Light was beginning to dawn; and it didn't look pretty. "Ellie, whom exactly did you assault?"

She shrugged. "I didn't assault anybody. All I did was kick this guy."

"This guy?" I prodded.

Ellie shrugged. "This, um, *cop.*"

Oh dear God.

"I didn't even kick him hard. And he charges me with assault—can you believe it? As if maybe I'd hit him with a baseball bat or something." She rolled her big blue eyes again. "I mean, really, what a crybaby!"

I shifted position in my chair. "Ellie, hon, you didn't happen to mention to him that he was a—"

Ellie lifted her chin defiantly. "I most certainly did. As soon as I kicked him, that idiot cop said that he could arrest me for assault, and I told him right then that he was a big, fat crybaby!"

Oh dear God in heaven.

Over the course of my children's lives, I've been making a mental list of Things I Never Thought I'd Have To Tell My Kids. Heading the list was: *Don't throw your shoes at the TV.* That one, I believe, is pretty self-explanatory. Also appearing pretty high on the list was: *Don't carry fire through the house.* This one I'd added one winter when seven-year-old Brian was so delighted to find out how easily a twig off the maple tree in our front yard could catch fire in the fireplace that he'd decided to run upstairs to show it to Ellie.

And now, I had something else to add to the list—something that should, no doubt, head the list: *Don't ever call a cop a crybaby.*

Ellie was rolling her eyes yet again. "Can you believe that cop arrested me for assault? I mean, is that the most preposterous thing you've ever heard?"

I just looked at her. I didn't want to say it out loud, but the fact was, oh my yes, I could believe it. What would've been hard to believe is if he had not arrested her.

I nodded my head, though. "Preposterous," I repeated. "Simply preposterous."

"Cops are such idiots," Ellie said. She ran her hand through her straight blond hair, and added, "Oh, I'm sorry, Mom. I didn't mean to say anything bad about somebody you're dating."

I nodded. "No problem," I said. I had a few bad things to say about him myself.

"Chris is really a neat guy," Ellie went on. "Wait until you meet him. You'll see."

"I have met him," I said. "Briefly, just outside in the hall. And, yes, he did seem like a nice person. Very concerned about you. He said to tell you to everything's going to be OK."

Ellie's reaction to Chris's reassurance was puzzling. Instead of smiling, she frowned. She stared at me for a couple of seconds, still frowning, then asked, "Mom, some-times, don't you think, the police can get sidetracked awfully easily? And can end up going after the wrong person?"

I thought about that for a moment. "Sure, I suppose that could happen." I wasn't sure what she was getting at. She'd just told me that she'd kicked the cop, so it looked to me as if, in this instance, they'd apprehended the right person.

Ellie nodded. "That's what I thought."

"In your case, though, I think they'll probably just release you later tonight on your own recognizance. Since what you did was a pretty minor offense. I really think—"

I stopped here, and just looked at Ellie. She was obvi-ously not listening to me. She wasn't even looking at me, anymore. She was just sitting there, staring at the top of the table between us, going over something in her mind. There was now something in her eyes I couldn't identify. Fear? Anger? Determination? I wasn't sure what it was, but I did know one thing.

It made my stomach hurt.

Chapter 5

•

Nan

I know I told Bert that the Jefferson County Jail was not so bad, but after spending about thirty seconds tops sitting on one of the hard, black plastic chairs thoughtfully provided for visitors, I realized something.

I'd lied.

Turkish prisons could actually beat out the Jefferson County Jail.

To begin with, the place stank. Literally. Turkish prisons probably smelled of exotic oils. The Jefferson County Jail smelled mainly of Lysol, an odor I can't say I've ever really liked. Beneath that dominant bad odor, there were even worse smells: urine, sweat, and, oh yes, that all-time favorite, vomit. If *Eau de County Jail* could be bottled, it could no doubt be used quite effectively in crime-prevention programs. Just one spray would be a major deterrent.

If the odor wasn't deterrent enough, you could throw in a couple of pictures of the place. The linoleum floor looked as if maybe, at one time, it had actually had a color, but after countless scrubbings, whatever shade it used to be had been reduced to a yellowed gray. The walls were the color of oatmeal, and like oatmeal, they had lumps. Patches were scattered here and there, which some enterprising soul had not bothered to smooth over. It made you wonder what had happened to the wall that would've required patching. Had somebody tried to kick their way out of here? Had they had a whiff of *Eau de Jail* and passed out, falling into the wall? Had a head been slammed into the uneven surface?

Some of the people around me certainly looked as if their heads might've been among those that had been bounced off the wall. Some of them looked as if it had happened more than once. Particularly the teenager with her hair in green-tipped spikes who couldn't seem to sit still. She got up and wandered past me again and again, humming to herself. I found myself actually hoping she was high on something, because if this was the way she acted normally, I was scared.

Also wandering around the room was an elderly geezer dressed in faded overalls, a stained undershirt, and flip-flops. Watching him stop every once in a while, and puke his guts into the nearest garbage can, narrowly missing the bib of his overalls—and, a couple of times, the tips of my Reeboks—was an adventure in itself.

I also couldn't help but notice the painfully thin woman with the swollen lip and the black eye who'd evidently brought clothes to whomever she'd come to see. From the nervous conversation she engaged in with the bald cop behind the desk next to me, I gleaned that the jailee under discussion was the woman's boyfriend. He was also, without a doubt, the guy who'd left behind the lovely tokens of his affection on her eye and lip. I decided he had to be the one when I heard the woman vehemently denying it to the desk cop. "I fell—that's how I got this. I fell down, that's all! Jimmy wouldn't never lay a hand on me. He ain't that sort."

Uh-huh.

I actually thought about grabbing the woman by her

skinny shoulders and shouting right in her face: "THINK!"
It would probably only scare her, though, and, Lord knows,
she looked scared enough. Also, thinking might not be her
strong suit.

There were about ten or twelve other people in the room,
but I tried not to stare at anybody. Mainly because there's
a saying I dimly recall that goes something like this: *When
you look into the abyss, the abyss looks back at you.* In
this case, the abyss was not only looking at me—it was
apparently trying to figure out how to steal my purse.

I noticed that both the spiked-hair teen and the elderly
drunk kept giving my Dooney & Bourke shoulder bag piercing stares. It was a purse I'd foolishly spent far too much
money on, so I was really in no mood to have the thing
snatched from me. I picked my purse up off the floor, looped
its strap across my shoulder, and put it on my lap.

I would have moved closer to the desk where the bald
cop was sitting, but I was already sitting in the chair closest
to him. Any closer, and I would've had to sit on his lap.
Which wasn't all that attractive a proposition. Have I mentioned that the bald cop at the desk had a double chin, a
beer belly, and a Robert De Niro mole on his left cheek?
Only I don't recall that De Niro had a big black hair growing
out of his.

As time went by, the desk cop managed to talk to just
about everybody there. He didn't start any of the conversa-
tions, but eventually, every single person in the room had
wandered up, and from what I could gather, pretty much
asked him the exact same thing and gotten the exact same
answer: Nobody can see anybody under arrest until they're
arraigned, and that happens upstairs, in the Hall of Justice.
If they are going to be released tonight, they will be exiting

the building upstairs. Visitors could go upstairs to one of the windows and check on the current status of anyone arrested.

I could be wrong, but it sounded to me as if "upstairs" was a recurring theme. It also sounded to me as if the desk cop was telling everybody that they were waiting on the wrong floor. In spite of being told this, however, nobody left. The fact that everybody would choose to stay down here, after being encouraged to go elsewhere, made me begin to fear for conditions upstairs.

Eventually, Desk Cop must've figured out that the only person he hadn't yet talked to was little ol' me. He got up, scratched the top of his bald head, and then sauntered over. "So," he said, "you're a twin, huh?"

I guess, considering the circumstances, it was a better conversation opener than: *Come here often?*

"I'm a twin, all right," I said. I tried to smile. I also tried not to look at that big black hair.

He grinned at me, looking me up and down. "Is that right?"

My smile felt pasted on. Oh, yes, this had all the earmarks of being hit on. "I kid you not," I said.

Desk Cop stuck out his hand. "I'm Ralph."

Usually, when somebody comes over to introduce himself, and I am definitely not interested, I give him a fake name. I was just about to say, "Glad to meet you. I'm Myrna," when I realized that this would not do. For one thing, this guy was a cop. Not exactly a good person to give a fake identity to. For another thing, he knew Hank. We may not have dated very long, but I believe Hank would remember that my name has never been Myrna.

I shook Ralph's hand. "I'm Nan," I said.

Ralph's hand was a little sweaty. I resisted the urge to wipe my hand on my jeans as Ralph said, "You're the one on the radio, huh?"

I nodded. I sort of expected him to start asking me about what it was like to be a disc jockey, which is what most people ask me, but Ralph had other things on his mind.

"You know," he said, "me and the guys can't get over Hank. Dating *twins*." He was grinning now, his eyes almost closing with the effort. "We never would've thought that Hank had it in him," Ralph said. "That sly dog."

He appeared to be laboring under a misconception. I hated to burst his bubble, but as I mentioned before, you shouldn't lie to a cop. "You know, Ralph, Hank didn't date both of us at the same time. He first dated me, and then— after he and I broke up—he started dating my sister."

Why I was explaining all this was beyond me. I probably should have just kept my mouth shut, because now everybody in the room seemed to be staring at me. Except, of course, for the geezer and the teenager. They were still staring at my purse.

"Hank dated you first, huh?" Ralph said. "And then changed his mind."

Once again, I tried to smile.

You could tell that Ralph was adding it all up in his mind. Let me see now: Hank is only dating one twin now, so that's two twins minus one twin. Let me see: carry the one—yep, that leaves just one twin. *This* one twin, as a matter of fact.

Ralph took a step closer, grinning. "I don't know how in the blue blazes Hank could ever have made up his mind between you two beautiful girls."

OK, I don't want to sound ungrateful here, but Bert and I are far from beautiful. We're not even within waving distance of beautiful. Also—and I know I sound a mite picky here—we're not girls. After living almost forty years, if Bert and I have not finally made it to womanhood, there's something very wrong.

I bit back what I might've said under other circumstances, however. You don't really want to be rude to a cop, any more than you want to lie to him. Particularly when jail is only a few steps away. My luck, I'd get arrested for resisting a date.

"You know," I said, "that's exactly what my boyfriend says." This time I had no trouble smiling.

Ralph's round face fell. I knew Hank would probably tell him different, but for right now, the lie had the hoped-for effect. "Well," Ralph said, his eyes kind of darting around, looking for something to say, "you tell your boyfriend he sure is a lucky man." Then he sort of shambled on back to his desk.

That last had been such a nice thing to say, I almost regretted getting rid of old Ralph. Because once he was gone, there wasn't a whole lot left to break the monotony.

I'd counted all the patches on the wall and about half the floor tiles when Bert finally showed up.

She looked as if she'd just walked a hundred miles.

"Bert, hon," I said, getting to my feet. "Are you OK?"

There are times when I'm grateful that I have escaped motherhood. True, there are not many times—especially since here lately it looks as if the escape might be permanent—but this was definitely one of them.

"Oh, yeah, I'm fine," Bert said, but her voice sounded distracted.

"And how's our little Public Enemy Number One?" I asked.

Usually, Bert laughs at my weak attempts at humor. This time she didn't. "It's not funny, Nan."

I shrugged. "Come on. It's not like Ellie murdered anybody."

Oh, yes, I actually said that. Out loud and everything.

"So what's the deal?" I went on. "Will she be released tonight?"

Bert filled me in then. I tried not to look proud, but to tell the truth, Ellie sounded sort of gutsy. My baby niece had hauled off and kicked a cop. She was, of course, completely insane, but it had been rather brave of her to do such a thing.

"Well," I said when Bert was through, "she didn't really hurt anybody. They're probably just going to scare her really bad, by going through the motions of arresting her, but I can't believe that—"

I stopped talking when I noticed that Bert was clearly not listening. She was staring past my right shoulder, frowning. "Oh, God," she muttered, "this is all I need."

I turned around to see what Bert needed, and lo and behold it was Jake Powell, Bert's ex, coming through the front double doors. A few months ago, he'd been wearing blue jeans, silver-tipped boots, a plaid shirt, and a feather earring. Bert had started calling him Tex behind his back.

Today, in a gray suit, a collarless shirt, and no tie, Jake looked more like Tom Cruise in *Rain Man*. Jake's hair was no longer pulled back into a ponytail—it was cut far too short for that now. It was, however, still combed straight back, in a style a lot of men seem to like these days. I've never seen one guy that this style looked good on, and Jake was no exception. It didn't help that he evidently managed to keep his hair combed straight back, pretty much defying gravity, by combing something through it that made it look distinctly greasy. Staring at him, I couldn't help but think of the Exxon *Valdez*.

Jake had made another change, too. He'd traded the feather earring for a diamond stud. It was sparkling in the dim light as he nodded hello to me and then looked at his ex-wife. "Bert, what in the world is going on? Is Ellie all right?"

While Bert filled Jake in on Ellie's crime spree, I watched the two of them. Body language is an interesting thing. Every time Jake leaned toward her, Bert leaned away, putting as much distance between her and him as she possibly could without moving her feet. Every time she did this, Bert sort of ducked her head, as if she were apologizing for the snub.

Whether Bert knows it or not, she feels a lot of guilt about Jake. After all, these days he appears to be eager to get the two of them reunited in the bonds of holy matrimony, and now it's Bert who's doing the balking. I know Bert sometimes feels as if she's the philanderer—not Jake.

Of course, that's exactly how Jake wants Bert to feel. He wants her to totally forget about the twentysomething secretary he took off with. Or the way, after Twentysomething had dumped him for a younger guy with a bigger paycheck, he'd actually tried to get Bert and me to join him in a threesome. I believe the quaint phrase he'd used was: ménage a trois.

To use a phrase popularized by Bugs Bunny, *What a maroon.*

What was amazing to me was that Jake had the audacity to show up and try to get Bert to forget any of it. Let alone, try to get her back. You'd think he'd be content simply to feel grateful that she hadn't shot him. Bert's face now looked drawn as she finished telling Jake about Ellie's predicament.

"Look, Bert, I'll go see if I can talk to the court clerk about bail right now," Jake said, patting Bert's hand.

Not too long ago, Jake would've had to go talk to a bail bondsman, but there's been a change in Kentucky statutes recently. I recalled the news story about it that aired on WCKI. Kentucky lawmakers had decided that posting bonds was sleazy and that it should be against the law for a private person to profit from such a thing—effectively wiping out the businesses of bail bondsmen across the commonwealth. Those same Kentucky lawmakers, however, must've thought that it was perfectly all right for the courts to be sleazy and make a buck or two off bail bonding, because they decided that the whole thing could be handled by a court clerk.

Jake smiled at Bert. "I'll see the clerk and have Ellie out in a jiffy."

Really. He actually said *jiffy*.

If Jake had expected Bert to clasp her hands together and murmur, *My hero*, he was sadly disappointed. "I don't know, Jake," she said. "I'm not sure the court clerk is available on a Sunday. Even if the clerk's office is open, it'll take hours. Ellie's going to be in that awful holding tank all night."

Jake held up his hand. "Now don't be jumping to conclu—"

Bert interrupted. "According to Ellie, she has to have a hearing and the bail set or the charges dismissed or the fine levied or whatever the judge hearing her case decides to do. And they only call the judge in every few hours. So it probably won't be until tomorrow morning before her case is even heard. She's going to be in this awful place forever." Bert's eyes began to fill with tears.

I put my arm around Bert's shoulders, before Jake could think to do it. "Hon, try not to worry, OK?" I said. It was a dumb thing to say, but hey, it was the best I could come up with on short notice.

"Yeah," Jake said, moving closer to Bert. He looked as if he'd really like to put his own arm around her, but I'd clearly gotten there before him. "It's going to be fine—it's just a little assault charge. Practically nothing."

"Nothing?" The voice was deep, male, and unmistakably irritated. None of us had heard Hank Goetzmann walk up behind us. He'd apparently walked out of the lockup area, down the same hall Bert had just traveled.

I stared at Goetzmann. My goodness, he looked terrible. He had circles under his eyes, and his shoulders were stooped with fatigue.

Although he answered Jake, his eyes traveled almost immediately to Bert. "I'd hardly call assaulting a police officer nothing. And now, well, it's gotten—"

"Excuse me?" Jake frowned. "Goetzmann, you're not actually trying to tell me that Ellie really assaulted an officer, are you? She kicked the guy in the shins! I hardly think that's an assault!"

Goetzmann stared at him for a long moment. "I'm not trying to tell you anything, Powell."

Isn't it cute how, when men can't stand each other, they only call each other by their last names?

Goetzmann was now turning to Bert. "I just talked to Ellie about the death of Franklin Haggerty, and I think you need to know that—"

Jake's frown deepened. "Excuse me, Goetzmann, but I believe I was talking. Now, I demand, as Ellie's father, that she be released immediately!"

Goetzmann turned to stare at Jake again for another long, long moment, then turned back to Bert. "As I was saying, Ellie has just told me something that—"

It was Bert who interrupted him this time. "Hank, why can't Ellie be released right now? Like Jake says," Bert said, her voice a little higher than normal. "You know as well as I do that this whole thing about her committing an assault is ridiculous," she added.

Goetzmann suddenly looked as if she'd slapped him. He took a deep breath and seemed about to say something. Before he could speak, though, Jake had moved to stand right next to Bert.

"I know you don't have kids of your own," Jake said, "but surely you can sympathize with the way we, as Ellie's parents, feel."

I had to hand it to him. In a single sentence, he'd grouped himself and Bert together and excluded Hank. Hey, I didn't call him Jake the Snake for nothing.

Bert reached out and put a hand on Goetzmann's arm. "You can do it, Hank. Please. Just tell that policeman Ellie kicked to drop the charges."

Goetzmann just shook his head, his eyes miserable. "Bert, I'm sorry but—"

Bert rushed on, her voice quavering a little. "Please, Hank. Ellie shouldn't have to spend the night in jail just because she lost her temper. Please let her go, Hank."

Goetzmann heaved a ragged sigh. "That's just not possible."

"Of course, it's possible," Bert said. She was beginning to sound angry. "You can talk to the police officer. You can tell him that she didn't mean anything." She paused, her eyes filling with tears again. "Please, Hank."

The unspoken phrase *for me* hung in the air. *Do it for me.* Hank looked sick.

After dating him, I never thought I'd ever feel this way, but I actually felt sorry for the guy. Goetzmann appeared to be caught between a rock and a hard place.

"Yeah, Goetzmann," Jake prodded. "You could do it if you really wanted to."

Goetzmann shook his head, his eyes still fixed on Bert. "OK, listen to me. I've been trying to tell you. That friend of Ellie's. Chris Mulholland? He was seen by several of the other antique dealers arriving at the fairgrounds for the show this morning. They saw Mulholland quarreling with the dead man, shortly before Haggerty was found shot to death, lying by his van. When we came to take Chris to headquarters for questioning, Ellie was with him, and she objected violently to the idea of Chris going to jail—to say the least. She insisted over and over that Chris couldn't have done it. That's when she kicked one of the police officers who was with me right in the shins—when he was taking Chris in for questioning about the murder. So we had no choice. We had to take her in, too."

"Goetzmann, we know all that," Jake interrupted. "So Ellie kicked a cop. Big deal. This is where you get our little girl a Get-Out-of-Jail-Free card." Jake managed to put an arm around Bert this time, his arm resting heavily on top of mine. "That is," Jake added, "if you really care anything about this family."

The challenge was not lost on Goetzmann. He took a step toward Jake, clenching and unclenching his fists. For a minute there, I really thought he was going to slug Jake right in the mouth, something which I personally would've paid good money to see. Then Goetzmann took a deep breath, opened his fists, and turned back to Bert. He took both her hands in his, something that was kind of difficult since both Jake and I were holding on to her. Still, Goetzmann managed.

"Bert, I can't do anything to get Ellie out of jail right now—and, believe me, I would if I could. But it's not that simple anymore. As of now, it's not going to be possible to bail Ellie out until her arraignment. And maybe not even then."

"What?" Bert's voice was just a whisper. Then she slowly pulled her hands out of his.

Goetzmann ran his hand over his eyes and looked back at Bert. I realized then that what I'd taken for fatigue in Goetzmann's face wasn't that, at all. It was, instead, worry.

"That's what I've been trying to tell you," Goetzmann said.

"Tell me what?" Bert asked. Under my arm, I could feel her shoulders tense.

"Ellie just confessed to the murder of Franklin Haggerty."

Chapter 6

●

Bert

My daughter does not kill people.

This is the first thing that went through my mind as I stood there, trying to make sense of what Hank had just said.

My daughter does not kill people.

I couldn't believe I was even thinking the words. You shouldn't ever have to think such a thing. It was just a given. A self-evident truth. My little girl didn't have it in her to take another person's life. This is, after all, the kid who cried all afternoon because she accidentally stepped on a frog in the yard. That day I'd told her again and again that the frog she'd killed had gone to frog heaven and was now happily playing leapfrog with all the other frog angels, and still Ellie had cried for hours. *Hours.*

Hank was now staring at me, his eyes worried, no doubt expecting me to say something, and all I could think of was frog angels.

It was laughable.

I looked over at Nan. One of the great things about having an identical twin sister who has shared so many things in your life is that if something awful happens, and your twin is not there to witness it, it doesn't seem quite so real. The day my divorce was final, I'd stood alone in front of the judge, and I'd thought, *This isn't really happening. Nan isn't seeing this, or hearing this, or feeling this. It's not really real.*

Standing next to me now, Nan looked as if she was in pain. She met my gaze, and her arm tightened a little around my shoulders.

Oh God. She was here. She was reacting to it. So it must have really happened. My little girl had actually told somebody out loud that she'd killed a man.

The horror of it was almost too much to grasp.

I heard Jake's voice as if from a distance. Which was pretty odd all by itself since he was standing right there. No surprise, Jake was behaving the way he always did when he was upset—he was yelling at the top of his lungs.

"Are you *nuts?*" Jake bellowed, waving his arms around like a madman. "Do you really think Ellie could murder somebody?"

Jake seemed to have forgotten that we were all standing in front of the double doors of the basement of the Hall of Justice, and there were quite a few people around us. When Jake started yelling, several of the people near us turned to stare. A sad-looking teenage girl with green spiked hair and big, bright eyes moved a little closer, no doubt to hear better. The poor thing looked as if she needed a good meal.

I knew, of course, why I was even thinking about this teenager, why I was looking around, instead of concentrating solely on what Hank and Jake were saying. I was trying to get some distance. I needed to step away, for just a second, from the awfulness of the moment so that I could think.

"Are you totally out of your mind? Ellie is not a killer!" Jake yelled.

A muscle jumped in Hank's jaw. "Powell, you'd better lower your voice."

Hank said this very quietly, with no emphasis at all. I stared at him. His eyes were dark with fury. So this was how Hank behaved when he was angry. Unlike Jake, who got louder and louder, Hank got very, very quiet.

I wasn't sure which was worse.

Hank's quiet was unnerving. Even Jake must've been a little rattled by it, because Jake did something then that he'd never done in all the years we'd been married. He actually lowered his voice. "Look, Goetzmann," Jake said barely above a whisper. I was amazed. Of course, Hank did have a gun. Maybe that's what I'd needed all those years. "All I'm saying is that Ellie could not possibly have shot anybody," Jake went on. "There's no way she could hurt a fly."

At least, Jake was saying something I agreed with. "Jake is right, Hank—"

"Ellie won't even kill bugs in the house," Nan said, interrupting me. "She scoops them up in a Kleenex, and deposits them outside."

This was true. Ellie wouldn't even spray insects with Raid, for God's sake. She called it "cruel and unusual punishment."

Hank nodded, as if to acknowledge that he had indeed heard what had been said, but what he was going to say was already written on his face before he even said it. "None of this matters—"

OK, it was at this point that I got a little angry myself. "What do you mean, none of this matters? Of course, it matters! It means that Ellie is lying!" I heard myself say this, and I couldn't believe it. I never thought I'd ever be trying to convince somebody that my daughter is a liar.

"She didn't do this, Hank," I said. "You've got the wrong person behind bars, and you need to be looking for the right one."

Hank was very quiet for a long, long moment. If anything, his eyes had gotten darker. "Bert," he finally said, "I don't need to be told how to do my job."

I stared right back at him. "Apparently you do if you believe Ellie's ridiculous story."

Hank was quiet again for what seemed like an interminable moment.

I shifted my weight from one foot to the other. This silent treatment could get really old, really fast.

"Ellie's story," Hank finally said, his voice so calm he could've been giving us financial advice, "is not all that ridiculous. It's very believable. She's claiming self-defense. She says that she went to talk to Haggerty after her boyfriend Chris Mulholland met her at his booth at the flea market. According to her, Mulholland had just spoken with Haggerty. Ellie says she wanted to talk to Haggerty because Mulholland was so upset."

"Did you ever stop to think," Jake interrupted, "what this Mulholland guy was so upset about? Maybe he was upset because he'd just killed somebody! That makes sense, doesn't it?"

Hank took almost as long to answer this time as before. By the time he finally spoke, I wanted to shake the words out of him. "Chris was upset, according to Ellie, because Haggerty was threatening to have Chris thrown out of the show. For interfering with the business of another dealer. Haggerty had told Chris that he was going to complain to the directors of the flea market about Chris. Ellie said she went over there because she thought she could talk some sense into Haggerty."

That sounded like Ellie. At her young age, she still thought that a few well-chosen words could fix any problem.

Hank sighed and went on. "Ellie says she found Haggerty still at his van, unloading some boxes of items he was bringing in to sell. He was putting the boxes on a dolly and was not in a mood to talk. She says he started yelling right away, then grabbed his gun. He threatened her with his gun, they struggled, and the gun went off. It hit Haggerty in the chest."

"And she didn't call the police?" I asked.

"Or an ambulance?" Nan added.

Hank sighed again. His sighs were getting almost as annoying as his long silences. "Ellie says she knew right away that Haggerty was dead. She panicked and ran back inside the flea market. She says she tried to act normal the rest of the day while she waited for Haggerty's body to be discovered."

Hank was right. Ellie's story was believable.

I just didn't happen to believe it.

"Goetzmann," Nan asked, "do *you* think that Ellie is telling the truth?"

Hank ran his hand through his hair. "I don't know what to believe. It's true there are some gaps in her story. And what she's told us corresponds to what she could've heard on the news. For instance, Ellie couldn't tell me where Haggerty got the gun in the first place. From his glove compartment, from behind the visor, from the floor, where? She says it was just all at once in his hand."

"See," Jake said, waving his arms again. "*See?* She's just

covering for that Mulholland guy—anybody with half a brain would know that."

Hank ignored that last. As a matter of fact, he ignored Jake altogether. Turning to me, he said, "Although it's true that the things Ellie knows are the same things that were on both the radio and television news, disclosing just those things would be a smart thing to do—if you really did commit the murder. Give out no more details than are public knowledge. That way, you can leave yourself a way out—a way to take it all back, if you want." He studied my face. "I know Ellie's smart. You told me once she'd graduated from high school fifth in her class, and she's making straight A's at UK."

Jake couldn't let that one go by. "Yeah, she's smart— she's smart enough not to kill anyone. She's also smart enough to make up a big lie to try to shield somebody else."

Hank sighed again. It was so annoying, I wanted to slap him. "Hank," I said, "you know Ellie." Even though she'd been at the University of Kentucky for almost the entire time we'd dated, Hank and I had driven to Lexington and taken Ellie and Brian out to dinner a number of times. She'd talked to him endlessly about different cases he'd worked on. She'd laughed at his jokes. And some of them had not been all that funny. "Do you really think she could shoot a man, Hank? The very idea is absurd."

Hank's eyes were miserable. "Bert, in every homicide I've ever worked, there has been somebody who says exactly what you just said. Sometimes it's a relative. Sometimes it's a friend. But they always say that the person under arrest could not possibly have done it. And yet, ninety-nine times out of a hundred the accused has been guilty. You just can't tell what people might do."

I couldn't keep the anger out of my voice. "This isn't every other homicide case you've worked. And it's not just *people*. This is Ellie."

Hank was silent yet again. It was all I could do to keep from screaming at him.

He must've known how angry I was, because when he finally spoke, he looked straight at Jake for once. "Look, I don't know if Ellie is lying or not," Hank said. His voice was infinitely patient, as if explaining something to someone a little slow. "Unfortunately, as a law-enforcement professional, I can't exactly ignore a confession. I can't just let her walk out of here. Surely, all of you can understand that." As Hank said this last, his eyes traveled to mine.

On one level, yes, I certainly did understand it. Hank was just doing his job.

On another level, however—the level where I was Ellie's mother—I didn't understand it at all. Not a bit. My little girl was going to spend tonight—and maybe many more nights—here in this awful place, and Hank was going to let it happen. He could let Ellie go home with me, but he chose not to.

I looked into the eyes of the man I thought I loved and, in that moment, I was sure I hated him. No wonder he'd decided to be a cop. He *enjoyed* pushing people around. He got a kick out of being the guy with the keys. The guy who could lock you up or let you go. And I'd thought Jake was a control freak. Hank could give him lessons.

I should have realized it before. No one but Jake could ever care as much for Ellie and Brian as I do. No one else could care as much as their parents.

My expression must've changed as all this was going through my mind because Hank looked a little taken aback.

He hurried on, not looking at me anymore. In fact, he didn't really look at anybody. He seemed to be staring at a spot on the discolored linoleum. "I do want you to know that we're continuing to investigate this homicide. Ellie's confession hasn't stopped that. We're continuing to talk to Chris Mulholland. And anyone else who had a grudge against the victim." He paused, and then added, "There's something else, too."

"Something else?" Nan asked.

"It may just be coincidence, but evidently while Haggerty was lying dead in the fairgrounds parking lot, the house he owned was being broken into. No one was at home at the time. Nothing seems to have been taken either. Just a simple break-in."

"Nothing was stolen?" Nan repeated.

"Haggerty's wife doesn't think so. Although it's hard to tell she says she really can't be absolutely sure." Hank scratched his head. "Whoever broke in sure left in a hurry— the Haggertys' silent alarm called the cops, who arrived just minutes later. Not much time to take anything. The place is being dusted for fingerprints, as we speak."

If Hank expected me to pat him on the back for the great detective work, he had another think coming. My daughter would still be spending the night in jail.

I took a deep breath. "I'd like to talk to Ellie again," I said, folding my arms across my chest. "And her *father* needs to talk to her with me." I couldn't help but emphasize the word *father*.

Jake looked a little startled that I'd included him in my request. "Why, Bert, that's—" he began.

"And Nan," I went on, interrupting whatever Jake had

been about to say. "I know Nan will also want to talk to Ellie with us."

Nan nodded.

I half expected Hank to refuse. He seemed to be on such a power trip. But he didn't. "The rules are one person at a time, but I'll arrange it. Maybe all of you can gang up on her and make her listen to reason. If Ellie really has confessed to a murder she didn't commit, someone needs to get across to her how stupid a stunt this is. And they'd better convince her pretty damn quick."

Jake squared his shoulders. "We'd like to see her right away." He could've been giving instructions to a man-servant. I half expected him to snap his fingers.

Hank just looked at Jake. He didn't say a word; he just gave him a look as he turned to leave.

It took Hank a little over thirty minutes to arrange things. I suppose it might've really taken that long, but I couldn't help but wonder if Hank had taken his time because Jake had instructed him to do it right away.

Whatever the reason, about a half hour later, Jake, Nan and I were shown into a small room down the hall from the lobby we'd been waiting in. The room had walls the color of butterscotch, a single overhead light with an assortment of dead bugs in the globe, and linoleum not quite as faded as that outside. It smelled like dirty socks. We all sat down at a scarred oak table, and in about ten minutes or so, Ellie walked through the door, accompanied by a short, stout female cop. Ellie looked a little whiter than when I saw her last, but she gave us all a big smile.

I was so glad to see her, I could've cried.

I wanted to give her a hug, but when I moved toward her, the female cop shook her head. "No physical contact," she said. Have I mentioned that the woman was short, fat, and in her uniform, she resembled a navy blue fireplug?

Ellie took a seat at the head of the table.

"Well, I guess I'm going to be here a while, huh?" was the first thing she said.

"Absolutely not," Jake said, his voice booming in the small room. "I'm going to get you the best attorney in Louisville. I know some people, and we're going to get this thing taken care of. Don't you worry."

"How are you doing, sweetheart?" I asked. "Are you OK?"

"I'm fine, Mom."

Nan, true to form, did not bother with the amenities. "So, Ellie, sweetie, why are you protecting Chris? Isn't he a big enough boy to take care of himself?"

Ellie had been smiling, but the smile vanished after that one. "I'm not protecting anybody," she said. "Chris has nothing to do with this."

Over the next half hour, she said that again and again. No matter what anybody said, Ellie continued to insist that she was telling the truth. She'd shot Haggerty in self-defense.

When the fireplug indicated that our visit was over, I let Jake and Nan leave me alone with Ellie.

"OK, nobody's here but you and me," I said. "So I want to ask you one more time, and I want you to tell me the absolute truth." What I really wanted to do was give her a good shaking, and perhaps shake some sense into her. I managed, somehow, to fight the feeling. "Ellie, did you kill that man?"

Ellie looked me straight in the eye, her expression open

and guileless. When she spoke, her words were deliberate and rang with sincerity.

"Mom, I'm so sorry. I really am," she said with a little catch in her voice. "I didn't mean to kill him. It—it just happened."

I nodded, not trusting myself to speak.

The fireplug came up then, and, taking hold of Ellie's arm, she escorted my beautiful daughter back to her cell.

I watched Ellie walk down the hallway, her back straight, her short blond hair bouncing a little as she took each step. At the end of the hallway, she turned back to me, before she rounded the corner. She gave me a shaky little smile, and then she was gone.

It was only then that my eyes welled with tears.

Ellie was her father's daughter—that was for sure. There was not a doubt in my mind that she was lying through her teeth.

Chapter 7

•

Nan

As a person who happens to have the exact same face, I believe I can say with absolute authority that Bert looked awful. When Bert had stayed behind to talk to Ellie alone, I'd known why, of course. It wasn't any strange twin telepathy, either. In fact, I think even Jake knew that Bert wanted to ask Ellie one more time if she really, really, really was telling the truth about shooting Haggerty. What Ellie's answer had been was written all over poor Bert's face as she came down the hall.

I noticed that Goetzmann took one look at Bert as she walked up to us and stood his ground. A very wise move, I might add. When Jake and I had come out of our own little meeting with Ellie a few minutes before, Goetzmann had immediately come up to me and asked just one question. "Any change in Ellie's story?"

Just like a cop.

When I shook my head no, he'd returned to the black plastic chair he'd been sitting in and continued to look down the hall, obviously watching for Bert.

Just like a guy in love.

Goetzmann had not acknowledged Jake in any way, and Jake had returned the favor by silently glaring at Goetzmann's back every few minutes or so.

Just like an idiot.

Deftly dodging the which-man-will-she-speak-to-first question, Bert ignored both Jake and Goetzmann and came straight over to me. She shook her head wearily. "Oh, Nan," Bert said, "what in the world are we going to do?"

Wouldn't you know? The anal-retentive guy in the room took that as something more than a rhetorical question.

"Well, first thing," Goetzmann said, moving to stand next to Bert, "Ellie's going to need an attorney to represent her. Now, I know a couple of very good criminal lawyers who—"

"Hey! I sell insurance, buddy," Jake said, walking over to stand on the other side of Bert, "so I think I know a criminal attorney or two."

Testosterone must've addled Jake's brain. He made it sound as if the insurance business and a life of crime were synonymous. Or could it be that he was just trying to let us know that a number of his clients had brought criminal charges against him? In which case, it seemed like an awful lot to divulge just to make a point.

All three of us just stared at Jake for a long moment.

Goetzmann finally shook his head, and said, "I don't know how to respond to that—"

"You don't have to respond, buddy," Jake said. "I can get my daughter an attorney—without your help. That's all you need to know."

The conversation might've gone even further downhill from there, but fortunately, we were all distracted by the tall, lanky young man who came running in through the double doors.

"Hey," Brian said to no one in particular.

I couldn't help staring. This was a new look. Up to now,

Brian had always showed up in crisply pressed Oxford cloth
shirts, khaki slacks, and shoes so highly polished, you could
see your face in them. I'd always thought he'd been like all
teenagers, rebelling against his dad. Only when Brian had
started rebelling, his dad had been in his Tex Ritter phase,
as I mentioned earlier. Jake's hair had been longer than
mine, his jeans had been so ragged, they'd looked as if they'd
been washed with razor blades, and his feather earring had
been so big, if you didn't look close, you might've thought
some birdlike creature had attacked his ear. Poor Brian had
had no choice. He couldn't dress like his dad, who was at
the time dressing like a teenager. The poor kid had been
forced to rebel by going clean-cut. He'd made IBM represen-
tatives look like sloppy dressers.

Nowadays, with his dad doing Tom Cruise, Brian must've
found it necessary to make a slight adjustment to continue
his rebellious ways. He was now dressed in ragged cutoffs
and a threadbare T-shirt with a faded, full-color illustration
of the *Titanic* on the front. Above the illustration was the
touching sentiment: *THE BOAT SANK. GET OVER IT.*
His tennis shoes had holes in both toes, and both socks were
a discolored gray.

It was Brian's hair, however, that really had me staring.
The last time I'd seen him, he'd worn it neatly trimmed, and
parted on one side. Now there was not enough of it to part.
It had been cut in a style I believe they call a buzz these
days, but back when Bert and I were little, we'd called it a
burr. Buzz or burr, Brian's hair couldn't have been more
than one quarter of a inch long all over his head. I looked
at him and wondered how many people had come up and
asked him how the chemotherapy was going.

"So, what's the deal? Is Ellie getting out tonight or what?" Brian's jaw looked muddy with five o'clock shadow.

Bert and Jake must've seen Brian's new look before, because they barely gave him a glance. Of course, it could be that one reason Bert wasn't looking at Brian was that she was now staring at Jake. "You called Brian?" she said.

Jake nodded. "Of course I did," he said. "When there's a problem with someone in the family, the whole family should help them out." He glanced over at Hank, no doubt to make sure that Hank had gotten the less-than-subtle message: Jake, Brian, Ellie, and Bert were a unit—a unit which did not include Hank.

"That's right," Brian said. "I'm here to help out. So, what's the deal?" Brian has always been laid-back. Once, when he was seven, he'd carried a stick on fire through the house, and when Bert had yelled at him, he hadn't quickened his pace. He'd just sauntered over to the sink, with the thing blazing away only inches from his hand, and turned on the water to douse it. Today, however, he seemed even more laid-back than usual. He actually started to smile right after Jake started filling him in on Ellie's confession.

"Brian." Bert sounded irritated. "This is hardly a laughing matter."

Brian ran his hand over his buzz. "I can't help it. Ellie confessing to murder? That's wild, isn't it? I mean, of all people—"

Talk about fanning the fire. Bert turned to glare at Hank. "Come to think of it, you're right. The idea that Ellie could hurt anybody *is* laughable—"

Off the hook, Brian grinned openly, looking around at the rest of us. "It's a hoot," he said.

"It's ridiculous—that's what it is," Jake put in, staring at Hank.

Hank stared back. "You don't need to tell me that. You need to tell Ellie," he said so quietly it was almost under his breath.

Brian was running his hand over his buzz again. "I don't get it. Why would Ellie confess to something she didn't do?"

That one took some explaining. Bert, Jake, and I all pretty much talked at once, trying to fill Brian in on the unbelievable mess his sister was in. Some time during the confusion of all of us talking at the same time, Goetzmann left us. Out of the corner of my eye, I saw him look for a long moment at Bert before he disappeared down the hall. If Bert noticed, she gave no sign.

When Jake and Brian left to arrange for legal representation for Ellie with one of those numerous criminal attorneys that Jake knew so well, Bert and I headed for my car. After we got inside, we just sat there for a long moment and stared at the windshield.

"Nan, Ellie's got to be lying," Bert finally said. "I just know it."

"No argument here," I said.

"Then we've got to do something to make her tell the truth."

"I guess we can assume that grounding her isn't going to do it," I said. Especially since jail was pretty much the mother of all groundings.

I was trying to lighten Bert's mood, but she acted as if she barely heard me. "Do you think there's a chance, if we go out to the flea market, that we could find someone who saw Haggerty alive after Ellie said she talked to him?" Bert said. "Maybe somebody at that flea market knows something about Haggerty that would point to his killer. Or maybe they saw something this morning."

"Sounds good to me," I said. I did not point out that the police had probably already covered these bases, because I knew Bert needed to feel like she was at least doing *something*. I also knew, of course, that what Bert really hoped to find out was something—anything—that would implicate anybody else other than Ellie.

When we got to the fairgrounds, the flea market had ended about an hour earlier, and the parking lot was emptied of most of the cars. The vans, trucks and station wagons left were probably those of dealers, still taking down their booths.

Kentucky was on daylight saving time, so even though it was pretty late, there was still enough light to see. I wondered if the police had drawn a chalk outline around Haggerty's body as it lay there on the parking-lot pavement. If they had, there was a chance we could find the spot where Haggerty was killed.

I don't know if it was morbid curiosity or just needing to see where Ellie was supposed to have shot Haggerty that made both Bert and me want to see the exact spot.

We found the outline under one of the metal poles that dotted the lot. The outline wasn't chalk, though. It was done in pieces of white tape. Some of the tape had been pulled up, but a lot of it was still there. Maybe the warmth of the pavement had caused the tape to adhere to the surface a little more than usual. The metal pole next to the outline was topped with a sign that read W16, supposedly erected to help people find their cars in the massive parking lot. Providing, of course, that they remembered to look for the closest marker. Judging from my own behavior, that didn't happen much. I preferred the seek-till-you're-weak approach. Looking around, I pictured the lot completely filled with cars.

"It's easy to see how his body could have lain here for a while, undiscovered." I said. "To everyone inside, a gunshot would've sounded like a backfire or something like that."

Inside the Left Wing of the fairgrounds, most of the dealers had just about finished packing up. People hurried past us, pushing dollies filled with taped-up cardboard cartons. As we walked through the massive room, some turkey, who seemed unnaturally enthusiastic for this late in the day, came on the public-announcement system pleading with dealers not to overlook signing up for Kentucky sales-tax numbers, if they didn't already have one.

Oh, sure, that was going to happen. These dealers would be absolutely thrilled to fork over six percent of their proceeds to the Commonwealth of Kentucky. Then the turkey added that failure to have sales-tax numbers on record would prevent them from participating in the flea market next month. I almost smiled. There you go. If at first you don't succeed, try, try a good threat.

Bert and I tracked down the flea-market office down a long corridor on the west side of the fairgrounds building after two botched attempts by dealers to give us directions. To be honest, the botching was not the fault of the dealers. Bert and I are what has been called directionally challenged, a much better word than *flaky*, which has also been applied to us.

Our problem with directions is probably related to our being mirror twins and never quite getting that whole right-left thing down pat. All I've got to say about our problems is this: You start out as one thing, growing along as merrily as you please, and then, out of the blue, turn into two things—one right-handed, one left-handed—and see how well you can tell right from left. I've always figured Bert and I were lucky we could tell up from down.

As we opened the door to the flea-market office, a man seated at a gray metal desk turned toward us. He was about our age, maybe a couple of years younger—it was hard to tell. He had shoulder-length blond hair, a tan George Hamilton would envy, and gorgeous green eyes. Oh my yes, this guy was pretty good-looking, in a Whole Earth sort of way.

Unfortunately, he was also the guy who had told me to be sure to mention the flea market on my radio program. Old Green Eyes himself. Mr. Finesse.

I cringed inwardly, as he flashed his pearly whites and rose to greet us, extending his hand. He'd seen Bert first. "Wow! It's Nan Tatum from WCKI!" he boomed at her, clearly delighted. "It's a pleasure to see you again! I'm Sam Grainger."

From the sound of his voice, I realized that he'd also been the turkey on the P.A. system. Without taking his extended hand, Bert glanced back at me. Courtesy was not going to be her strong suit until we got Ellie out of jail. She frowned at me. "You know this guy?"

"We've met," I said. "Briefly."

About that time, Sam's green eyes had started doing the twin-bounce, looking first at me, then back to Bert, bouncing back and forth. "Wow," he said, "you two really do look alike." Looking at me, he added, "I already knew you were a twin, of course, from listening to your radio program, but—wow!"

If he said *wow* one more time, I might be the second person in the family in jail for murder.

"I'd thought, when we met before, that you were a dealer," I said.

Sam grinned. "Hey, I am! I have a booth here, and I also manage the entire market. Most of the time the managers of flea markets are also dealers. We're just one big, happy family!"

"No kidding," I said, thinking that at least one member of the big, happy family—Franklin Haggerty—wasn't so happy anymore.

At this point, Bert must've decided enough with the small talk. She artfully maneuvered the conversation around to the murdered dealer. "We want to know about Franklin Haggerty," she blurted.

"What's to know?" Sam said. He was still grinning. Cheshire cats had nothing on the man. "Haggerty was a jerk." He gestured to a group of folding chairs, and we all sat down. I couldn't help but notice that he made sure he sat down next to me.

"Did he have any enemies?" Bert asked.

"Wow, he had plenty of enemies," Sam said. "Like I said, he was a jerk."

"Anyone who might want to see him dead?" I asked.

"Wow. I don't know about that," Sam said, running his hand through his blond hair. "*Dead* is kind of a strong word. What's your interest in the guy anyway?" Without waiting for us to answer, he hurried on. "Oh, wait a sec. This is for the news on WCKI, isn't it? Oh, wow. You're not planning to switch to anchoring the news, are you?"

Hell, no, I thought, *and get up at four o'clock in the morning? Why don't I just stick pins in my eyes?* But I just smiled and shrugged my shoulders without answering, trying to give the impression that he'd caught me.

"Oh, wow, I really hope you don't go to news. I enjoy your show, you know. I'm quite a fan."

"Thanks," I said, batting my baby browns at him.

"Why did you let Haggerty have a booth if he was such a jerk?" Bert asked.

Sam seemed a little startled as he turned to look at her. "We didn't have much choice. Sure, there were complaints about Haggerty's temper tantrums, even about some of the deals he made. You know—complaints that his merchandise was falsely represented, that kind of thing. But when we denied him entrance in one of the shows, we got more complaints about that. Apparently, some collectors would deal with the devil himself, just as long as he had what they're looking for."

Sam shook his head as he added, "And Haggerty had the merchandise, too. He found the items they wanted. He had a great memory and went to all the estate sales and was constantly bringing in new items. He scoured the obituaries, just to be first to look at estates in the better parts of Louisville. Even looked at the obits in Chicago, St. Louis, Indianapolis—anywhere he could get to fairly easily."

"A regular ghoul," I commented.

"Hey, ain't we all?" Sam said cheerfully. "When you think about it, antiques by definition had to have been owned by somebody sometime who probably didn't survive the experience."

What could I say? He had a point.

"Could you possibly give us a list of the people who complained about Haggerty?" I asked.

Sam grinned. "Anything for you," he said smoothly. He walked over to his desk, sat down, tore a page off a legal pad, and began to write. I noticed his fountain pen was a

Mont Blanc—a pen that starts at a hundred dollars and goes up. Beanie Babies, T-shirts, and antique toys apparently brought in the big bucks.

Bert was already on her feet. "While you do that, do you mind if we go talk to some of your dealers about Haggerty?"

"Please?" I added. Can you imagine? Me, being the more polite of the Tatum twins—would wonders never cease?

"No problem," Sam said, smiling at me. "I'll have this ready when you get back."

We made the rounds of the tables, finding Haggerty's booth easily as it was the only one that had not been packed up. Lace covers were draped over his merchandise, and two folding chairs blocked the way into the booth.

Talking to the other dealers pretty much yielded nothing. Except that everyone's lips got a little tight as soon as we said Haggerty's name. A couple of people actually grimaced. Haggerty was one unloved guy.

As one gentleman, who was wearing denim overalls and had a huge gap where his front teeth should be, said, "There are some people that just piss other people off. Not that they deserve to be dead, or nothin'. I'm just sayin'."

That pretty much summed up everyone else's thoughts. No one had heard the shot. No one had seen anything out of the ordinary. And no one really missed Haggerty.

When we returned to Grainger's office, there were about a dozen people gathered in the outer office. Sam was standing in front of the group, his hands out, palms up. "Hey, it's not my call," he was saying.

"You told us to come back in a couple of hours," one of the men called out. "So here we are—now what's the word on Haggerty's stuff?"

Sam spotted us in the back of the crowd and motioned

us forward. "I'll be right with you," he said, when we were standing right next to him.

"What's this about?" I asked.

He shrugged with a sheepish grin. "They all want to know what's going to happen to the dead man's inventory—specifically, the unsold items left in his booth. Like I said before, he had a lot of HTF."

"HTF?" I asked.

"Hard-to-find items," Sam said. "Several of these people are dealers from the flea market, and a few are customers who'd apparently been wrangling with Haggerty about buying some of his antiques. Haggerty sometimes came down on his prices—so everyone got a different price. A lot of these folks were still haggling with him right up to when he was killed."

"Ghouls," Bert muttered.

I looked around at the group.

One of the men, his angular jaw jutting out no doubt at the indignity of dealing with commoners, was wearing an ascot. The lady with him was dressed in a crisp white linen suit and carrying a tiny Yorkie puppy in her arms. Another elderly lady wearing a black lace shawl was standing with a man dressed like a chauffeur, right down to the leather-billed cap, knee-high black boots and double-breasted uniform. Several of the other couples were very nicely dressed in what looked to be designer outfits.

Looking at the group, I was a little taken aback. Apparently, ghouls did all right for themselves.

Sam raised his voice, addressing the group. "Okay. I've done some checking and Mrs. Franklin Haggerty—Sheila—is going to take possession of the items left in the booth. Nothing is to be sold without her involvement. And, I've got to level with you, she's probably going to decide to auction the items."

There was an audible groan from the group. One man said, "You mean, you can't honor one of your dealers' commitments—you're the flea-market director, aren't you?"

"Do you have anything from Haggerty in writing?" Sam asked.

"Come on, Grainger. You know that Franklin didn't operate that way."

Sam held up a hand. "Then that's it, guys. You'll need to speak to Mrs. Haggerty about any arrangements you might've had with Franklin. She's the person with whom you'll have to deal."

The man with the ascot spoke quietly. His question pretty much covered what I was thinking.

"Where," he asked with great dignity, "may we find Mrs. Haggerty?"

Chapter 8

●

Bert

The Haggertys turned out to be neighbors of mine and Nan's. They, too, lived in the Highlands, on Willow Avenue, only a few miles from our own Napoleon Boulevard. The Haggerty residence was one of those huge, turn-of-the-century Victorian homes that are always being bought by speculators for a song, renovated, and then sold for outlandish prices. Looking at the house as we drove up, I wondered if Haggerty had been in on the song part or the outlandish price part.

Somebody told me once that the reason this area is known as the Highlands is that this is the only part of Louisville that stayed dry during the infamous 1937 flood, when the Ohio River overflowed its banks and put most of the city underwater. I suspect, though—since there hasn't been a flood like that since—that the reason the name continues to be used is that nowadays it pretty accurately reflects the prices real estate commands around here.

Nan parallel-parked at the curb, and we walked up the sidewalk. Cracks in the foundation of the wraparound front porch were evident as we climbed the steps, and paint was peeling on the molding around the front door. One pane in the stained-glass windows of the front door was missing, but it had been replaced by a piece of cardboard cut to the correct shape.

While Nan rang the doorbell, I just stood there, taking a good look around. This Victorian house didn't look particularly renovated. In fact, it looked as if no money had been spent on upkeep in years. Maybe Haggerty had not been as successful in his antiques business as he would've led people to believe.

I'd expected Sheila Haggerty to look like a woman who'd spent the last twenty years or so living with—if you'll excuse the expression—an asshole. I stood there on her somewhat dilapidated porch, waiting to meet a beaten-down, thin, mousy little woman, with a hunted look in her eyes. Basically, someone who jumped at every sharp sound, who was constantly looking over her shoulder, and who maybe had a facial tic or two. Considering Haggerty's constant yelling, I also thought there was a distinct possibility that she might be partially deaf.

In fact, without actually voicing it to myself, I guess I was secretly hoping that Mrs. Haggerty would be the sort who'd taken abuse for years and then finally snapped. I didn't think her being a murderer was all that outlandish, particularly since Hank had quoted to me more than once all those statistics that clearly indicated that wives and husbands were the most likely to kill each other.

Recalling my marriage to Jake, I was not about to argue with the authority of statistics.

As the front door slowly opened, I guess I was already picturing petite, mousy old Sheila plugging Haggerty, if for no other reason than to just finally shut his big mouth on a permanent basis.

The woman, however, who opened the door was not at

all petite. And certainly not mousy. She was at least six feet tall, closing in on two hundred pounds, with shoulders like a linebacker's. She wore no makeup, had streaks of gray through her ponytail, and had on one of those shapeless flowered dresses that back in the sixties they used to call muumuus—probably because they make whoever wears them look like cows. Sheila Haggerty's biceps would've made Hulk Hogan proud.

Nan and I exchanged surprised looks. This broad wouldn't have had to shoot Haggerty, at all. She could've bench-pressed the man, then pulled him apart like a Thanksgiving wishbone.

"Whaddya want?" Sheila yelled, even though she was standing only a few inches away. She did a double take then, looking first at me, then over at Nan, and then back to me again. "You guys twins or what?" she bellowed. It was not so much a question as an accusation. As if maybe Nan and I had become twins just to annoy her.

I stood there, pretty much openmouthed. Thank God, Nan was not so tongue-tied. "Why, yes, we are twins. How nice of you to notice," Nan said, with a smile that looked glued on. Nan introduced us, then hurried on. "Mrs. Haggerty, first of all, we want to express our profound sympathy for your loss. We realize this is a difficult—"

Mrs. Haggerty interrupted. "Yadda, yadda, yadda!" she boomed, and waved her hand in a hurry-up gesture. Besides pegging her as a Seinfeld fan, the rude gesture indicated she had probably been a good match for the ill-mannered, ill-tempered Haggerty. "For God's sake, get on with it!"

Nan glared at the woman, at which point I thought I'd better take up the slack. "Mrs. Haggerty—"

"Sheila!" she bellowed. "Mrs. Haggerty was my late husband's mother!"

"Sheila, we had a business deal going with your husband,"
I lied, "and we were wondering—"

"You and the rest of the city of Louisville!" she interrupted again.

"I beg your pardon?"

"You're the fourth one today! Beanie Babies are going
to be the death of me yet!" Sheila stood there, blocking the
doorway, hands on her hips, staring at us, looking even more
irritated than ever.

Nan was no longer glaring, and I guess I must've looked
a bit taken aback. Nan took over then. Without voicing it
aloud, we'd apparently decided that the only way to get
through this was to do tag-team questioning.

"If we could have just a moment of your time," Nan said,
"I'm sure—"

"Oh, well, I guess you might as well come on inside!"
Sheila yelled. "No use flapping our gums out here on the
porch!"

I was beginning to understand Haggerty's tendency to
raise his voice. If he'd wanted to get a word in edgewise in
this household, he'd have needed a megaphone. As we followed Sheila Haggerty into the house, I looked for some
sign of a hearing aid in the woman's ears. There was none.

We moved through a narrow hall and turned left into
what at one time must've been the parlor. The sound of
Sheila's elephantine steps on the hardwood floors resounded
in the room. I glanced down at the woman's feet. She was
wearing what looked like black orthopedic shoes with thick,
ribbed soles and black socks. The white of her legs looked

deathly pale against the socks. Very stylish with a muu-muu.

"Take a load off!" Mrs. Haggerty commanded, gesturing toward a couple of antique occasional chairs that I was pretty sure could not support her weight or Haggerty's. Sure enough, when we sat down, little clouds of dust wafted around us. The room smelled old, a mixture of mildew and dust.

A small piece of paper on a string fluttered as I sat down. It dangled from the wooden armrest. I leaned closer for a better look. It was a price tag reading: "$350 for the pair."

I looked around. Everything in the room had small white tags attached to it—lamps, tables, chairs, figurines. You name it, it was for sale. The fifties coffee table in front of us had a small sticker pasted on the glass top: $75. To the left of my chair, an armoire decorated with hand-painted birds and flowers so lifelike, they looked almost real, had a tag that said $875. The entire room was marked with a price—including the rugs. I turned to look at Sheila with real sympathy. Hank had said Mrs. Haggerty couldn't really tell if anything had been stolen during the break-in. No wonder.

Had this poor woman lived every day with everything she owned constantly being up for sale? No wonder she was yelling. You wouldn't know what chair you were sitting in from day to day. Goodness, you wouldn't even know if you were sitting at all.

Her entire household was in a constant state of flux. Now that I thought about it, this could also be a pretty good motive for murder. This poor woman had just wanted to hang on to a few of her things, instead of having that old skinflint sell them out from under her.

My God. What a way to live.

"You certainly have a lovely home," I told Sheila. "I've always loved Willow Avenue, with its lovely old Victorian houses."

Sheila cleared her throat, and glanced around as if seeing the room for the first time. "This place?" She shrugged her massive shoulders. "Yeah, it's nice, I guess! It's got a lot of room for goods!" The volume of her voice hadn't lowered even a decibel.

"Goods?" Nan repeated.

She gave an exasperated noise. "Goods! Goods!" She gestured around the room. "You know: what I sell. Goods! Haggerty kept filling this place to the rafters with goods, so I gotta move this crap!"

"Of course." I hoped what was on my face was an understanding smile, but, to be perfectly honest, I was shocked. She was the one selling the stuff. At the very least, she was in on the pillaging of her home, every bit as much as Haggerty.

I tried not to show my disappointment, because there went a perfectly good motive for murder.

"Now I'm gonna to have to sell all this junk by myself!" Sheila sighed heavily, looking around. "I'll have to do all the buys now, too—at least, Frankie was some help in that department. Not much, but some. Always had to be on him and on him to keep the goods moving! Otherwise, man, you couldn't walk through this place! Now with him gone . . ." She allowed her words to trail off.

I looked at her. If they had not found the man's body, I might've found myself wondering if Haggerty had been murdered, after all. Having met the missus, I thought it seemed far more likely that he was simply in hiding.

Sheila turned back to us. "So what exactly was my husband selling you two?" she asked. "A tandem bicycle?" She chuckled loudly at her joke, the whole of her body shaking with mirth. But I noticed she still watched us for the answer. The expression on her face was now almost eager.

Nan and I blinked at each other a couple of times. Like idiots, we really hadn't gone over that part of the story. Nan raised her eyebrows and widened her eyes at me. Which pretty much said, you're on your own.

I tried to remember some of the things Ellie had pointed out to me in Haggerty's booth. "Well, there was only one item, really," I said. "I saw it in your husband's booth. A fifties stuffed vinyl Horsman baby doll in its original box," I said.

I recalled the tagged price of $85. When Ellie had been telling me about Chris and his business, Ellie had mentioned that ten percent discounts were pretty much standard. "We were still dickering on the price," I went on. "He'd quoted me a price of $77, and I was coming back earlier today to actually buy it when I found out that your husband had been—" I wasn't sure where to go with this. *Shot* seemed to be a bit understated. *Murdered* sounded macabre. Fortunately, Mrs. Haggerty seemed to know what I was getting at. She nodded and made another one of those motions for me to hurry up and finish. I cleared my throat. "So, is the doll still available?" I really hoped I wasn't actually going to have to buy the item.

"See what I mean—Frankie was a fool!" Her eyes had taken on a crafty look.

"Excuse me?"

"Seventy-seven dollars? That's just giving it away! Franklin was such an idiot about the business."

"I beg your pardon?"

"That Frankie was always discounting prices. That M-I-B is one twenty-five—take it or leave it!"

"M-I-B?" Nan asked.

"Mint in box," Sheila snapped in Nan's direction. Her eyes, however, were still on me. I was reminded of a snake, staring down its prey.

"One hundred twenty-five dollars! Take it or leave it!" she repeated to me.

"One hundred and twenty-five dollars?" Now it was my turn to raise my voice. Good Lord. That was a fortune to pay for an old doll. Even if it was M-I-B, which it certainly wasn't. I remembered the dress on the doll was torn, and the hair on one side looked as if a child had played beauty parlor with it and given it a trim. I couldn't believe Sheila Haggerty would actually charge more than her husband. "That's almost twice what your husband quoted me," I said. "And that price isn't even what the tag said."

"Well, it's what the tag says now!" she bellowed.

I crossed my arms across my chest. "I'll have to think about it," I said.

"Probably that's what you said to Franklin on Saturday! And now look where you are. You should know that the whole shebang is going up for auction day after tomorrow. You must want that doll pretty darn bad to come all the way over here! So, if you want it, better get it now!"

Her small eyes looked lit from some kind of inner flame. Wow. Old Sheila was obviously enjoying herself. "OK, how's this?" Sheila went on. "You buy the doll today, and I'll throw in a vintage doll dress. Free for nothing." She smiled at me, revealing crooked lower teeth. Leaning toward me, she repeated, "Free for nothing."

Free for one hundred and twenty-five dollars. That's how I'd heard it.

Sheila's leaning in my direction was giving me the feeling she was about to make a grab for my purse. Lord. She was worse than her husband had ever thought of being.

Nan jumped in before I could say something rash. "Have you any idea who might've killed your husband?"

"What?" Sheila blinked a couple of times, and with obvious reluctance, took her eyes off my face to look over at Nan. "Well, yeah, now that you mention it, I do."

We sat there staring at her. After a second, both Nan and I asked in unison, "Who?"

"The cops have this little chippy in custody who's already confessed. Said something about her and her boyfriend arguing with my Frankie."

Chippy? This awful woman was talking about my Ellie. I felt my face flush with anger. I'd tell her a thing or two about her Frankie, but somehow I didn't think she'd think he did anything wrong.

I tried to control my voice as I said, "Actually, we heard that the girl's confession is all a mistake—someone else killed your husband. Not the chippy."

"Well, I ain't heard that. But that little girl did it, all right—someone saw a woman talking to Frankie in the parking lot that morning. Couldn't identify her because they was too faraway. But it had to be her—you know the type. Spoiled little brat messing with a man trying to make an honest living—"

That did it. I was on my feet. "Did you say *honest*? Are you kidding? We heard that Mr. Haggerty put old dolls in new boxes and sold them like they were mint. We heard your husband quoted different prices to different people—

raising the price to people he didn't like. We also heard your husband was a crook, trying to pass off merchandise as something it wasn't."

"Where did you hear these things?" Sheila was on her feet now, too. "Have you been going around asking questions about my Frankie? Have you? What gives you the right to go around badmouthing my poor dead husband? Who the hell do you think you are?"

"Just somebody trying to find out the truth," I said.

Nan apparently had tired of sitting there, looking up at Sheila and me. She rose heavily to her feet.

"The truth?" Sheila repeated. Her voice, amazingly enough, was quiet for once. "You ain't interested in no doll then?" A frown formed on her face, like a thunderstorm gathering steam. "DAMN. Then this has all been one big trick, ain't it? WHO ARE YOU?"

I took a deep breath. "Well, since you ask, I'll tell you. I am," I said, raising my head high, "the little chippy's mother."

We might have made a really elegant exit right then, except that when Nan and I started to move toward the door, Sheila started to move right after us.

Seeing her gaining on us, Nan and I broke with decorum and just ran for the front door.

Chapter 9

●

Nan

Being perky on the radio is pretty damn difficult when your niece is in the slammer, being held for murder. Not to mention, it's even more difficult when your twin sister has spent the entire night before phoning you just about every hour on the hour, worrying out loud. I guess I should've expected it, because Bert had not exactly been a happy camper on the way home from Sheila Haggerty's.

"I guess they really are going to keep Ellie downtown tonight, huh?" she asked. "Ellie really is going to have to stay in that awful place all night, huh?"

I didn't say a word. I just kept right on driving. Of course, what was going through my mind was: *Well, yes, Bert, I hate to break it to you, but generally, the police do like to keep those people behind bars who have recently confessed to murder. Cops are picky that way.*

Being my twin, Bert didn't seem to need me to put that little thought into words. She just made this little disgusted sound back in her throat and folded her arms across her chest.

We were almost home before she spoke again. "You know what I'm tempted to do? I'm tempted just to go right back

downtown, and when they bring Ellie in to see me, I'm going
to just grab her and hurry her right out of there."

It was kind of a good thing I was driving, because I could
just keep right on looking straight ahead. I didn't have to
look over at Bert at all. I knew, of course, that if I even
glanced her way, I'd be giving her my *are-you-nucking-
futs?* look. This little phrase is how Bert describes the looks
I give her when she says something so crazy, I can't believe
what I'm hearing. In this case, I knew if I looked at her that
way, it would be cruel and unusual punishment. After all,
Bert was just terribly worried about Ellie. As any mother
would be. If she was talking like a lunatic, you could overlook
it. Sort of.

Bert must've picked up on my general lack of enthusiasm
for her latest strategy. "OK," she said, "so I guess you'd
say that my going back downtown to get Ellie isn't a good
idea."

"No, Bert," I said, keeping my eyes dead ahead, "I'd say
that breaking Ellie out of jail is a great idea. Truly terrific.
A wonderful way to get yourself shot. And maybe Ellie, too.
What a great idea that is."

Bert was silent after that—until I was pulling into my
driveway. "I can't tell you how mad I am at Hank for doing
this to Ellie."

I hated to stick up for Goetzmann, but it did seem as if
Bert was not being entirely fair. "Bert, hon, I'm not sure
he could do anything about it."

Bert frowned, and tossed her hair. A sure sign she was
not about to listen to a silly little thing called reason. "Non-
sense," she said, got out of the car, and marched over to her
side of our duplex without once looking back at me.

I'd thought that was pretty much all Bert had to say for

the evening. I was, unfortunately, very wrong. Bert had something to say about five more times throughout the night. The first time was just minutes after I drifted off to sleep. The telephone jangled me awake, and as soon as I picked up the receiver, Bert said, "Nan, do you think Ellie is safe? The police won't let anything happen to her, will they?"

It took me fifteen minutes to convince Bert that the kind of things she'd seen in the movie *Escape from Alcatraz* pretty much only happened at Alcatraz, which wasn't even open for business anymore.

During the phone call I got about two hours later, I believe the movie we discussed was *Women in Chains*. A couple hours after that, it was *The Great Escape*. I actually had to say out loud that, no, even though Steve McQueen was held in solitary confinement, without bathroom privileges, and eating slop, that probably was not happening, as we spoke, to Ellie. I was pretty sure, in fact, that the Louisville jail didn't even have solitary confinement, that it probably encouraged its residents to use the bathroom on a regular basis, and that slop was not served in the middle of the night, anyway.

When, a mere sixty-two minutes later, Bert called again to ask me one more question, I'd had it. My clock said it was more than an hour since I'd last talked to her, but my eyes were saying they'd only just shut.

It wasn't that I didn't feel sympathetic. I did. In fact, I was pretty damn upset about Ellie being in jail, too.

I will admit, however, that the way I felt was obviously not exactly the same as the way Bert felt. Bert had that whole protective-mom thing going. Sure, I would've liked to have protected my niece, but I guess it just wasn't the same as wanting to protect a daughter. There had to be a

major difference between those two things. For one thing,
I could sleep. At least, I could if the phone would stop ringing.

"Nan," Bert said this last time, "do you think they've
given her a toothbrush?"

Like I said, I'd had it. "Bert," I said, "I have to work
tomorrow." I hate to admit it, but my voice was not kind.
"I need some sleep. I am sure Ellie has a toothbrush. What's
more, if you phone me again, I'm going to come over there
and kill you with mine. It'll be in all the papers—TWIN
KILLS TWIN IN TOOTHBRUSH STABBING. Then there
will be a record of homicide in the family. And that won't
do Ellie's case any good."

Bert took all that well. She hung up on me. If I hadn't
been so worried about her, I would never have phoned her
back. As it was, though, since it was clear that she was
nearly ready to be outfitted in one of those very stylish
jackets with the extra long sleeves that tie in the back, I
immediately dialed her phone number as fast as I could.

Once she answered, and I heard how shaky her voice
sounded, I felt like a jerk. A sleepy jerk maybe, but a jerk
nevertheless. I ended up staying on the phone with her for
the next hour, trying to think of something to do to help
get Ellie out of this mess. When we finally had a plan—and
I was pretty much convinced that Bert was indeed going to
get through the night without doing anything that would
get her a cell next to her daughter—I finally told her, "Hon,
I gotta get some sleep."

"Oh," Bert said. "Sure." She actually sounded surprised.
But then again, I'd heard that the insane don't need a whole
lot of shut-eye.

The next morning, when I dragged myself into the radio
station, I had bags under my eyes that I could've carried

groceries home in. Somehow, I managed to get through my Monday show. Although my eyes were shut most of the time, I must say in all modesty that I did an unbelievably terrific job of acting as if playing tunes by Garth Brooks and Reba McEntire was all I really lived for. Especially when you consider that, at the time, all I really lived for was a nap.

Before I went on the air, I'd staggered into Charlie Belcher's office to tell him that he had to get some other announcer to take over my production, at least for a while. Production is what people in the radio biz call making commercials.

I was so tired, I didn't have the strength to be subtle. I just came right out and told Charlie that I needed some time off to help Bert help Ellie. Or, at the very least, to help Bert keep from going stark raving mad.

"Take all the time you need, Nan," Charlie had said, leaning back in his chair and putting his feet on his desk. I hadn't even sat down yet, or begun to plead or anything. "As far as your production is concerned, we've got everything under control," Charlie said. "Don't worry about a thing."

I would've asked him if he felt all right, but if he were having some kind of fit, I didn't want to do anything to alert him to the problem. He might try to find a cure. "Thanks a lot, Charlie," I said. "I really do appreciate it." I turned and started to head out of his office.

"Take all the time you need," he repeated. "And, if you want," he said, right before I grabbed the doorknob to make my escape, "feel free to talk about your niece's case on the air—hey, if you want to generate public sympathy for her, go for it. The station is behind you all the way. We'd love to help."

Okay, so Charlie had a teeny, tiny ulterior motive. I was not going to let it bother me. What was important was he'd given me the time off—at least until it seeped into Charlie's equally teeny, tiny brain that I had no intention of parading Ellie's troubles in front of all of Louisville in order to boost WCKI ratings. Hell, I was thanking my lucky stars that Ellie's arrest had not made the *Louisville Courier-Journal* yet. I wasn't sure that anybody would make the connection and start calling me at the station to talk about it, but there was always that chance. I didn't even have to think twice to know what Bert would think of that little scenario.

No, thank you, Charlie. If it was publicity I wanted, I'd just do it up big and phone Jerry Springer. Maybe Sheila Haggerty could wrestle me and Bert in front of a national audience.

If I'd had the strength, I would've run out of the control room as soon as the intro to the news came on at three o'clock. As it was, I sort of lurched toward the front lobby.

As planned, Bert was waiting. She jumped to her feet as soon as I came through the door. She looked a lot like one of those thoroughbreds in the Kentucky Derby—just raring to go. She, unfortunately, was a thoroughbred that hadn't gotten much more sleep than I had in the last twenty-four hours. To use a horsey phrase our granddaddy used to use all the time, Bert looked as if she'd been ridden hard and put away wet.

She handed me an icy, canned Coke to match the one she'd just gotten out of the machine in the hall. We popped tops in unison as we headed for my car.

The plan we'd come up with in the wee hours of the morning was pretty simple. Since we hadn't been able to get anything out of Sheila Haggerty except possible acute hearing loss, Bert and I were going to talk to the people whose names were on the Haggerty complaint list—the one that Mr. Grainger of flea-market fame had given me after he got rid of the crowd of ghouls that had been outside his office.

Bert had the list spread out on her lap on the passenger's side even before I slid behind the wheel. In typical Bert-like fashion, she'd sorted them according to location to minimize our drive time.

It was a fun afternoon—if you like hearing people whine.

Apparently, the dearly departed Haggerty had given a lot of people a lot of reasons to whine, too. We told the people we called on that we were following up on their complaints about Franklin Haggerty, kind of implying that we represented the flea-market director. Hey, we had his list, didn't we? No one seemed to question why we'd be following up a complaint against a dead man.

A black gentleman by the name of Ezekiel Johnson, who lived on Portland Avenue, gave us homemade sugar cookies on a pink Depression-glass plate and an earful. While we munched on the treats, Ezekiel called Haggerty a racist pig who charged more to black folks than he did white people. "Don't get me wrong—he overcharged white folks, too. Just not as much." Ezekiel shook his gray head. "Franklin Haggerty was not a very nice man," he'd said, taking a bite out of one of his truly scrumptious cookies.

That seemed like a pretty clear indictment. However, when we asked Ezekiel how recently he'd bought anything from Haggerty, he promptly replied, "Why, I guess that would be the evening before he died."

A woman by the name of Rose King, who lived on Fourth Street, near the Louisville Library, was the dealer whose booth had been located right next to Haggerty's, month after month after miserable month. Rose told us that Haggerty had actually followed customers into her booth and told them her items were damaged and that his identical pieces were cheaper and better quality. Rose, however, also admitted to recently buying items from Haggerty herself.

A Miss Edna Parslett, who lived in a subdivision off of the Outer Loop, told us that Haggerty had called her to say a doll—an American Character Sweet Sue doll, whatever *that* was—that she'd bought from him was broken. "He drove out here and stood right there where you are and showed me tiny white spots on the legs and told me the material the doll was made of was falling apart," the woman said without even drawing a breath. "He said he'd known about the defect when he sold the doll to me, and it had been bothering him, taking advantage of me that way. He hadn't been able to sleep, knowing he'd done such a thing." Haggerty had asked her to return the doll, then refunded her payment in full on the spot.

I'd just stared at her. Like in Paul Harvey's tales, something told me there had to be a *rest of the story*. "So why did you complain?" I asked.

The woman had snorted—not her most attractive moment, by the way. "Because I later found out that he'd gotten an offer for the doll over three times what I paid. Without knowing the connection, Haggerty actually resold it to my boss at work. Turns out there was nothing wrong with that doll at all—those white spots were just the usual aging for dolls that old—Franklin Haggerty had only wanted to make a bigger profit on the sale."

After a couple of hours of listening to these people, I began to wonder why no one had shot Haggerty any sooner than this. I think Bert thought the same thing. We really weren't making any progress—any of these people seemed to have as much reason as the next one to have plugged Haggerty. As we neared the end of the list, Bert became quieter and quieter, which I knew meant she was getting more and more depressed. We rode in silence to the next address on the list—a Mrs. Margaret Smith-Williams, 48501 Windsor Avenue in St. Matthews.

As it turned out, Margaret took the Haggerty complaint prize. In her early sixties, she answered the door wearing a soft white silk blouse with an artist's bow at the neck, a pleated navy linen skirt, pearl drop earrings—and white fluffy slippers with ears that looked like bunny rabbits. "A gift from my grandchildren," she explained with a chuckle when she noticed the way Bert and I were staring at her feet.

She also carried a book in one hand, her place marked by a black ribbon—something by John Steinbeck that actually looked as if it could be a first edition. Reading glasses hung from a beaded chain around her neck.

From the looks of her house, with its stately pillars out front, Margaret didn't look as if she needed to make another dime; but, according to our list, she, too, was a dealer.

I quickly explained why we'd dropped by, and Margaret graciously invited us in. "Taking part in the flea market with my antiques is just something I do as a hobby since Alfred— my husband—passed away," she explained. "It keeps me from getting maudlin."

Anyone who could wear bunny slippers and actually use the word *maudlin* in a sentence was my kind of woman.

Bert and I followed her down a foyer with wood floors polished to such a high sheen, they almost glowed. In the living room, I looked around, noting the parquet floors and the various pieces of antique furniture that filled the room. Unlike Haggerty's house, where antiques of every kind filled every inch of space, these pieces looked to be from the same period and looked especially chosen to complement each other. I had a feeling the carved pigeonhole desk in the corner may have cost as much as all my furniture put together.

Margaret perched on a woven cane chair that looked as if it couldn't support a sparrow. "Please do sit down—why, you're twins, how delightful!"

Delightfully, Bert and I just stood there. I knew Bert was doing the same thing as I was—trying to figure out where we could sit without harming any of these obviously expensive pieces. The only time I'd ever seen anything this old was in a museum; and there'd been small printed signs all over the place, reading: *Please do not sit on the furniture.* The signs had not added: —*you heathen;* but I believe that was understood.

Margaret gestured toward a sofa that looked as if only half of the back was there. As we sat down, I figured the woman was probably taking no chances. She wanted us to sit on something that was broken already.

"That's a fainting couch," Margaret said, "made in the late 1800s for women to swoon on, should they be so inclined."

"No kidding? There was a lot of that going around back then," I said, looking at the couch.

I caught Bert's disapproving look in the corner of my eye. If the coffee table in front of us had hidden her legs, she'd probably have kicked me. Bert always gets on her very ultrabest behavior in the presence of wealth. I, on the other hand, agree with whoever it was who said, no matter how much money you've got, you still put your pants on the same way as everybody else. Of course, if you've got major bucks, you might have a lot of volunteers eager to assist you in taking them on and off.

"So how can I help you?" Margaret Smith-Williams asked. When we explained the whole thing, and told her we needed to hear anything she had to tell us, she gave a huge sigh. "That man! Franklin Haggerty was the rudest person I ever met in my life. Why, if Alfred were alive today, he would have simply throttled that awful man." She glanced over at the oil portrait in a gilded frame hanging over the fireplace.

Bert and I followed her gaze. The guy in the portrait was bald, wore oval wire glasses, and had a gentle smile. He also had a face with more lines than a road map and a body so thin, he'd have made Don Knotts look portly. If that little guy was Alfred, he couldn't have throttled a gnat. All Haggerty would have had to do was breathe on the little guy, and he'd have spun across the room.

Margaret was warming to her subject. "I have a lot of the same items as Mr. Haggerty did—old tin toys, dolls, and such. And my prices are much lower. Because, well, I don't have to make a huge profit. I just want to charge what's fair." Margaret frowned. "Can you believe, more than once, that horrible man came into my booth before I arrived on the first day of the flea market and took all my tags off, so people wouldn't know how much my things were? I'd have to spend the entire morning retagging things, instead of greeting customers; and I know I lost a lot of sales. When I complained to the management, Mr. Haggerty swore he was innocent—even though other dealers said he'd also done the same thing to them." Her cheeks had turned a shade pinker as she told the story.

"Well, I finally did get even with him." Margaret smiled now as she went on. "When Alfred died, Haggerty came to the auction to buy some of the things I'd decided to part with. I refused to let that man bid on a single item—and I was perfectly within my rights, you know. I'd heard about how Haggerty cheated some of the people he bought estates from. Well, he wasn't going to get a thing owned by my Alfred—I made sure of that."

Bert sat up a little straighter. "He cheated some of the owners of the estates he bought?"

"Oh, my dear, I wasn't the only one he treated so cavalierly."

"Cavalierly?" I repeated. I wasn't sure I'd ever heard anyone use that word in conversation.

Mrs. Smith-Williams adjusted the bow at her neck and nodded, folding her hands in her lap. "I've heard several of the other dealers talk about how Haggerty would convince some poor grieving soul that she didn't have much of anything in the things left to her. Then that awful Mr. Haggerty would pay her a pittance of what the whole lot was worth. Well, many of these poor dears are having to get cash together rather quickly to pay inheritance taxes or probate lawyers or some such."

She made it sound as if needing cash quickly was as remote to her as catching malaria.

"Why, the poor dears would take whatever they could get and not get a second estimate. That awful man would take advantage of their desperate situations."

Bert glanced at me, and I could read her look. Now we were getting somewhere. Finally, here was a reason for

murder. Not just some little quarrel with a disgruntled customer, or doing something underhanded to a fellow dealer,
but cheating a grieving survivor out of their inheritance.

"Do you have any names?" Bert asked a little breath-
lessly. "Anyone whom we could talk to who sold their estates
to Haggerty?"

Mrs. Smith-Williams frowned. "Oh, my dear, I don't think
I know any names. I just heard the talk at the flea market.
This is a tiny circle, you know, at least of the antique dealers.
We all see each other at auctions all the time, and we hear
things. Then we tell each other—we're terrible gossips, I'm
afraid. Now let me see—who was it who told me about
Haggerty buying estates?"

She turned and studied the portrait over the fireplace,
as if maybe Alfred knew the answer. After a moment, she
brightened. "Wait a minute. I know. It was the lady who
has her booth next to mine. She told me there was actually
a dealer at the flea market who'd had his family's estate
bought by Franklin Haggerty. As I remember, Haggerty
bought it from the executrix, who was the dealer's sister, I
believe. Haggerty really snookered her, too—paid far, far
less than what the collection was worth—at least, that's
what people are saying. Now, what was that dealer's name?"

She tapped her finger against her temple as if that would
help her remember. "Millhaven, Millhardin—something like
that."

Bert and I turned to look at each other.

"Mulholland?" we asked in unison. "Christopher Mulholland?"

"Oh, yes, that's it," Margaret said. She looked at us, her
eyes doing the twin-bounce. She looked first at me, then at
Bert, then back over at me. "Oh. Do you know him?"

Chapter 10

●

Bert

I felt as if someone had just thrown ice water on me.

Mrs. Smith-Williams sat there, continuing to do the twin-bounce with her eyes, waiting for one of us to answer her question.

Did I know Chris Mulholland? The answer that immediately leapt to mind was: "Apparently not as well as I should."

I knew, of course, that my daughter seemed to be pretty crazy about the guy. But did I happen to know that his parents' estate was sold to the man my daughter was accused of murdering? And that this particular sale gave Chris an excellent motive himself to kill Franklin Haggerty? Why no, as a matter of fact, that little tidbit had never come up. Strangely enough.

I could feel the ice water changing to steam. I wasn't sure whom I was most mad at—Ellie or Hank for not telling me. Of course, maybe Hank had not known. That seemed unlikely, though. Surely, the policeman in charge of the case would've found out about the connection between Chris Mulholland and Franklin Haggerty even sooner than Nan and I had. If Hank had known, then he'd deliberately chosen to keep the information to himself.

My daughter was in jail, and there was the distinct possibility that Hank was not being totally honest with me? I sat there on Mrs. Smith-Williams's fainting couch, and I could feel myself getting more and more angry. How dared Hank do such a thing? Did he think I was some kind of child to be shielded from the truth? How insulting could you get?

Nan had been looking over at me, more or less waiting for me to answer Mrs. Smith-Williams's question. I had so much going through my mind, though, that I must've looked as if I wasn't going to answer anytime this century.

Turning to face Mrs. Smith-Williams again, Nan cleared her throat. "Well, no, I've never met Chris Mulholland," she said. "Bert's daughter is a friend of his, though."

"Oh," was all Mrs. Smith-Williams said. Her bright eyes, however, turned to stare pointedly at me. I wasn't sure what that look meant, but I got the feeling that for a little old lady, Margaret Smith-Williams didn't miss much. "Well, I hate to be saying bad things about the dead," she went on, "but I do believe that Mr. Haggerty enjoyed snookering people. It made him feel like a big man."

"Not that he needed any help," Nan added.

Mrs. Smith-Williams paused for a moment, and then she made a tiny little snuffling sound, holding her small, bony hand to her mouth, as if trying to stifle the sound. It took me a moment to realize that she was laughing.

When she got herself under control, Mrs. Smith-Williams hurried on. "Again, not to speak ill of the dead, but Mr. Haggerty really did seem to get a charge out of goading someone to the point of losing his or her temper. It was all a game to Mr. Haggerty."

"He lost," Nan said.

Mrs. Smith-Williams snuffled behind her hand again. Evidently, she thought Nan was a real laugh riot.

I, on the other hand, wished Nan would stop interrupting what Mrs. Smith-Williams had to say. I mean, it was nice that the old woman found Nan so entertaining, but—excuse me—my daughter continued to be accused of murder. I wasn't exactly in a laughing mood.

"Mr. Haggerty was certainly very rude," Mrs. Smith-Williams was going on. "And did you ever meet his wife? My goodness, they were two peas in a pod."

We continued to speak ill of the dead for a short while longer, not really saying anything different, just more or less repeating what Nan and I already knew. This must've occurred to Nan about the same time as it occurred to me, because she abruptly got to her feet. "Well, we really need to be going," she said.

I just stared at Nan. Bulls in china shops are probably more subtle.

This is typical Nan, though. She is so rude around rich people. Really, it's a kind of reverse discrimination. I don't know if Nan is envious, or irritated, or what, but she seems to feel that it's her big chance to show them that she is not the least bit impressed.

And yet, if somebody's wealth didn't make any difference to her, why not treat them the way you'd treat anybody else?

"What my sister means," I said, "is that we have a pressing engagement elsewhere and, unfortunately, we simply can't stay any longer." I got to my feet. "Thank you so much, though, for taking the time to chat with us."

Mrs. Smith-Williams was gracious enough to walk us to the door. "I'm sorry I wasn't able to tell you anything more," she said. "Do come back and visit. Anytime." Her tone seemed a little wistful.

She actually waved at us as we pulled away.

It was clear now why Mrs. Smith-Williams took part in flea markets when she didn't really need the money. With her husband gone, she was lonely. Money really didn't solve everything.

Like, for example, it didn't keep your daughter from confessing to murder.

"Makes you wonder, doesn't it?" I said, as I got into Nan's Neon.

Nan looked over at me. "You mean, about what it's like for that poor lady to grow old all alone? In that big house without her Alfred?" She looked back over at the house. "I imagine, with all the money she has, she could find a few ways to ease the pain. Go to Europe. Take a cruise. You know what they say. Money can't buy happiness. But it can sure rent it."

I blinked. And they say twins are supposed to be psychically linked. "No, Nan, I meant about Chris. This is probably why Chris has so little money these days. Haggerty bought his parents' estate and paid him far less than it was worth."

Nan started the car and pulled into traffic. "So you think that Chris confronted Haggerty, they argued, and Chris shot him?"

I glanced over at her. "Sounds reasonable, doesn't it?"

"Except for the fact that it took Chris several months to do it."

I shrugged. "Maybe Chris was a procrastinator."

That possibility didn't seem all that outlandish to me, but Nan rolled her eyes. "You mean, he meant to kill Haggerty, but he just couldn't get around to it? It was on his list of Things to Do Today, but he just kept putting it off, and putting it off, and putting it off?"

Derision can be so ugly. And such a waste of time. I interrupted. "Why don't we go and talk to—"

"Chris's sister," Nan finished for me.

OK, so our psyches may not be linked, but sometimes, they certainly seem in sync.

We stopped at the first gas station we passed that had a telephone booth. Actually, I should say we stopped at the first station that had both a booth *and* a telephone book, because we'd passed three on Shelbyville Road that had outside telephones but not a book in sight. The phone booths still had the chains that the books had hung from, but no book.

I've always wondered why in the world people steal entire phone books. Are they using them as doorstops? Are they being taken by weight lifters, who practice tearing them in half? Is there a warehouse somewhere filled to the rafters with hot phone books waiting to be sold on the phone-book black market?

At the fourth gas station we passed, the phone book was luckily still there. Even luckier still, there were only two Mulhollands listed: a Christopher Mulholland and a K. Mulholland.

"You think that's his sister?" Nan said.

The address was on Alta Avenue, a little over ten minutes away.

"One way to find out," I said. I dialed the number.

The phone was busy. It continued to be busy for the next ten minutes.

"It would be faster just to drive over there," Nan said. "Besides, at least, we know somebody will be home."

She drove down Shelbyville Road for a few miles, then turned on to the Watterson Expressway. The Watterson has been voted one of the most dangerous expressways in the United States. What can I say? Things like this make you proud to be a Louisville native.

They also make the blood drain from your face. Nan narrowly avoided certain death by deftly dodging an oncoming semi, and then scooting at a diagonal into the middle lane. She was going almost seventy-five by then, but some thoughtful soul in a red Ford Bronco must've decided that Nan was taking liberties, moving that slow on his own personal expressway. The idiot actually honked.

It was then that I realized just how stressed I was. Before I could stop myself, I'd rolled down the window on my side, and given the guy the finger. I continued to salute him, as he returned the lovely gesture, picked up speed, and whipped past us.

I think Nan was even more surprised than I was to see me do such a thing. Her eyes were like saucers as I rolled up the window.

"Bert." She said my name as if she wasn't really sure it was me.

I shrugged. "Well, he deserved it."

Nan nodded, but she kept darting looks at me all the way to Alta Avenue. As if maybe trying to figure out if the Body Snatchers were in town.

The Mulholland home was located in a truly lovely residential area of Louisville adjacent to Cherokee Park—a place where I'd always dreamed of living. The two-story brick house with its multiple gables and quaint wooden shutters was small compared to its neighbors, but it still looked

like a place Nathaniel Hawthorne might write about. A small
metal sign in the front yard said:

FOR SALE
Contact Schuyler Ridgway, Realtor
at Arndoerfer Realty
502-892-2222

We rang the doorbell and listened to Westminster chimes
echoing in the house. No one came to the door.

Nan and I looked at each other and then at the late-
model Nissan that stood in the driveway. Surely, someone
was home.

We rang the bell again.

On the third ring, the door was yanked open by a tall
blonde in her mid-twenties wearing a small white terry-cloth
bathrobe. She had a dark tan, long curly hair, and very large
brown eyes. She would've been very pretty if she had not
been wearing that big frown. "OK, what?" she demanded,
glaring at us. "And this had better be important!"

She teetered a little and grabbed hold of the doorjamb
to keep from falling. I looked down.

The young woman was barefoot, standing on her heels,
each of her toenails gleaming a very wet ruby red. Those
little pink sponges that keep your toes separated when
you're painting your nails were stuck between the toes of
each foot. From this vantage point, she looked as if both
feet had sprouted extra pink toes.

I also noticed that she was holding on to the doorjamb
with the very tips of her fingers, being careful not to touch
the surface of her gleaming ruby red fingernails either.

"Are you K. Mulholland?" Nan asked.

"Not Kaye. *Kaitlin.* I'm Kaitlin Joan Mulholland. What's it to you?" she said. Her tone was not kind. "And can you make it snappy? I'm a little busy here. I've got a party to go to tonight." She flapped her hands around, in a futile effort to dry her nails, and nearly lost her balance again.

I just looked at her. Her brother was under suspicion of murder, and she was going to a party?

"We're here about your brother," I said, "and Franklin Haggerty."

"Who?" Kaitlin asked.

"Franklin Haggerty," Nan said.

"Not him," Kaitlin said. "I know Franklin Haggerty—he bought my parents' estate. But you said, my *brother.* As a matter of fact, I don't have—"

"May we come in?" I asked.

Kaitlin was shaking her head no before I even finished. "Look, I don't know what you want, but I don't have time to waste."

Well, now, that was something we had in common. I pushed past Kaitlin and walked inside.

"Bert!" I heard Nan say, but I didn't slow down. With Ellie whiling away every second sitting in that awful jail, I was in no mood for making nice.

"Hey!" Kaitlin said, hopping after me on her heels. "Wait a minute! What the hell are you doing? Who are you anyway?"

I let Nan introduce us, while I led the way through the foyer to the living room. Once there, I came to an abrupt halt. Maybe there was a reason Kaitlin hadn't invited us in. There didn't seem to be anything in the living room to sit on. There was nothing but a half dozen gigantic throw pillows in shades of orange, pink, and green. They looked extremely out of place against the cherry-paneled walls and the ornately carved fireplace.

"Look," I said, "we need some answers." I tried to sound official. "We've been asked to look into the death of a Mr. Franklin Haggerty, and your name came up."

That got old Kaitlin's attention. "You're private detectives?" she said. "*Twin* private detectives?" Can you believe she sounded skeptical?

I tried to look tough—which is pretty hard to do when you're wearing a flowered summer dress and little white heels. Nan, for once, was dressed far more appropriately. In jeans and T-shirt, she seemed to be going for a Serpico look. "Yeah, well," I told Kaitlin, trying to sound like Humphrey Bogart in *The Big Sleep*, "in this business, it takes all kinds." I would've liked to have had a trench coat on, so I could shove my hands in its pockets. I had to be satisfied with just putting my hands in the slit pockets of my dress.

I could feel Nan's eyes boring into me. I glanced over at her, and immediately decided that it would be best not to look over at her again until her eyes weren't quite so round.

Kaitlin shrugged. "Y'all might as well sit down," she said with a shrug. She herself sank onto one of the pillows, then put both her feet up on a low rattan table in the center of the pillows, wiggling her toes as if that would hasten the drying process. She noticed our look—no, make that a stare—at the room and shrugged again.

"Mom and Daddy had all this crappy old stuff," Kaitlin said. "I sold all of that boring old junk to Mr. Haggerty and finally got something I liked. I'm going to take all this good stuff to a new apartment, once I sell this dumb old house."

This little airhead thought this lovely old house was dumb? I sank down on a hot pink pillow, and Nan sat on an orange one. This had to be what being eaten by a giant marshmallow would feel like.

From where I sat, I could see down the hallway, where the wooden frame of a futon, minus the mattress, leaned against one wall. Volumes of an *Encyclopedia Britannica* were stacked against the opposite wall, no doubt taken from bookcases that had been sold. On the walls around me could barely be seen faint rectangular outlines where pictures once hung.

Kaitlin noticed my look at the outlines and shrugged. "Those were some crappy oil paintings my folks had—weird flowers and farm scenes and stuff. I sold those, too—you wouldn't believe what Haggerty paid me for those crappy old paintings." She grinned, as if she'd really pulled one over on the man.

I sincerely hoped the crappy old artists hadn't been Sargent or Monet. When Kaitlin finally regained her sanity, she was going to remember all that crappy old stuff she sold and probably feel a lot like Native Americans do when they think about Manhattan.

"So you two are twins, huh?" Kaitlin asked, finally looking at us rather than at her nails. "That's cool. I sure wish I'd had a twin—we could've hung together against everybody else."

Hanging together against everybody else wasn't exactly what I would've immediately thought of, but at least the young woman wasn't snapping at us anymore.

"We were wondering what you know about your brother's relationship with Franklin Haggerty," Nan asked.

Kaitlin answered with another shrug. "That's what I've been trying to tell you," Kaitlin said, blowing on her nails. "I don't have a brother."

I nearly slid off my pillow at that one. Had Nan and I made a mistake?

"Chris Mulholland is not your brother?" Nan asked.

Kaitlin shrugged. "Nope, he sure isn't. Mom and Dad had Chris living with us—as a foster child or something— since I was five. But he wasn't my brother. He was like an abandoned baby or an orphan or something."

Like an abandoned baby?

"But he isn't real family—my folks got him from some orphanage." Kaitlin made it sound like they'd picked him up at the grocery. "Mom and Dad just let him use their name because he didn't know what his real name was." Kaitlin's tone indicated that this was some kind of failing on his part.

I stared at the young woman, trying to understand what she was saying. "Chris isn't your brother? Then who got the proceeds from your parents' estate?"

Kaitlin sighed elaborately. "Didn't I just tell you that? *I* did. *I* sold the estate to Mr. Haggerty. Chris didn't have a blessed thing to do with any of it." She rearranged herself on the pillow, making herself more comfortable while carefully watching her wet nails. "I mean, it wasn't like Chris was an heir or anything. My parents died without a will, so I was the only one who inherited anything—you know, like it should be. After all, I was their only biological child."

I blinked. "Your parents didn't leave a will?"

Kaitlin shrugged, a now-familiar gesture of hers. "Why would they make a will? Who would've expected them to die so young? They were only in their early fifties. They died suddenly—Daddy lost control of their car during a snowstorm. It went over an embankment."

She said it so casually, it might have been the story of

someone else's parents. Where were this young woman's feelings?

"And your parents didn't adopt Chris?"

She shrugged. "Guess they never got around to it. He's no relation to me now, legal or otherwise." Kaitlin certainly seemed quite content with that arrangement.

Nan and I glanced at each other. I was sure she knew what I was thinking. Talk about sibling rivalry. I could just picture what a fun family the Mulhollands must have been. They must've put the fun in *dysfunctional*. After years of resenting her brother, Kaitlin had finally found a loophole in the family bond. And she was using that loophole to cut Chris out of her parents' estate.

Kaitlin blew on her nails again. "I mean, I read about Mr. Haggerty's death in the *Courier-Journal*, but I sure don't know what it has to do with me. The guy bought the estate, and he did a great job. Who you guys need to talk to is Chris—he and Haggerty did flea markets together, I think."

Nan took a deep breath. "Actually, Miss Mulholland, we wanted to talk to you because some people are saying that Franklin Haggerty cheated you. That he paid you a pittance for what your parents' estate was worth. Which might give you a motive for shooting him."

Kaitlin sat up straight, no easy task on that soft pillow. "Oh, that's just a bunch of bull doo-doo!"

Nan and I exchanged a look. *Bull doo-doo?* What a delicate flower this woman was.

"I've told you how happy I was with what Mr. Haggerty paid me," Kaitlin went on. "You should've seen all that old junk I sold him."

I was glad I couldn't. I might've wept.

I thought about Chris, and what Ellie had said about how his sister wouldn't help him if he were in trouble. Ellie certainly had been right. When their parents died, Kaitlin had turned Chris out of the only home he'd known since he was a baby and left him penniless. Staring at the young woman, I finally couldn't help myself—I had to ask. "Kaitlin, don't you think your parents would have wanted Chris to have something?"

Kaitlin didn't even seem to consider the matter a second. She shrugged. "They loved him, I guess. But not like a real biological child—not like they loved me. I told you— he wasn't their real child. *I* was." She looked at Nan and then at me, finally sensing our disapproval. It seemed to make her irritated. "Look," she added, "I've had it pretty rough, too, you know. I've just been trying to get over the sudden loss of my mother and father—it hasn't been easy."

Right, I thought, what with all the parties to go to.

Kaitlin went on. "I had to hear about their car accident all alone. Chris was supposed to have been here that day, too—he was supposed to be home from college that weekend. But, no, I was all by myself when the police called. My father died in that car accident instantly; but Mom lingered for two awful days. Chris didn't even show up at the hospital until late that night."

Kaitlin glanced around the paneled room with a kind of satisfaction. "So, no, I don't think Mom and Daddy wanted him to have anything. I always thought of Chris as kind of taking advantage—just trying to get close to my folks so he could get something out of them."

It was very hard to imagine a baby taking advantage of anyone. It wasn't hard, however, to imagine the resentment this woman had felt as a little girl when a new baby—a boy—came into the home. I wondered if she'd been angry at her parents ever since.

Kaitlin went on, her eyes flashing. "Well, he's not going to get a penny from them. Besides, I still don't know where Chris had been that day. He's certainly never told me where he was—to my satisfaction, anyway." She paused, her dark brown eyes narrowing. "Daddy was a very careful driver, too."

I stared at her.

Was she implying what I thought she was implying?

I turned to look at Nan, who sat openmouthed on her pillow.

Yep, she certainly was.

Chapter 11

•

Nan

OK. I admit it. Kaitlin Mulholland was getting on my nerves.

She actually had a look of satisfaction on her pretty face. She was accusing her foster brother of killing her own parents, and she looked positively tickled to be saying such things. She looked particularly delighted to see my and Bert's jaws drop.

I leaned forward. "Was there any evidence found that would indicate that your parents' car had been tampered with in some way?"

Kaitlin shrugged. "Nope. The police looked it over and didn't find a thing." She blew on the fingernails of her right hand. "But that doesn't mean anything."

I just looked at her. It doesn't mean anything other than maybe you're just making wild accusations, totally unsubstantiated by fact.

"Had Chris ever threatened your parents?"

Kaitlin shrugged again. "Nope."

"Did your parents ever indicate that they were afraid of him?"

Yet another shrug. "Nope."

"So what makes you say that Chris could've caused the car accident that killed them?" Bert asked.

Kaitlin's big eyes got even bigger, as she looked over at Bert and then back at me. "Oh, I never said THAT. All I said was that I didn't know where Chris was that day, and that Daddy was a careful driver. That's *all* I said."

Bert and I exchanged a look. Evidently, Kaitlin had no intention of being sued for slander.

"Then you really don't think Chris murdered your parents?"

Kaitlin's eyes looked sly. "Now, I didn't say *that* either."

Have I mentioned that when somebody gets on my nerves, sometimes I am not a nice person? I really needed to go before I went for Kaitlin's throat.

With some effort, I extricated myself from the dumb floor pillow and got to my feet. "Well, we really appreciate your taking the time to talk to us," I said.

Bert looked a little surprised at my sudden decision to leave, but she managed somehow to get off her pillow and on her feet, too. "Yes," she echoed uncertainly, looking over at me. "Thanks."

I reached for Kaitlin's hand. In fact, I took considerable satisfaction in grabbing Kaitlin's wet little fingertips in a hearty grip, looking her right in her big, brown, vacant eyes, and saying, "Oh my yes. Thank you so much for all your help."

The horrified look on Kaitlin's face was something to press in one's memory book. "Hey!" was her thoughtful response, as she tried to wrench her hand away. "Hey! HEY!"

Bert and I left Kaitlin groaning over the smears in her fingernail polish. I would've stepped on her wet toenails, too, but she sidestepped me as I went past her and headed out the front door.

Once out of that little bitch's house, I found myself taking deep breaths of fresh air.

What a horrible little twit! Not only did it seem as if Kaitlin had not given a hoot about her own parents, but she actively hated her erstwhile brother—enough to toss the guy out on his ear once her parents weren't around to prevent it.

All I can say is: Wow. I've been called a man-hater in my time, but Kaitlin made me look like a pussycat. Hell, she made Lucrezia Borgia look like a pussycat. At least, old Lucrezia had put her men *out* of their misery. Kaitlin Mulholland seemed to take satisfaction in seeing her former family member left homeless without a dime.

I was beginning to understand why Ellie felt so protective of Chris. I felt sorry for him myself.

I glanced at Bert as I unlocked the passenger side of my Neon. Frowning, she was already grumbling as I climbed into the driver's seat.

"The worst thing about all this," Bert said, "is that it now looks as if Chris doesn't have a motive to murder Haggerty anymore. Chris wasn't going to get any of the estate anyway, so what did he care if Haggerty undervalued it? In fact, he might actually be glad to see Kaitlin taken to the cleaners." She frowned again. "Damn."

I couldn't help but stare. Had Bert actually said what I thought she just said? Good Lord. First, she gives some guy the finger, and now she's cursing? I could only conclude one thing. Either Bert had recently undergone a personality transplant, or she was slowly but surely losing her mind.

She was staring back at me now, looking definitely distraught. "It really does look as if Chris didn't kill Haggerty."

I reached over and patted Bert's knee. "Look on the

bright side, hon," I said. "At least Ellie hasn't been dating a cold-blooded killer."

I was trying to be upbeat, but Bert did not seem to appreciate my effort. She glared at me.

"OK," I hurried on, "maybe Chris still does have a motive. He had argued with Haggerty that very day." I pulled out of the driveway. "Of course, if you listen to his charming sister, Chris also did away with his foster parents. So these last few months have been pretty much of a murderfest for the boy."

Bert frowned. "Do you think it's really possible that he could have set up the accident that took the elder Mulhollands' lives?" Bert had gone nuts. She actually sounded hopeful.

"Sure, it's possible," I said. "Of course, Kaitlin herself could have done it, too. Personally, I think the Mulhollands must've been your typical nuclear family—always ready to explode."

Bert sat up a little straighter as she buckled her seat belt. "I guess we need to talk to Ellie again," she said. "She has to be told what Kaitlin said about Chris. Pull over at the next phone booth, and I'll call Jake to see if he's got her out of jail yet. I'll—I'll be right—"

I was pretty sure Bert had meant to say, "I'll be right back," but her voice trailed off. She sat there, taking deep breaths, and then all at once her eyes filled with tears. "Man, I can't believe what I just said." Bert wiped at her damp cheek with the back of her hand. "I'm actually having to find out if my daughter is still behind bars."

Bert never cried. Particularly not in a car parked in front of somebody's house. Where anybody could walk by and possibly see her. "Bert," I said gently, "it's going to be OK."

I believed it, too. It had to be OK—Ellie could not have killed that man—and sooner or later everyone would know. I only hoped, for Bert and Ellie's sake, it was sooner.

I leaned over and gave Bert a hug.

Bert stopped crying right away, brushing the tears away with an irritated motion. "This is stupid," she said, straightening up. "My bawling isn't helping anybody. All it's going to do is make me dehydrated."

I had to smile. "And dehydration is a very big concern."

Bert smiled a little, too. "When this is all over, though, I'm going to give myself a very, very long cry. I've earned it, I deserve it, and I'm going to have it."

"Dehydration be damned," I said.

Bert smiled a little more, blinked hard, and took another deep breath. "OK, let's find a phone."

We found one a lot faster this time, since all that was required was for the phone to work. And for it not to look too disgusting. The phone at an Amoco station a couple miles away met both these stringent requirements. As soon as I pulled up, Bert was out of the car.

She returned, looking as if she might cry all over again. "I can't believe it," she said, getting back into the car. "Jake says he offered to post the equity in his house as collateral for Ellie's bond. But Ellie—my brain-dead, lovesick daughter—is refusing to let Jake post bail until they drop all charges against Chris. Can you imagine?"

Actually, I could. I put it under the category of *Stupid Things Smart Women Do When They're In Love*. Things like trusting him when he says, "I'm only going to bars to drink." (Which, if true, is a whole other problem). Or "She's only a friend." Or "Keep the motor running. I'll be in the bank for just a second."

"Boy," I said. "Ellie must be crazy about the guy."

"Nan, I think we better talk to Chris at the jail before we talk to Ellie—we've got to convince him to get her to stop this lunacy," Bert said.

I just looked at her. "Even if we convince him, how is he going to convince *her?* I'm not sure they'll let prisoners visit each other—"

"We'll have him write her a note. Or give her a phone call," Bert said. She stared at me with growing exasperation. "Just drive, OK?"

Man. Having your daughter in a jail cell can make you a little touchy. I did, however, as I was told. I drove.

It was around seven-thirty in the evening when we walked into the basement of the Jefferson County Jail. Louisville, however, is on daylight saving time, so we still had a lot of daylight left. Apparently, someone else had been putting in a long day, too. We met Hank Goetzmann in the corridor as we were heading down the hall toward a window marked INFORMATION. He was coming from the opposite direction, and he stopped dead in his tracks, his eyes fixed on Bert, as we approached.

I really would've left them alone to speak in private, but Bert immediately latched on to my arm like she wished we'd been born Siamese twins.

When we got close enough, Goetzmann asked, "How are you holding up?" Right away, I knew that he wasn't addressing me. Mainly because he hadn't looked my way since he'd spotted us.

By this time, Bert was in no mood for sympathetic questions. Or maybe she was afraid she'd start crying again. At any rate, she didn't even answer his question.

She just planted herself, with me attached, right in front

of him. "Hank, we want to talk to Chris Mulholland. And don't start telling me about what the rules for visitors are and that we're not his attorney or his immediate family or anything. We have to get Chris to talk some reason into Ellie."

Halfway into her speech, Goetzmann was already shaking his head no. "Bert, you can't. He's—"

"Don't tell me what I can or can't do, Hank," Bert interrupted. "This is my daughter we're talking about. We have to get into the jail to see Chris, and we need to do it ASA—"

"Bert, that's what I'm trying to tell you. He's not here. Chris Mulholland was released around five this afternoon."

Bert's and my identical mouths dropped open. "What do you mean, he's been released?" I asked.

Hank held his hands out to Bert as if pleading for understanding—a futile gesture, I might add. "We couldn't hold him. The public defender assigned to him got Chris released."

"Damn!" Bert burst out.

Hank's eyes widened. Evidently, he, too, realized hearing Bert curse was right up there with hearing radio waves from another planet. "Now, Bert," he said, "don't get upset. We tried everything we could think of to keep him. It wasn't an accident, you know, to have Chris walk by you in the hallway that time. Those cops stopped just so he'd recognize you and maybe say something he didn't mean to say."

Bert blinked. "Well, that didn't exactly work, did it?" Her tone was scornful. "And now Ellie's still in jail, and the guy who probably really did kill Haggerty gets to go on home, free as a bird. And you're telling me not to get upset? Are you crazy? Of course I'm upset!"

Hank's jaw tightened. I'd seen that look on his face

before, and I could tell it was taking a real effort on Hank's part not to lose his temper. "Bert, Chris Mulholland said he didn't have anything to do with Haggerty's killing, and we don't have any evidence otherwise."

"But you don't have any evidence against Ellie either," Bert argued.

Goetzmann gave her a pointed look. "You mean, other than the fact that she confessed?"

Bert stared him down. "As if you really believe her. Ellie didn't do it, Hank—and I think you know it."

Goetzmann sighed, but when he spoke, there was an edge in his voice. "Even if I wanted to, I couldn't just let her go. She's *confessed*. Don't you understand what that means? Law-enforcement personnel tend to take confession to a crime pretty seriously. Particularly when there're lots of witnesses that say you just argued with the guy. We're funny that way."

I could've told Goetzmann that sarcasm wasn't the route to go with Bert in her present mood. She was already huffing and puffing when he was no more than halfway through his little speech. "Whom do you think you're talking to, Hank Goetzmann?" Bert asked.

This did not seem like an answer I wanted to hear. Bert had released her grip somewhat on my wrist, but as I tried to edge away, Bert tightened up again.

"I am talking to a distraught mother who is not making much sense," Hank said.

Bert's eyes looked as if a couple of flares had gone off behind them. "You could let her go if you wanted to, Hank," Bert said, drawing me closer.

"No," Hank said, "I couldn't. How would that look to the people I work for? Excuse me, guys, but go ahead and let this confessed murderess go because I say so. I can vouch for her because I've been dating her mother. Do you really think that would work?"

Bert apparently missed a significant portion of what Hank had just said. What she did hear was the first part. "How would it LOOK? Is that what you're concerned about? How all this looks?"

Goetzmann did what a lot of men do in this situation. He repeated what he'd already said. "Bert, Ellie confessed. Understand?"

"No, I don't understand. All you have is Ellie's confession," Bert said, "and, believe me, she's about to change her story."

Goetzmann sighed again, and I could tell whatever he was about to say was not going to be good news. "As a matter of fact, we now have a witness who says she saw Haggerty talking with a blond woman in the parking lot that morning—at approximately the time he was killed."

After a long moment, while she digested this latest bombshell, Bert found her voice. "The woman wasn't Ellie. Do you hear me? It WAS NOT Ellie. There are a lot of blond women in the world. Can the witness identify the woman she saw? Did she say it was Ellie?"

Hank sighed. "She says she didn't see the person clearly—but she would swear it was a woman, not a man. And that she was blond. That's all we have."

Bert stared at Hank for an even longer moment; then she squared her shoulders. "We need to see Ellie now. Both of us, Hank. Can you arrange it?"

He could and did.

Fifteen minutes later, Hank escorted us into what was probably an interrogation room in the jail. The room was relatively bare except for some chairs and a table, and a slightly open door at the rear of the room revealing what looked like a sink and toilet in there. No doubt, for those people kept confined in this room so long that they needed to answer nature's call. Or maybe the bathroom was provided so that, once they confessed, they could go in there and throw up.

I also noticed that there was one of those large mirrors on one wall—no doubt, one of those two-way jobs you see on television all the time. I had to fight the urge to wiggle my fingers at whoever was watching us on the other side of the glass. A few minutes later, Hank brought Ellie in and then vamoosed.

I took one long look at Ellie and came to a quick conclusion. Orange is not Ellie's color.

The orange jumpsuit worn by all inmates of the Jefferson County Jail made Ellie's blond hair look greenish and her pale skin sallow. Not only that, but the lack of a blow-dryer and designer shampoo had made her short blond hair look limp and lifeless.

The three of us sat on metal folding chairs drawn up to a metal table. Bert couldn't seem to let Ellie's hands go. "Boy," Bert said, "I'm so glad they're letting us see you without some policewoman standing around."

Ellie looked close to tears, but she smiled and nodded her agreement.

Bert kept on holding Ellie's hands in hers as she told her about the witness who'd seen a woman with Haggerty just before he was killed.

Ellie's eyes widened.

"So I guess, Ellie," I put in, "somebody saw you there, just before, you know, it happened—"

Ellie's eyes widened even more, as she looked over at me. "Somebody has identified *me*? Really?"

I shrugged. "Well, I don't know if they identified you specifically, but they did say it was definitely a woman."

Bert shrugged. "I guess that's one of the reasons they let Chris go, because someone came forward and said that—"

"Wha-a-t?" Ellie said.

I stared at her. Ellie's face looked white. It was a moment before she could speak. "Did you say that they released Chris?"

Bert nodded. "They released him a little while ago."

Ellie's color did not improve. Shaking her head as if trying to wake up, she rose and started walking around the room. Her eyes looked bewildered. "How could they let him go? What about his confession?"

Bert blinked. "What confession?"

Oh God. What I was thinking made me feel a little sick. "Ellie dear," I said, "Chris never did confess. The police just took him in for questioning. They held him for as long as they could, but since they didn't have any evidence against him, they let him go."

Ellie stopped pacing, and turned to face us. Her cheeks were bright pink. "But he was supposed to confess! We agreed. After we found out about Haggerty being killed, Chris was afraid the police might think that he did it—you know, because the two of them had argued."

I glanced over at Bert. She looked almost as pale as Ellie.

Ellie hurried on. "We talked about it and decided that if the police came for Chris, he and I would both confess to the murder so that the police couldn't charge either one of us. It was the perfect plan."

Perfect for Chris. Not so perfect for Ellie.

Ellie's hand suddenly went to her mouth. "Oh my God," she said. "If I'm the only one who confessed, then I'm—I'm in real trouble."

Oh, yes, that pretty much summed it up.

Ellie's blue eyes looked enormous. Turning to face her mom and me, she said, "I didn't kill Mr. Haggerty. I didn't kill anybody."

What a surprise.

"But the police might actually believe that I did it."

"That is generally the way confessions work," I said.

"But I have to tell them," Ellie said. "I have to tell them I didn't do it, and they have to let me go."

Bert squeezed her hand. "Even if they wanted to," Bert said, "they can't just let you go. You *confessed.* Do you understand what that means? Law-enforcement personnel tend to take confession to a crime kind of seriously. They're funny that way."

I turned to stare at Bert. She didn't even seem to realize she'd repeated almost word for word what Goetzmann had just told us.

"Oh, Mom, what am I going to do?"

If it weren't for the fact that we were sitting in a jail, it would've been a lovely moment. It had been years since Ellie had thought her mother—or older people, in general— knew more than she did.

Ellie's eyes were brimming with tears.

Bert got up and hugged her. They stayed like that for a long time, with Bert holding Ellie close and stroking her hair. I felt a little strange, as if I were intruding on a mother-daughter moment.

Finally, Bert said, "Now let me see. First, we're going to call your dad, and he's going to contact your attorney.

Then your attorney is going to tell you what you need to do about recanting your confession." If Bert's voice had not been shaking, you'd have never known how upset she was.

"Now, go in the bathroom and wash your face. Then come back out here and tell me and Nan one more time exactly what happened," Bert said. "Including every single thing you did the day Mr. Haggerty died. And this time, I don't want to hear anything but the truth."

I didn't know about Ellie, but Bert was beginning to scare me. Her voice was getting colder by the minute.

Ellie teared up again. "Oh, Mom, Nan, I'm so sorry I lied to you. It's just that Chris told me—"

I nodded. "If I had a dollar for every time some guy talked me into doing something that was not exactly bright, I'd be a rich woman today."

I'd meant that to sound comforting, but Ellie's lower lip trembled. She turned and all but ran into the bathroom.

While Ellie was out of the room, Bert looked over at me, her eyes like black steel. "Once Jake gets here," she whispered, "you and I are going to pay a little visit to Chris Mulholland."

Oh, yes, Bert was starting to scare me, all right.

Chapter 12

●

Bert

I really did try to calm down as Nan and I left the jail.

Really, I did.

As soon as Jake had arrived with Ellie's attorney in tow, Nan and I headed for Chris's apartment. I had no intention of making a fuss. All I wanted to do was to convince Chris to tell the police that he'd put Ellie up to confessing. That was all. I wasn't going to make any personal judgments about what kind of low-life scumbag would do such a thing. I was just going to get him to explain to the authorities how it had happened that Ellie had ended up confessing to a murder she didn't commit.

After all, I told myself, there were a lot of reasons I should feel sorry for Chris. A foster child hated by his foster sister. A person not even important enough to his foster parents to be remembered in a will. If those things weren't enough, as soon as we drove up to his house, I could certainly see that he had fallen on hard times.

Chris Mulholland lived in a renovated, three-story stone house on Elm Street in Old Louisville near the university. Many of the massive two- and three-story houses in this area had been grand homes to several generations of one family in the twenties and thirties. Now they'd been reno-

vated to become several small apartments and rented out
to college kids who'd rather live just about anywhere than
in the college dorms.

Most of the houses have an abundance of ancient charm,
with wraparound porches, stained-glass insets, and cupolas
like witches' hats sitting on the roofs. Chris's house, however, did not have an abundance of charm. What it had an
abundance of was decay.

The cracks crisscrossing the sidewalk that led up from
the curb were home to anemic-looking dandelions. Paint had
flaked off the building's trim and shutters so much that it
looked as if the place had a bad case of dandruff. Two stone
cardinals that, I guess, were supposed to be perky end posts
to the stone railing that went around the covered porch had
large chips missing out of their wings and beaks. One of the
birds had broken off altogether and teetered on its side,
ready to fall and crush the toes of the next person who tried
to use it as a handhold.

Nan and I exchanged glances, and I knew she was recalling, just as I was, Kaitlin's beautiful house—floor pillows,
notwithstanding—with its multiple gables and manicured
lawn.

Chris's apartment was the downstairs unit on the left,
with its own front entrance. At our ring, Chris opened the
door and blinked at us through the screen door. I was struck
again with how handsome he was—strong, honorable jaw,
guileless blue eyes, and a self-effacing air. Dressed in khaki
slacks and a blue chambray shirt, he was the boy next door—
if the boy next door happened to be a dead ringer for Brad
Pitt.

"Oh, hi," Chris said, glancing first at Nan, then back at
me.

"Hello, Chris," Nan said. Her voice sounded no-nonsense, all business. "We'd like to speak with you for a minute."

Chris managed to look puzzled, as if he had no idea why on earth the two of us might want to talk with him. "Uh, sure," he said. "Come on in." He opened the screen door to let us pass by him. "Which one of you is Ellie's mom?"

I made a little wave of my hand as I went by.

He smiled at me. "It's good to see you again," Chris said. "So, how's Ellie?"

My answer was, I believe, a bigger surprise to me than it was to Chris.

I hauled off and belted him right in the mouth.

The only thing I could think of at the time was this little creep had actually convinced my daughter to confess to murder, on the promise that he would do the same. Just to confound the police. Sure, Ellie was a gullible idiot— there was no doubt about that—but this guy was a snake.

He'd talked Ellie into doing something incredibly dumb, and then he'd reneged on the deal.

And now, he had the colossal gall to ask how she was?

Chris grabbed his mouth, his eyes bright with hurt and surprise. Despite the pain in my hand, I was rearing back to slug him again, when Nan grabbed my arm.

Chris was holding his lip and gaping at me. "Are you nuts? What did you do that for?" he asked.

I stared back at him. I have always been amazed at how some men can do the very worst to you and then still be surprised that you're annoyed. Chris, with his good looks, had no doubt been getting away with a great deal ever since he'd reached puberty.

"What's the matter with you?" he was now asking.

I didn't trust myself to answer, and Nan must not have

either. She jumped right in with what Ellie had told us, as we followed Chris farther into his apartment. He headed straight for a tiny kitchenette and opened the freezer door of his fridge.

"But that's all wrong," Chris said, when Nan finished. I felt my teeth clench. I really and truly hoped he didn't do what I was afraid he was going to do.

His voice sounded as if he were talking through foam rubber, mainly because he already had the beginnings of a pretty large swollen lip. Chris shook a plastic tray of ice cubes into his kitchen sink and grabbed up a couple of cubes, pressing them to his lip.

"Look," he said, turning around to face me. "You've got to believe me. Ellie's making this whole thing up. I never told her to confess, and I certainly wouldn't confess to anything like that myself. What an idiotic thing to do!"

I nodded as he talked. Yep, he was going to do it. He was going to call my very stupid, very wonderful daughter a liar.

So, naturally, I slugged him again.

This time I managed to get a couple of really good blows to the top of his head, even though Chris crouched and put both arms up to protect himself. I would've hit him even more if Nan had not grabbed me around the waist and pulled me backward.

Have I mentioned that Nan is stronger than me? It didn't occur to me at the time that Chris probably was, too. He could certainly have hit me back. But, then again, he was a coward; or he wouldn't have had Ellie take the fall for him.

Not to mention, at the moment, I didn't care how big the guy was. I swear I could've beaten him to a pulp.

My arms and legs were flailing about, trying to break

loose from Nan's hold. We must have looked ridiculous, like
two cartoon characters, Daffy Duck being held back by Bugs
Bunny. But all I could think of was, how dared that little
creep lie about it! How dared he even think we would take
his word over Ellie's!

Chris was yelling, still crouched down, arms still above
his head. "But I didn't do it, I tell you—I didn't tell Ellie
to confess!"

Nan tightened her arms around my waist as I struggled
to get to him. In my defense, I would like to add that I
was overwrought. I would also like to add that I have not
assaulted anybody since.

Nan yanked me backward. "I suggest that you stop saying that, Chris, or I'm going to let go of my sister again."

I was brought up short by that one. Goodness. Nan made
me sound like a pit bull on a leash.

Chris got up and backed away from me, holding his hands
out as if to ward me off. He was still holding the ice cubes,
and he slumped back against the kitchen counter as he
pressed them to his lip again. "Look, I'm sorry about Ellie.
I'm really worried about her being in jail and all."

Oh yes, he looked worried, all right. He looked very
worried about his swollen lip.

"But I haven't done anything wrong," Chris went on.
"I'm a victim here, too. If you don't believe me, just go talk
to my sister. You'll see what's been done to me. Kaitlin has
stolen everything that's rightfully mine."

I glared back at him. I was really glad he didn't have any
sharp instruments around his kitchen, because I wouldn't want
to find out what I was capable of right then. "Sister?" I asked.
"You mean foster sister, don't you?"

"Chris, we have talked to Kaitlin," Nan said. "So you

were a foster child and your foster parents left no will when they died. That's a real shame, but it doesn't give you the right to implicate an innocent person in a murder."

"You'll notice you're not in jail," I said. "You'll notice you're standing right here, free as a bird—unlike some people I believe I have already mentioned."

Chris ignored everything except what Nan had said about his parents. "My parents did so leave a will. Kaitlin stole it or destroyed it or something. I know they left one, though—I saw the will with my own eyes. My mother showed it to me."

"Yeah, right," Nan said. "And we can believe this, like we can believe everything else you've said?"

"I don't care what you believe," Chris said. "It's the truth. I was supposed to get half. That's what Mom told me."

I stared at him, noticing that he never referred to his parents as foster parents. Maybe they had never treated him like a foster child. Maybe the only person who treated him like a foster child had been Kaitlin.

Chris was going on, his voice muffled by the ice cubes. "My mother put the will in this trompe l'oeil armoire that my parents owned."

"Trump what?" Nan asked.

"Trompe l'oeil," I said. "It's French for 'fool the eye.' If I remember my high school French correctly."

Chris nodded. "That's right. The trompe l'oeil armoire was the thing I was arguing with Haggerty about—other than him being a scam artist, of course. Haggerty bought that armoire from Kaitlin."

I just looked at him, remembering Sheila Haggerty's house and the large armoire I'd noticed there, its doors covered with realistic birds and flowers. Was this the armoire Chris was talking about?

Chris went on. "I was trying to convince Haggerty to let me search inside the armoire. There's a hidden recess built into one of the drawers—one of those things old cabinetmakers used to do—where Mom put the will. But Haggerty was being stubborn about letting me look, for some reason."

"He wouldn't let you examine the armoire?" Nan asked.

"Haggerty insisted the armoire was empty, but the way he acted—" Chris shrugged. "I always felt like he was hiding something."

Nan and I looked at each other. Much as I hated to admit it, this little snake was making sense. Maybe Kaitlin hadn't wanted to share her parents' estate with a foster brother. Maybe she'd wanted it all. Maybe she had found her parents' will and destroyed it. Or maybe she couldn't find it, and that's why she'd decided to sell every single piece of her parents' things.

Or maybe Haggerty had found the will among the things Kaitlin had sold him, and tried to make a deal with Kaitlin. He'd keep quiet about the will for a price. Was he blackmailing her? Everything I'd heard about Haggerty certainly made me think that he was capable of blackmail.

The real question was, however, could Kaitlin have killed Haggerty to keep his mouth shut about the will?

I sighed. Chris was still a snake, but maybe he really was a victimized snake.

Chris held his hands out in a silent appeal. "I've even asked Mrs. Haggerty to let me search through my parents' things; but she's even worse than her husband. That bitch wanted to charge me $5,000 for the privilege. Hell, I don't have that kind of money. Her wanting to charge me that much, though, made me think she has to know something."

"How do we know," I asked Chris, "that you didn't kill Haggerty to get the will?"

Chris looked first at me, and then very slowly looked around the room. I followed his gaze, noting the chipped sink, the fifties refrigerator, the gas range with its broken and missing knobs. "Would I still be living in this dump if I had that will?" he asked.

He had a point.

Of course, considering what a fine young man he was, it could still be that Chris himself had killed Haggerty for the will and just hadn't taken legal action yet. Chris could be waiting until Ellie was convicted of the murder. It was also still very possible that Chris had killed Haggerty in the argument over the armoire.

I met Nan's eyes and knew she was thinking what I was. If we had that will, at least, we could prove someone else had a motive to kill Haggerty. I really didn't care if it was Chris or Kaitlin. Or the Pillsbury Doughboy. Just someone other than Ellie.

"OK," Nan said, leaning against the kitchen counter, "Now tell us again. Exactly where did you see that will?"

Chris stood there, pressing the ice to his mouth, looking as if answering that question might be even more painful than my punching him in the mouth.

Chapter 13

•

Nan

I honestly don't know what made me decide to do what we did when we got to Sheila Haggerty's house.

Or why in the world Bert went along with it.

Maybe it was the sight of Bert actually honest-to-God belting someone in the chops. That whole belting thing was so unlike law-abiding, rule-following Bert. I mean, she never even cut class in high school. She was a virgin when she got married, for goodness' sake. If you gave Bert the word *assault* in a word association game, she'd say *a pepper*. Well, you get the idea.

I'm not saying that Bert has never, ever hit anyone before—she has. She clobbered somebody with her purse once, when she thought that somebody was trying to kill me. But that was an extreme case. And she'd used her purse. This time when she'd belted Chris, it had been with her bare hands.

Of course, I did have to hold Bert back, more's the pity— Chris could easily have decked her with one blow. I wouldn't have put it past him, either. If he'd enticed Ellie to confess to murder for him, he certainly wouldn't be above hitting a woman.

The whole time I was preventing Bert from going after

him, though, I'd felt like applauding. There is something so exhilarating about seeing a very good-looking, very smooth-talking guy getting hit right in the mouth.

Yes, yes, I realized that I needed to run, not walk, to the nearest psychiatrist's office and work out my not-so-latent hostilities toward the opposite sex. I would hazard a guess, though, that the number of women who might find such a scene exhilarating would number in the thousands. And that would just be in Louisville alone. Hell, we could make a parade heading into the old psychiatrist's office to work all that hostility out of our little systems.

Of course, I've always wondered why it is that we women are always the ones who end up in psychiatrists' offices, poring over "self-esteem issues." Men don't seem to be worrying about their self-esteem. Apparently, lying to women and treating them badly doesn't hurt a guy's self-esteem at all.

Watching Bert pound on Chris, I've got to say, was pretty much of an eye-opener. Now I realize that it would save a lot of money and time—and do a woman's self-esteem a world of good—if, when you caught your man in a lie, you just hauled off and belted him right in the mouth.

At any rate, Bert and I had left that exhilarating scene behind us, and we were planning to mosey on over to Sheila Haggerty's house. While one of us chatted with the lovely woman, the other one would rifle through the Mulholland furniture and look for the missing will—if, indeed, it existed in the first place, Chris not being what I would call a totally reliable source.

For an unreliable source, however, he'd given us a pretty good description of the furniture and other items in the

Mulholland estate that had been sold to Haggerty. Bert, of course, being Bert, had made a list—with notations.

Anyway, that was the plan.

I'd driven about halfway to Willow Avenue when it occurred to me what time it was. "You know, Bert," I said, looking over at her, "it *is* after nine o'clock."

Bert didn't even look my way. "And your point?"

The old rule-centric Bert would never have called on someone after 9 P.M. without phoning first. I couldn't help but stare at her. Years of learning social graces at our mama's knee had apparently been wiped away by one over-riding urge of maternal protection. I suppressed a grin. "Nothing," I said. "We just need to hurry before Sheila goes to bed."

"So which one of us wants to talk to her?" Bert asked, glancing quickly over at me and then back at the road. She was leaning forward, as if that would make my Neon go even faster.

"Oh, why don't you do it?" I said, trying to sound casual. "You do small talk so much better than me." Frankly, I had no idea which one of us did small talk better, but the very idea of listening at length to that bullhorn that passed itself off as a woman made my ears ache.

"Are you kidding? You're the best talker—goodness, you do it for a living," Bert said, in the same oh-so-casual tone.

It occurred to me then that the possibility of impending deafness had occurred to Bert, too. In the end, we decided the question the same way we settled the question of "Who was It?" when we were kids. We recited that time-honored rhyme: "One Potato, Two Potato." For the record, I ended up being "Seven Potato," and Bert ended up being "More."

In other words, she was It, the one who got to talk to the bullhorn.

As it turned out, though, talking to Sheila turned out not to be an option, after all.

When I pulled my Neon up to the curb, all the windows in the Haggerty house were dark. "Drat! She's already gone to bed," I said.

"Well, let's wake her up!" Bert said. She was already out of the Neon and marching up the steps by the time I got out and locked up my car. I stared after her again. Man, this was one determined female.

I joined Bert on the porch as she rang the doorbell. Inside, we could hear the doorbell echoing through the hallways; although, Lord knows, with all the pieces of upholstered furniture and heavy draperies inside, it was a wonder the sound wasn't completely absorbed two seconds after the button was pushed.

After about thirty seconds, tops, Bert rang the bell again, tapping her foot impatiently.

I glanced at the empty driveway alongside the house. "Bert—" I began.

By that time she was really leaning on the bell. Evidently, when Bert is determined to annihilate a few social graces, nothing's going to get in her way.

"Hon," I said, "I don't think she's home."

This time Bert looked over at the driveway, too. She sighed. "Great. Just great. Now what?"

Her crestfallen face was more than I could bear. At least, I'd like to think that's what was going through my mind. A heartfelt sympathy for my beloved sister, who only wanted to get her daughter out of the hoosegow.

On the other hand, it might've been the thrill of doing

something we really shouldn't. Exhilarated by watching Bert do something she shouldn't to Chris, I now felt terribly inclined to do something myself that I shouldn't.

I tried the front door, as Bert's eyes widened. The door was locked, of course. "You know," I said, "the windows in these old houses don't always lock very tight. One little push and up they go."

Bert's eyes got even wider. "That's breaking and entering, isn't it?"

I shook my head. "Not at all. We wouldn't be breaking— we'd just be entering."

Bert stared back at me for a split second. Then she headed off the porch, taking the steps two at a time. She moved quickly around to the rear of the building.

I took a fast look around. There didn't seem to be anybody outside, and I could see no one standing at their windows, looking this way. I caught up with Bert and snagged her arm as she was removing the screen from one of the windows on the ground floor. "Listen," I whispered, "one of us should stay out here and stand watch in case Sheila comes home." I was whispering just in case Sheila's neighbors still had any hearing left—a remote possibility, but still a possibility.

"OK," Bert whispered back. Having put the screen down, she was now tugging at the window sash. "You can stand watch." Her face contorted with the effort of trying to lift the window.

The damn thing held.

I moved on to the window next to hers, lifting out the screen. "Oh, no, you don't," I whispered back, grunting with the effort to lift that window, too. "I've got a lot more experience with hunting for things in messy places. Like my home, for example. You stand watch."

"But I've got a lot more experience hunting for lost things. Years of experience with two kids who were constantly losing stuff," Bert countered. "So you stand watch."

We continued arguing about it as we made our way slowly around the house, trying to lift every damn window we came to. Those suckers had to have been locked and then painted shut. Not one of the windows would even budge.

"Damn!" Bert said.

I guess I was getting used to her potty mouth by now. I didn't even glance at her. Instead, I moved directly to the back door and tried the doorknob. It was locked tight. The dead bolt, in fact, looked pretty invincible.

Next to me, Bert had picked up a large stone. "Look," she whispered, "as long as we're doing the entering, we might as well go with the breaking, too."

OK, that time I stared. Bert was getting to be a wild woman.

Bert caught my look, and shrugged. "Hey, I'll leave Sheila some money to get her window fixed." She frowned, testing the rock's weight in her hand. "You see another rock around here? This one is a lot lighter than it looks."

I looked down at the ground. A door key lay in the spot where Bert's rock had been. Well, whaddya know? Dear, thoughtful Sheila had left us her door key, hidden under one of those fake hide-a-key rocks. I reached down and picked up the key. Having locked myself out a few times, I'd actually been considering getting myself one of those hide-a-key rocks. Now I could see that a potential robber might do the exact same thing that Bert had just done. I didn't want to rain on anybody's parade, but it seemed to me that this was a major flaw in the whole fake-rock concept. Maybe what the fake-rock people should manufacture instead were fake snakes.

When I showed the key to Bert, she almost let out a whoop, stopping herself just in time. "Wonderful!" she whispered, dropping the rock.

I unlocked the back door, and Bert immediately tried to edge past me, saying, "OK, you stand watch."

I grabbed her arm, pulling her back. "Bert, for one thing, you lost at 'One Potato.' Remember? And, you're the one dating a cop—think of the crap that will hit the fan if we get caught. And, finally—and I think this pretty much ends all discussion—I found the key."

I don't know which argument prevailed, but Bert frowned, handed me her annotated list, crossed her arms, and stepped aside. "I'll come get you if I see anyone coming."

"Right," I said. Hurrying through the back door, I shut it softly behind me.

Moving around in dark, crowded rooms filled with wall-to-wall furniture is not as easy as it sounds. I'd banged my knees and shins about half a dozen times before I decided that using the small penlight on my key chain would probably be OK. After all, the woman had heavy drapes at most of the windows—how likely was it that a light that small could be seen from the road?

I searched the armoire first. Bert had said trompe l'oeil meant "fool the eye." Well, it didn't fool my eye—it looked like someone had painted a window and a bunch of birds and flowers on a couple of doors. The inside of the armoire didn't fool my eye, either—it was completely empty, including the so-called hidden recess in the drawer.

I glanced around the room. From the list, I had a pretty good idea of what furniture pieces I was looking for. What

I didn't count on, though, was how many pieces might fit that description. A "long walnut buffet" could be any one of four pieces. A "heavy carved mahogany writing desk" could be one of three. I pulled out the top drawer of the desk nearest to the armoire and flicked my penlight around. It was exactly the same as the armoire—empty.

I'd worked my way through about three-quarters of the list when my attention was caught by a shadow in the rear of a drawer in the "carved walnut liquor cabinet." My heart actually began to pound. A liquor cabinet was exactly the place I'd hide my own will. I'd need several stiff drinks if I were contemplating my own death and going over the pathetically small amount of stuff I had to show for a lifetime. I reached in and pulled out a packet of papers, held together with a large rubber band, that had been pushed all the way to the back of the top drawer.

I removed the rubber band, my heart pounding even louder, only to discover that the whole bundle was just a stack of ancient, professional-looking photographs in brown cardboard display folders. You know the kind—sepia-toned shots of unsmiling people in dark clothes sitting very stiffly and looking as if they were in great pain. Which, come to think of it, they probably were, considering how long it took to expose film back then.

These particular photos, though, were probably considered cheesecake in those days. I pictured some old guy sitting, having a drink and leering at these pictures—their version of popping a beer and looking at the latest *Playboy* magazine. The photographs were all of the same person in various poses—some tall woman, here looking coyly over her shoulder, there her ruffled lace collar dropping off a bare shoulder, all with her thick blond hair piled high in a Gibson-girl style over a rather angular face. In several of the pictures, she wore a see-through negligee, bra and panties, and what looked like silk stockings. These, no doubt, got some turn-of-the-century dude's heart pounding, but they were pretty mild by today's standards. I looked at one of the pictures a little closer, shining the penlight directly on the photo.

I could swear the face was familiar somehow—maybe a long-dead relative of Kaitlin's? And yet, other than hair color, I couldn't honestly say that I could see any family resemblance.

I was about to toss the photos back in the drawer when I heard someone moving in behind me.

"Bert?" I whispered as loud as I dared. "Is someone coming?"

There was no answer.

I started to turn around.

That, however, was pretty much the last thing I remember. Except, of course, for that sudden and very sharp pain on the back of my head.

And, oh, yes, all that blackness, rushing up and pulling me into it.

Chapter 14

•

Bert

I awoke, lying on my back in dew-covered grass, staring up at a starry black sky. Crickets chirping, and frogs croaking, and other night sounds all around me made my head throb from the incessant racket. For a second, I wondered if the sparkling stars that appeared above me were the same stars I'd seen right before everything went black. Those particular stars, though, I was pretty sure hadn't had that big white moon in the middle of them.

I struggled to my feet, my head protesting with sharp jabs of pain every time I made the slightest move. When I'd managed to stand fully upright—no small task—I looked around, trying to place where in God's name I was. A sidewalk, a door, a rosebush swam in front of me. Then I saw the fake rock on the ground.

And it all came back to me.

I'd been standing just outside the open door, feeling a little bored and a lot worried about Ellie. There had been a soft rustle of movement just behind me. Before I could even turn around, though, there had come an excruciating pain and then—total darkness. Even as I'd dropped into the void of black, I could still hear Nan through the open door, moving around inside the house.

The back door was closed.

Oh my God—Nan!

I reached for the door, as a wave of nausea washed over me, and the world began to blur again. After that, I guess I opened it, moved inside, and groped my way through the dark house. I say, I guess I did all this, because I don't remember any of it. Everything was a dark blur until I found myself kneeling at Nan's side.

She lay there, in front of an antique liquor cabinet, flat on her back, her eyes closed, her face so pale it looked like it should be illuminating the room.

"Nan?"

My voice sounded shaky. It also sounded like I was yelling at the top of my lungs, as my head rocked with another stab of pain.

I leaned unsteadily closer, feeling for a pulse in Nan's throat. Thank God I felt it immediately. If anything, Nan's heartbeat seemed a little stronger than my own. It was significantly slower, though. I felt tears spring to my eyes, I was so relieved.

Once I'd done the pulse thing, though, I wasn't sure what else to do. The house was very dark, even with moonlight streaming in the window. I knew I should probably go find some water to sprinkle on Nan's face to help her come to, but the truth was, I didn't want to leave her. I also wasn't sure just how steady on my feet I was myself.

My luck, I'd lose consciousness again somewhere in the house. And Sheila Haggerty would come home and trip over the two of us.

The thought of Sheila returning home added urgency to the task at hand. "Nan!" I said. "Wake up, for God's sake!" As I said this, I took hold of Nan's limp hand, patting it like

I'd seen people do on TV. I've never known why they do that—maybe the sensation is so annoying it wakes people up—but it was the only thing I could think of to do that did not require my getting up and going anywhere without Nan.

"Nan?" I said again. "Honey?"

She didn't move.

With my head aching, I tried to think what else to do—which only made my head hurt worse. I shouldn't move her, should I? Nan really didn't look good—should I even try to wake her? An ambulance—that was it. I should call an ambulance. In fact, twin ambulances. I sat back on my heels, looking around for a telephone, still holding on to Nan's hand, when all at once she groaned.

"Oh, Nan!" I said. "You're awake!" As it turned out, that might have been an overstatement.

Nan groaned again, and put the back of her hand to her eyes.

I couldn't tell if she was trying to get her eyes open, or to keep them closed. "Nan, listen to me," I said, leaning closer to her ear. "We've got to get out of here."

Her eyes fluttered open; and, almost immediately, she started trying to sit up.

"Oh, Nan, are you all right?" I asked, helping prop her up.

Nan turned her head toward me, her eyes squinting with pain, and I winced in return just watching her do it. Talk about twins feeling each other's pain—of course, it helps a whole lot if you've both been conked on the head.

Nan just sat there and blinked at me a couple of times, and then looked around again, peering into the dark. Slowly, she put her hand up to the back of her head, grimacing at the touch.

I moved closer, peering at her. She hadn't spoken yet. Maybe she didn't know me. Maybe she didn't know herself.

"Nan," I said, waving two fingers in front of her eyes. "How many fingers do you see? Come on, Nan," I said. "How many?"

Nan turned slowly to look at me. Then, finally, she spoke. "I see just one," she said, gingerly touching the back of her head again.

I had a moment of alarm, and then Nan added, "Just one idiot."

We both smiled at each other.

"Thank you so much for that unsolicited testimonial," I said.

"Do you know what time it is?" Nan asked. Her voice sounded a little woozy.

I shook my head, a motion I immediately regretted. The world dipped and swirled for a moment. I grabbed my head, waiting for the pain to subside. "Can't see my watch," I said. "Too dark."

Nan was struggling to her feet now, grasping the edge of the liquor cabinet to steady herself. "Oh man, what hit me?"

"You mean, what hit *us?*" I said, getting to my feet in the same painfully slow manner.

Nan turned to watch my painful ascent. "You too?"

I told her then what had happened. Halfway through my tale of the good, the bad, and the really, really painful, Nan lost interest. Been there, done that was written all over her face. She started looking down at the floor and all around her feet. "Oh, great," she said, "just great. They're gone."

"What's gone? What are you talking about?" I, too,

started looking at the floor, as if I'd actually recognize whatever it was, if I saw it.

"The pictures."

Nan went on to describe the photographs she'd found of some ancestral bimbo making like Mae West. While she talked, I took a good look at the room around us. My eyes had adjusted to the gloom, and what I was looking at was not pretty.

All around us, drawers were pulled out and emptied, their contents strewn on the carpet. Lids on chests were raised, and glass doors to bookcases stood wide open. Books had been pulled out into heaps on the floor.

"Oh my," I said.

I knew Sheila was not exactly the best housekeeper in the world, but even she would not have left the room like this. In fact, the room looked as if it had been thoroughly searched. Well, more like thoroughly ransacked.

"Good Lord, Nan, you really should've been more careful about making this mess. Now we're going to have to clean all this—"

Nan's really icky-sounding snort cut me off. "Bert, I didn't do this. I didn't have time to do all this." She looked around again—a motion, I could tell, that she, too, immediately regretted. "Whoever did this must've been looking for something a lot more interesting than vintage cheesecake."

I would have nodded my agreement, but I'd already found that to be a bad idea. "Like a will, maybe?" I said, keeping my head as motionless as possible. "I wonder if they found it."

"Let's get out of here," Nan said. I'm sure it was her intention to walk purposefully out the back door; but a scant two steps later, she had to grab hold of a ladderback chair to keep from toppling over.

I felt the same queasy sensation when I tried to walk. So Nan and I ended up putting our arms around each other's shoulders and making our wobbly way out the back door— no doubt, resembling two drunken sailors after an extensive shore leave.

It took a lot longer than it should've to get outside. Knowing that we had to get out of there, however, helped keep us moving. Neither of us had any idea how long we'd been unconscious. Sheila could be back any moment, although it was beginning to look more and more like she was away for the night—perhaps on a buying trip. God knows, she needed more stuff to clutter her living room.

I didn't mention it to Nan, but it wasn't just Sheila showing up that worried me. I really did not want to be arrested for breaking and entering—minus the breaking—or for vandalizing a home, regardless of whether we did it or not. It seemed to take us forever, but eventually, we made it to Nan's car.

On the way home Nan and I discussed the value of immediate medical attention for both of us. "No way, Jose," I believe, was Nan's reaction. We also talked over the appropriateness of informing the police about the Haggerty break-in.

"Which one?" Nan had asked, glancing over at me.

Goodness, she had a point. There was the break-in we'd done and the break-in that had been done after us.

In the end, we decided to play it safe and stop at a pay phone. We'd dial 911 and notify the police anonymously that the house had been trashed. That way, if they traced the phone call, it couldn't be traced to Nan or me.

I dialed the phone, wearing the wool driving gloves that Nan was still carrying around in her glove compartment.

The woman cop who answered the call asked me my name and address right away. Instead, I gave her Sheila's address, I described what had happened there, and I hung up.

That little chore done, all I really wanted was to get home and inhale a bottle of Excedrin tablets.

Maybe soak in a nice, relaxing tub.

When Nan pulled into her driveway, though, the first thing I saw was the car sitting behind mine in my driveway. My heart sank, and my head began to beat a very rapid rhythm on my skull.

Nan saw the car, too. "Uh-oh," she said, turning off the ignition.

The car was Jake's Lexus.

Jake got out of his car just as Nan and I got out, still moving very carefully from the pain. Nan took one look at Jake, standing next to his car, obviously waiting for me, and asked, "Want me to come over with you?" She tried to sound like she would be glad to accompany me, but her eyes begged me to tell her no.

I sighed. "Oh no, that's not necessary," I said. "Besides, I really do need to talk to him." I told Nan I'd be over a little later so that we could compare our ability to focus our eyes. I also insisted that she phone me if she started feeling any worse.

"I'm OK," Nan insisted. "I'm fine. Are you all right?"

"I'm fine, too," I said.

To prove it, we both moved unsteadily toward our front doors.

"Where the hell have you been?" were Jake's first words.

His tone definitely had the usual "you're-an-idiot" ring to it; but this time, wonder of wonders, Jake actually seemed to hear himself. "I mean," he hastily amended, "are you all right, Bert? You look like you're in pain, or something."

No kidding.

Jake, on the other hand, looked as if he'd just showered, shaved, put on a clean white Ralph Lauren polo shirt with the neck open and tan Dockers, and—was that cologne he was wearing?

Oh, God. It was the cologne he knew was my favorite—Aramis. I really didn't feel up to this.

"What happened?" Jake asked.

"It's a long story, Jake," I said, my tone weary. A story involving illegal activity and unconsciousness. A story I had no intention of ever sharing with him. I changed the subject. "So how's Ellie? What did the lawyer say?"

"That's what I've been waiting here so long to tell you," Jake said.

I waited, but it was clear he was not going to launch into it standing out here on my tiny porch. I turned then, and began trying to fit my key into my front door lock.

This last almost immediately began to seem like an impossible task. Mostly, I guess, because I couldn't quite figure out which of the three locks that swam in front of me was the right one.

After I missed the lock a couple of times, Jake put his hand gently over mine and took the key from me. "Here, let me do that," he said softly, one arm going casually around my shoulders as he leaned around me to insert the key.

The tone in his voice made me glance at him quickly, just in time to see a tiny smirk at the corner of his mouth. Oh, God, the man was actually thinking that his nearness was rattling me so badly, I couldn't unlock my own front door. I mean, really, Jake, can you say "egomaniac"?

Of course, at one time, I guess he'd had that kind of power over me, but that had been a long, long, long time ago. I would've laughed out loud, but I knew the effort would make my head hurt too badly. Besides, it was good to have someone helping me just then. Even if it did happen to be Jake.

"Thanks, Jake," I said, after he'd unlocked and opened the front door for me.

"My pleasure," he said, handing me my key. He took a deep breath then, and added, his words coming in a rush, "I might as well tell you the worst right off. The judge may not grant bail for Ellie."

"What?" I stared at him, trying not to wince, as my head throbbed. "But why not?"

Jake held up one hand. "Hey, I'm not saying he won't. It's just that this judge doesn't generally grant bail in murder cases—that's what the lawyer says anyway."

"But she didn't do it!" I said.

Jake was nodding, moving smoothly around me to step inside my apartment. I had no choice but to follow him inside. "I know that. You know that. But, unfortunately, the judge doesn't know that." He snapped my foyer lights on and went into my living room, turning on the lamps on my end tables. He turned to face me. "There's that dumb confession, you see."

The very thought of Ellie sitting in that awful jail cell made me feel a little sick. This was a nightmare. "Oh, Jake, what in the world are we going to do?" Tears welled in my eyes, and I blinked them away.

Jake needed no more encouragement than that. He was

at my side in a heartbeat, putting his arms around me, cradling my head against his shoulder. The feel of him was familiar, and surprisingly comforting. "We're going to fight this," he said against my hair. "Together. Tomorrow there's going to be a bail hearing, and the lawyer is going to submit the recantation of Ellie's confession. After that's done, all the police have against her is circumstantial—a blond woman seen arguing with Haggerty in the parking lot the morning he died. Ellie and Chris seen quarreling with Haggerty at the flea market—that's pretty much it."

I nodded, mutely, and started to pull away from his embrace.

His arms tightened around me. "Oh, Bert," he said. He took a long, shuddering breath. "I have dreamed of having you in my arms again."

I just looked at him. That sounded a lot like a nightmare to me.

"Please," Jake said. "Hear me out, OK?"

I closed my eyes. There really didn't seem to be any way to avoid hearing what he had to say.

"Bert, you know that I want to come back," Jake said. "Please let me. We're a family. You and me and Ellie and Brian. No one will ever care about our kids as much as I do."

I looked up at him, and he slowly began to lower his face to mine for a kiss.

It would have been so easy to just kiss him and see where it went from there. So easy. God knows I needed a little comfort then—especially since Hank had seemed to have let me down so badly. And yet, as Jake's mouth moved toward mine, the sparkle of that silly diamond stud in his ear caught my eye.

I couldn't help it.

At the very last second, I turned my head away.

Then I said to him what Jake had to have gotten used to hearing me say by now—especially toward the very end of our marriage, after I'd heard about him and his aerobic exercises with his secretary.

"Jake," I said, "I have a headache."

Then I escorted him to the door.

Jake turned to me at the doorstep. "Just promise me you'll think about it, OK? I want us to be a family again."

He looked so pitiful that I nodded. "All right, Jake, I'll think about it."

Jake leaned toward me, and kissed me softly on the cheek.

Over Jake's shoulder, I noticed a familiar car driving slowly by on the street in front of the house, its turn signal blinking to indicate its intention to turn into my driveway. The driver turned to look at me; and, in the light from the streetlamp, I saw his face clearly for a split second. I saw his eyes narrow, his mouth set in a tight, thin line. Then the driver looked quickly back at the road, gunned the motor, and drove past us, down the road and out of sight.

It was Hank.

He didn't look happy.

Chapter 15

•

Nan

I awoke the next morning, wondering whether that horrible
pounding I was hearing was someone knocking on my door,
or if the noise was all in my poor, aching head. I was pretty
sure jackhammers weren't that loud. I pulled my pillow over
my head and waited for the pounding to go away.

It didn't.

OK, so maybe there really was somebody at my front
door. I blinked at the digital clock on my bedside table—
half past eight. In the frigging morning, for God's sake.

I yanked on a pair of jersey knit shorts over my bikini
panties and pulled on a T-shirt that read "WCKI—All Up
and Down the Ohio River"—a slogan, by the way, that I've
always thought could've been either for a radio station or a
waste-disposal plant. I yelled, "I'm coming already! Hold
your horses!" As the pounding in my head seemed to rattle
my teeth, I ran down the hallway to my front door.

Needless to say, I was not in my best mood. My throbbing
head felt like I had the world's worst hangover, and I hadn't
even had so much as a lemonade the night before.

I threw open my door without even looking through the
peephole. "OK, OK, what?" I demanded, putting up a hand

to shield my eyes from the brutal onslaught of the bright August morning.

Sam Grainger stood on my porch step.

When my eyes focused, I had to admit that he looked pretty good—for a guy with a job title that had the word *flea* in it. Blond ponytail, nice tan, and wearing one of those white cotton, no-collar shirts, faded blue jeans, and cowboy boots. He gave me a sheepish smile, ducking his head apologetically.

"Wow, I'm really sorry to have to drop in this way," he began. His eyes began a slow excursion down my body to my bare feet. "Oh, wow, did I get you up?"

"Not at all," I said, "I always look like I've slept in my clothes."

I watched his eyes start the return trip and stop at my chest, no doubt in search of an answer to that age-old masculine question: Is she, or is she not, wearing a bra?

The answer? She most definitely was *not*.

I wasn't trying to be sexy or anything—I just hadn't thought to put the damn thing on, what with all the racket going on in my head.

I never sleep in a bra. Not since I read in some women's magazine that, back in the thirties, Howard Hughes had advised the actresses he'd dated to sleep in bras so that their perfect breasts wouldn't drop to their knees. Once I read *that*, I started going out of my way never to fall asleep in a bra. It's a personal rule never to take the advice of men with fingernails longer than mine.

"I'm really sorry to wake you up," Grainger said to my chest. "I was on my way to work, and I thought surely you—"

I snapped my fingers, and he looked up, but he didn't look the least bit embarrassed. He just smiled at me, then reached out and brushed a strand of dark hair out of my eyes. "Wow," he said. "Most women definitely do not look this good first thing in the morning."

I squinted at him, for the first time noting that the blond golden-boy hair had streaks of gray in it. Well, that explained it. He was older than I'd first thought, and his eyes were going.

"On behalf of all the women you've just maligned, thanks a whole bunch," I said. Like I said, I was not in my best mood.

Sam didn't seem to care that I was being so grouchy. He just grinned again. "On behalf of myself, you're welcome." His cheery demeanor was unnerving. So was the way his eyes met mine, and held. "So," he finally said. "I guess I better tell you the reason I came over—"

"Look, I've got to have a Coke," I interrupted. "I need caffeine right now, and I don't like coffee. You want something to drink?" Without waiting for an answer, I turned and headed for my kitchen. I could hear Grainger's boots clip-clopping after me.

"You drink Coca-Cola in the morning?" Grainger asked, leaning against my kitchen counter as I pulled a two-liter bottle out of my refrigerator.

I shrugged. "I figured it was a choice between the sweet brown stuff with caffeine or the bitter brown stuff with caffeine," I said, putting ice cubes in a couple of glasses and then pouring the Coke over them. I handed Grainger a frosty glass and took a long, long sip of mine. "I chose sweet," I said, with a sigh. Once the icy cola began to clear the cobwebs and put the pain in my head at a distance, I turned to look at Grainger. He was drinking his Coke and looking oddly uncomfortable all of a sudden.

"So," I said, "what's up?"

Grainger met my eyes. "Wow. Like I said, I'm really sorry to have to do this."

"Do what?"

He shrugged. "Tell you about the complaints I've been getting."

I was in the middle of another long sip. Swallowing, I said, "Complaints?"

"Right. Some very important people are not very pleased that I gave you and your sister their names and addresses. I'm afraid that they don't exactly appreciate being asked a bunch of questions. Harassment, they're calling it. And invasion of privacy. So I'm going to have to ask you and your sister to please stop questioning people about their problems with Franklin Haggerty."

I almost laughed in his face. For one thing, we'd pretty much worked our way through his precious list, and it had been largely a bust. In fact, it had been such a royal failure that I couldn't see Bert or me ever having to bother any of those people again.

On the other hand, now that I thought about it, why had our questions made anyone upset? Why would anyone care if we asked a couple of harmless questions if they didn't have anything to hide?

"Which of the people that we interviewed have complained about us?" I asked, taking another sip of Coke.

Grainger glanced away. "What does it really matter who complained? Let's just say they were in that crowd of people waiting to see me the other day."

Now why did I think he was trying to be evasive? I tried to picture which of that group might have been really important people. Most of the group had looked pretty unimportant. Of course, if *important* equated with *wealthy*—

which, I had a sneaking suspicion, was what the wow-guy here really meant—there'd been that old lady with the chauffeur. And then there was the short broad carrying the tiny Yorkshire terrier and some dork with an ascot, if I recalled correctly.

"So which ones were they?" I asked again. "Did we go out and question them that very day?"

Grainger cleared his throat, looking at me again. "Well, actually—it's not anyone you've talked to. Not yet. And, to tell the truth, it's just this one couple. They apparently heard from some of the others that you two were going around, interviewing people; and they wanted to make sure you did not come to see them. They called me at home last night, insisting that I tell you personally that you are not to use the names and addresses that I gave you any longer."

I stared at him, trying to picture them more clearly. "These people are saying that we're harassing them and we haven't even talked to them yet? You don't think that's kind of strange?"

Grainger shrugged. "Not if you know the type of people they are. Extremely rich, and extremely protective of their privacy. They certainly don't want to be involved in the investigation of a murder. Especially the murder of someone who was almost a stranger to them. They said it's—what was the word they used?—*unseemly.*" He took another sip of his Coke. "Some of the very rich are like that."

"Oh, really?" I said. "I wouldn't know."

"Wow, me neither," he said, grinning. "Look, Nan, I don't understand it, either. But these people apparently have some very important friends. Friends who, by the way, can get the business permit for the flea market pulled, if they want to. I'm just conveying the message to please leave these people alone."

I looked at him for a long minute. Then, without a word, I marched into the living room and got my purse off the sofa, where I'd left it last night. I opened my purse and pulled out the list of names that Grainger had given us. There were only a few people left on the list that we hadn't already seen.

Heading back into the kitchen, I started naming them off. "Mr. and Mrs. Wayne Brown. Sandie and Mark Ellsworth. Rita and—"

Grainger stared at me. "What are you doing?"

I smiled sweetly at him, my eyes wide. "Well, you can't very well expect us to be sure to avoid these people if we don't know which ones they are, can you?"

Grainger blinked a couple of times, but then he told me their names. "Mr. and Mrs. Leonard Hutcheson Welch, III. The complaint had been filed by Mr. Welch." I checked the list for their address: 45111 Brownsboro Road.

With my promise that Nan and I would not, in any way, harass the privacy-mad, filthy-rich couple still ringing, no doubt, in his ears, I hustled Sam Grainger out the door. I made sure that he did not see me crossing my fingers behind my back as I made my promise.

As soon as he left, I put on a pair of black jeans, a black bra, a black T-shirt, black socks, and black high-top Keds— an ensemble in keeping with the whole big, black lie color scheme. Then I called Charlie Belcher at the station and told him I might be just a teeny bit late.

"Because of your niece's murder case?" he asked eagerly.

When I reluctantly told him yes, Charlie bent so far backward to help me, he was probably standing behind him-

self. "Take all the time you need—all day, if you have to
have it," Charlie said. "Don't worry. We can cover for you."
At this point he took a deep breath. "I'm sure you'll want
to tell your listeners all about it when you feel you can," he
broadly hinted.

I made noncommittal noises and hung up in a hurry.

Then I hurried over to Bert's apartment. If Bert and I
continued to hurry, we could go see this twice-shy couple
before Charlie had to cover for me on the air for very long.

"So tell me again what we're doing?" Bert asked, as she
climbed into the passenger side of my Neon. This, after I'd
just explained it all to her, while she dressed.

I glanced over at her. Ever since Ellie was arrested,
Bert had been looking less and less like her prim, extremely
neat self, and more and more like me. It was scary. In fact,
that morning, she looked more like me than I did. She'd
pulled on faded ragged jeans, tennis shoes, a white T-shirt
with a hole in the sleeve, and a denim jacket. Her hair was
barely combed, and a dab of lipstick was her only makeup.

I could tell from how she squinted in the morning light
that her head felt a whole lot like mine. Only, I don't think
Bert had gotten nearly as much sleep the previous night as
I had. She looked bleary-eyed and totally exhausted. If we
didn't spring Ellie soon, Bert was going to be comatose.

"Do you feel like doing this?" I asked. "You know, I could
go see Mr. and Mrs. Welch by myself."

For an answer, I got a steely-eyed glare. I hurried to fill
Bert in—for the second time—on what Grainger had said. "It
just seems to me that if the Welches don't want to talk to us,
well, they are the very ones we ought to talk to right away."

Bert nodded, but I wondered if she was following what

I was saying. She looked as if she might have to feel better to die.

Mr. and Mrs. Leonard Hutcheson Welch, III, it turned out, lived in a colonial home with white columns out front. It was the kind of house you see a lot of in Louisville—a Tara wannabe. I believe one reason you see so many Tara wannabes in this city is that Louisville is a South wannabe. Every year when the Derby rolls around, this lovely city tries to convince visitors from all over the world that they've just arrived in the South. If anybody checked a map, though, they'd find that Louisville is not in the South at all. It's in almost the exact middle—not really in the North, not really in the South. This is no doubt why the state was divided during the Civil War, half siding with the Union, half siding with the Confederacy—back then somebody must've actually thought to look at a map.

The Welches' Tara wannabe was so big that when I first saw it, I thought maybe it was a church. It was situated on several acres of what looked to be a perfect weed-free lawn fronting the road. The Welches had a three-car detached garage, a bubbling stone fountain in the side yard, and a redwood privacy fence all around the back. A white-haired man with East Side Lawn Service emblazoned on the back of his T-shirt was just loading a lawn tractor onto a trailer, preparing to leave, when I turned into the winding driveway.

I pulled directly in front of the massive front door. The smell of new-mown grass filled the air as Bert and I got out of my Neon and walked up the fake cobblestone sidewalk. I knocked, using a brass door knocker so big and ornate, it would've made Marley's Ghost proud. The second she answered the door, I recognized Mrs. Welch. She was the blond woman with the Yorkie. Mrs. Welch's heavily mascaraed eyes widened as she looked from Bert to me and back again. Either she was surprised to see us, especially after she and her husband had specifically told us via Grainger not to come, or she was shocked to find two people so badly dressed on her doorstep.

Mrs. Welch, on the other hand, was wearing beige linen slacks, a beige sweater set made of what looked like genuine cashmere, and beige slippers. A strand of perfectly matched pearls hung around her neck. In her arms, the little York-shire terrier barked just twice, and then settled against its mistress's chest, its job apparently done.

The dog's topknot was tied with a beige ribbon, which perfectly matched its mistress's outfit, and its toenails were polished an icy pearl, the identical shade of Mrs. Welch's own nails. I couldn't help but stare. Lord, the woman evidently carried the Yorkie around so much, she and the mutt had to be color-coordinated.

"Yes?" the woman said, smiling. She had evidently recovered from her initial surprise and gone into gracious-hostess mode.

Bert returned her smile and introduced us. "My sister and I would like to speak to Mr. Welch."

Mrs. Welch smiled, but the smile didn't quite make it to her eyes. "I'm Edna Welch, his wife. What was it you wanted to see him about? He's a very busy man." She said this last as if it were something we should've known without being told.

"It's a private matter," I said. "Could you tell us where we might find him?"

Edna's eyes widened even more. "He's in the morning room," she said.

Of course, I thought. *Where else would he be this time of day?*

Edna went on. "I'll just go and—" She hesitated, and then evidently changed her mind regarding what she'd been about to say. "That is, I'll take you in to see him."

I wondered if perhaps she was one of those women who don't trust their husbands alone with other women. Whatever the reason, Bert and I followed her dutifully down a spacious hall.

The morning room looked a whole lot like what the people in my socioeconomic stratum would call a family room, with love seats and overstuffed chairs, and, in a corner, a small table and chairs. The furniture mostly faced the one wall that was pretty much nothing more than a giant window, looking out on the acres of manicured lawn and rose gardens that was the Welch backyard.

Leonard Welch's back was to us as he sat in a wing chair, staring out the enormous window—taking in the view, no doubt. He rose, however, when his wife entered, unfolding himself with an easy grace, and turned toward all of us as we came into the room. He was dressed in a white dress shirt, navy cardigan, and navy pleated dress slacks. Good Lord, these people dressed better when they were just hanging around the house than I did when I attended a wedding.

Leonard Welch took one look at us, bringing up his wife's rear, so to speak; and his eyes widened.

It was with some effort that I kept my own eyes from widening.

Oh my God.

I believe I was now feeling every bit as surprised as Mrs. Welch had been when she'd first spotted Bert and me on her doorstep. Because, what do you know, I'd just recognized Leonard. Not as somebody I'd seen standing outside the flea-market office. Oh no, I could easily picture tall, graceful Leonard in a Gibson-girl blond wig and a lacy collar, his slim body striking a feminine pose.

He was, without a doubt, the so-called woman in the photographs I'd found last night at the Haggerty house. Looking at him, I now realized that the only thing in those pictures that had given his true sex away was that angular jaw.

Well, well, well. Old Leonard must've had some photographer make sepia-toned photos of him in antique clothes—like those studios do that you see in shopping malls sometimes, where you can dress up like Bonnie and Clyde, or a 1900s dance hall queen, or even a Playboy bunny, and get your picture made.

Now that I thought about it, though, I doubted that Leonard would've wanted to parade around in his frilly negligees in front of a stranger. He'd probably been both subject and photographer—with some kind of timer on the camera to snap the photo, and his own darkroom to develop and print the results.

It sort of made one wonder how the late and not-at-all-lamented Franklin Haggerty had gotten hold of the pictures that Leonard had made of himself in drag.

I took a quick step backward as another thought occurred to me. If it had been Leonard in those pictures, then did it necessarily follow that it had also been Leonard who'd been so kind as to give me and Bert identical headaches last night? Had he been forcibly taking back what was rightfully his?

Or had it been someone else? Someone who'd seen the photos, recognized Leonard, and taken them to blackmail him?

That last seemed considerably more farfetched. Goetz-mann had told me once that, in criminal investigations, the simplest explanation is usually the right one. In this case, the simplest explanation was that it had been Leonard last night. If so, no wonder the Welches had not wanted Bert and me to drop by for a visit. They must've been worried that the twin who'd seen the photos might recognize Miz Leonard. Hell, they must've phoned Grainger with their demand that we cease and desist right after they'd left Haggerty's house.

The real question, at this point, had to be: Would Leonard commit murder to hide his cross-dressing secret? Or did he stop at just conking people over the head?

All this ran through my mind as I realized that Leonard was looking straight at me. I tried to smile as if I had no idea what he might look like in a filmy negligee. Not the easiest thing in the world to do, I might add. Leonard must've been satisfied that I didn't recognize him because his eyes traveled on to Bert.

She was in the middle of introducing us. "My sister and I are following up on some complaints lodged against Franklin Haggerty."

It seemed to me that finding out if Leonard drew the line at head-conking was not something Bert and I really needed to know. The police, however, really did need to know that he had an excellent motive for murder.

"We just wanted to know about the complaint you filed against Franklin Haggerty," Bert was saying in her best no-nonsense voice.

Leonard sighed and nodded. "Yes, well—would you two like to sit down?"

Edna bristled. "No, Leonard, they would *not* like to sit down. They're leaving."

Frankly, I was all for that idea.

Leonard sighed again. "Now, Edna—" he said. The way he said it made you realize that he'd said those two words many, many times before. "There's no reason to be impolite—"

Edna stared at her husband, incredulous. "Are you joking? Of course, there's a reason. We told Mr. Grainger at the flea market that we did not want to participate in any interviews like this one." She turned back to me and Bert. "And now these two show up, anyway. Didn't we make ourselves clear?"

I nodded. "You certainly did. And you're right. We'll be going right now." I turned to leave, but Bert stayed right where she was. She also shot me a look that said: *You wimp, why are you giving up so easily?*

Not at all wimplike, Bert turned back to Leonard. She said, "It does look suspicious that you won't even discuss the problem you'd had with Haggerty. It could make some people think you had something to hide."

"Or not," I added. "It could just be that you value your privacy. Which we certainly understand." Moving closer to Bert, I grabbed her hand. "We're terribly sorry for barging in like this. Come on, Bert."

Bert frowned at me, and shook off my hand. Turning back to Leonard, she hurried on, "You know, we've talked to several other people about Haggerty, and all of them have been eager"—this was a gross exaggeration, but Bert hurried on, anyway—"to tell us all about what their problem with Haggerty had been. It's really odd that you two are the only ones who do not even want to discuss it."

Leonard's eyes were now doing the twin-bounce. I wondered if he was looking first at one of us, and then at the other, just like everybody else who sees us together for the first time. Or was old Leonard here trying to figure out which twin had been the one inside the Haggerty house last night—the one who'd seen his Playmate of the Month photos.

I also wondered if our attacker could've been Edna. She certainly looked as if hitting somebody over the head might be something she'd enjoy. In fact, she was beginning to look as if she might enjoy it just then.

"Let me see if I have this right," Edna said, as she slowly scratched her Yorkie behind its ears. "You two are looking into complaints against a dead man." She cleared her throat. "Just for the record, how exactly do you plan to censure him if you find out that he's been in the wrong?"

What could I say? I'd been wondering why nobody else had ever brought this up before. "You know, you're absolutely right," I said. "There isn't much we can do at this point, is there?" I took a deep breath, and turned to Bert. "We *really* ought to be going."

Bert stared back at me. Finally. I could see from the look on her face that at last it had gotten through to her very tired brain that—what a surprise—I was definitely in the mood to leave. "Yes," Bert said slowly, turning back to Leonard. "We'd like to apologize for the intrusion. We'll just be on our way then."

Leonard waved his hand in the air. "No problem," he said.

We both turned, then, intending to head for the front door.

That, of course, is when we saw Edna Welch.

She wasn't carrying the Yorkie anymore. She'd traded in the little dog for a big gun, and she was pointing it in the general direction of Bert and me.

Chapter 16

•

Bert

Funniest thing: When a gun is pointed at you, it instantly becomes the most fascinating thing you've ever seen in your life. I couldn't take my eyes off it. The weapon looked like it had to be an antique—it had a wooden grip, a mottled gray metal body, and a very long, narrow barrel.

Apparently, Nan and I were about to be killed with a collectible.

I can't say it was a thrill.

Edna stood there in the doorway of her morning room, blocking Nan's and my way, holding the gun out in front of her with both hands. Like somebody taking aim in a shooting gallery.

Her little dog was seated, panting, between her feet. The Yorkie looked as scared as I felt. Of course, he was probably just scared because this was the first time in years his feet had actually touched the floor. The poor little thing was probably frightened to discover that he still had legs.

Beside me, Nan slowly raised her hands. Edna had not yet told us to do that, and I wasn't sure it was all that great an idea. It seemed to me that all raising my hands would do was give old Edna a clean shot at my chest. I would've preferred to cross my arms in front of my chest, and maybe even press my purse to that area, just to make sure that a bullet had a lot of stuff to go through before it hit my heart. While I was trying to make up my mind whether I should follow Nan's lead, Edna made it up for me.

"GET THEM UP!" she yelled at me.

I got them up.

Across the room, Leonard managed to look even more frightened than me, Nan, and the Yorkie put together. "Edna! My God! What are you doing? Have you lost your mind?"

I was not about to say it out loud, but that concept would get my vote.

"Ladies," Leonard said, turning to Nan and me, "I'm so sorry. Please forgive Edna. She doesn't know what she's doing. She hasn't been herself."

Edna may not have been herself, but whoever she happened to be at the moment was still pointing a gun in Nan and my direction.

"I know exactly what I'm doing, you fool," Edna said, glaring at her husband. She motioned toward us, indicating both Nan and me with a broad sweep of a very, very long gun barrel. "They know, idiot. They *know.*"

"What?" I asked. "What are we supposed to know?"

Edna sneered. Not a good look for her, I might add. "Don't give me that," she said. "You know exactly what I'm talking about."

Leonard moved closer. "Edna, please put that gun down! You can't do this. You can't!"

I, of course, nodded my agreement. Nan, I noticed, nodded, too.

Edna scowled. "Of course, I can. I can do anything I want."

Ordinarily, I would've applauded her can-do attitude.
And the way she was standing up to her husband. Good for
her. Nobody was going to mistake Edna for a doormat.
However, in this case, I didn't feel the least bit supportive.
Oddly enough. I wrenched my eyes away from the gun for
a moment and glanced over at Leonard, willing him to start
acting like a male chauvinist pig and order his wife to obey
him.

"This is not something you want to do, Edna, honey,"
Leonard said. His tone was cajoling. "This is crazy, sweetheart. Now put that pistol down."

"Don't you 'sweetheart' me, Leonard. We don't have a
choice," Edna replied. "We can't let them leave here with
what they know."

"Sure we can," Leonard said. "They don't know anything."

"But they do," Edna answered. "They do!" She sounded
as if she were about to cry.

I started looking around for something heavy to throw
at Edna, just in case the conversation started to take a really
ugly turn. Nan's eyes, I noticed, were also traveling around
the room, no doubt looking for the same thing.

"Leonard," Edna was now saying, her tone ultrareason-
able, "we simply cannot have people knowing about you. We
can't take the chance of it ever getting out about your—
your—"

Apparently, whatever she was thinking about was so
repugnant, she couldn't voice it aloud. "We have our position
in the community to consider," Edna hurried on. "My family
has never had this kind of scandal. NEVER."

Scandal? Did she say scandal? I glanced over at Nan to

see if she was taking all this in, and I discovered a very interesting thing.

Nan knew exactly what Edna was talking about.

When you're looking at a face as familiar as your own—mainly, because it *is* your own—it's not hard to read. The second Nan's eyes met mine, I knew that she was well aware of exactly what was going on here. She immediately looked away, back toward Leonard and Edna, but I'd already seen it on her face.

I rather hoped I'd live to have her explain it to me.

"Why, we'd be laughingstocks if people found out." Edna almost sounded matter-of-fact as the barrel of the gun kept doing the same twin-bounce that people's eyes often do. It bounced first in Nan's direction, then in mine, then back to Nan.

Leonard stared at his wife. "Are you quite insane?" he asked. "Do you really think it would be better for people to know that you've shot two women in our own home, than to find out about my little, well, indulgence?"

Edna fluttered her left hand at him, as if she were ridding herself of some pesky insect. The gun in her right hand kept right on doing the twin-bounce. "Indulgence? Is that what you call it? An indulgence?"

Leonard sighed. I believe we could assume that this was a topic that had been discussed several times. "Edna, it was just that one time. Just once. That's all. Just for a lark. I've never done it since, and I'll never do it again."

I couldn't help staring at Leonard. Did men take some kind of class to learn how to lie to their wives so that they all ended up saying the same thing? I had no idea what Leonard was lying about, but I couldn't help noticing that

Leonard sounded just like Jake, after I'd found out about his carrying on with his secretary.

Edna looked disgusted. "Once is entirely too many times, Leonard. Particularly if there are pictures. Which these women have seen. They've seen *you*." Her mouth twisted with distaste.

"Excuse me? I hate to interrupt," I said, putting up a finger. "But I haven't seen a thing. I don't know anything about any pictures."

"Me neither," Nan said. I knew Nan was lying, but I had to hand it to her. She sounded more sincere than I did.

"I don't know what you're talking about," I added.

"I certainly don't know, either," Nan added.

Edna's eyes were doing the twin-bounce now, along with her gun. "Good try, girls, but I know what I know. You wouldn't have been so anxious to leave if you hadn't recognized Leonard the second you got a good look at him."

"Edna," Leonard said, "please. Think what you're doing—"

Edna sniffed. "If you'd thought what you were doing, we'd never have been in this mess. Or if you'd told me sooner what you'd locked inside that stupid liquor cabinet, I'd never have sold it to Franklin Haggerty."

Leonard's long, angular jaw looked even longer. "Who would've thought you'd suddenly decide to sell that old cabinet?"

Edna bristled. "It was mine! Like everything else in this house. I could do with it whatever I wanted."

Leonard sighed again.

I was beginning to wish they'd pick another time to have this little discussion. Edna seemed to be getting more upset by the minute. It was not the sort of thing you wanted to see in a woman pointing a gun at you.

"If you'd only told me what you'd hidden in the cabinet, I would never have sold it. But, no! You didn't tell me a thing," Edna said petulantly. The gun was doing the twin-bounce with a vengeance now. "That cabinet was old and beaten-up. Really ugly." She looked over at me and Nan. "And you couldn't use it for anything. *He*"—she gave a vague nod in her husband's general direction—"said he'd lost the key. You would have sold it, too."

"No doubt," Nan said agreeably.

"Most certainly," I added.

Edna shrugged. "You would've sold it to Haggerty, too—even if he was a perfectly odious man. He was an antique dealer." She made it sound as if it were the equivalent to royalty. Apparently, she'd never heard the saying: If you scratch an antique dealer, you'll find a junk man.

"After all," Edna went on, "I couldn't very well just put an ad in the *Courier-Journal*, could I? And have God-knows-what riffraff show up at our front door? I think not."

I was pretty sure that Edna considered Nan and me prime examples of God-knows-what riffraff, but I tried to look sympathetic, nevertheless. "Of course you couldn't place an ad," I said.

"Oh no," Nan said.

"Edna, for God's sake," Leonard said wearily. "We've been over all this before."

Edna didn't even pause. "How could I know you had a hobby? How was I to know that you hid those horrible photographs in that old locked cabinet? I thought the damn thing was empty. I didn't even know there were any photographs in the first place. Until that awful Mr. Haggerty phoned."

Leonard's sigh this time was voluminous. "What can I say but I'm sorry, Edna? I thought it was harmless. How could I have known that Haggerty would have a collection of old keys, and that one of them would unlock that cabinet? That he would find those pictures, and that one day he'd—"

"Blackmail you?" Nan put in.

Edna winced. "See? She knows everything!"

Leonard grimaced as if he'd been slapped.

"Is that why you killed Haggerty?" Nan asked. "Because he was blackmailing you?"

I wouldn't have thought it possible, but Leonard looked even more horrified. "Me? Kill him? Oh, my goodness no. There was no reason for violence. He and I had worked out a perfectly acceptable price for which I would purchase the photographs."

I stared at Leonard. "An acceptable price?"

Leonard shrugged. "The price was steep, of course, but fair, I thought. I was getting what I deserved for causing my wife such distress. Of course, as it happened, Haggerty died before I'd even had to make one payment."

"And before you had a chance to get the pictures back," Edna added.

Leonard cleared his throat. "Edna, it's not my fault the man got himself killed. I did all I could do to get the pictures back."

Edna scoffed. "If you'd done all you could, you would've gotten the pictures. And now they're out there somewhere. Anybody could have them. Even these two." She used the gun barrel as a pointer, gesturing toward Nan and me.

"You didn't get the pictures back last night?" Nan asked.

I realized then what she was really asking: *You didn't hit both of us over the head and cause us extreme pain?*

Leonard and Edna just stared at us. "What are you talking about?" Leonard asked.

"Didn't you break into the Haggerty house last night and take back your pictures?" Nan asked.

Edna looked affronted. "Us? Are you actually accusing us of breaking into somebody's house?" Her chin went even higher. "I'll have you know I have never broken into anybody's house in my life! And neither has my husband!"

Evidently, holding a gun on someone was a lot classier thing to do than breaking and entering.

Leonard was shaking his head. "Someone has stolen the pictures?" He actually sounded alarmed.

Nan nodded. While Edna's gun bounced from Nan to me and back again, Nan explained that she'd heard from a policeman acquaintance that Haggerty's house had been broken into again, and that some photographs had been stolen.

As Nan talked, Leonard edged quietly closer to Edna.

"And according to my friend, all this happened just last night," Nan finished.

Edna rolled her eyes. "Do you really expect me to believe that? That some shadowy figure now has the pictures? And that you yourself have never seen them?" A smile curled her lip. "I'm not stupid, you know."

Unfortunately for her, she was mistaken. She *was* stupid—stupid enough to have let Leonard get too close. He was now almost next to her. Edna must've seen him out of the corner of her eyes, because she wheeled toward him just as he lunged for her.

Nan and I immediately responded to this sudden turn

of events with a demonstration of the kind of courage for which, I believe, we are very well known.

We dived behind the nearest love seat.

As we huddled back there, we could hear, on the other side of the love seat, several scuffling noises, the Yorkshire terrier yipping excitedly, and then a heavy thunk on the floor.

I peeked out. Leonard had his wife by the wrist, and the gun she'd been pointing at us was now in Leonard's hand. "Leonard, let go of me!" Edna was saying. "I mean it. That hurts!"

He didn't budge.

"Leonard, you will let me go," Edna said with authority, "or you know what will happen."

He dropped her arm as if she'd slapped him.

"You are such a fool, Leonard," Edna said, glaring at him and rubbing her wrist. She took a deep breath, and lifted her chin. "I wasn't actually going to shoot anyone," she went on. "I was just trying to scare them. So they'd keep quiet about everything. Really, Leonard, do you honestly think I could shoot somebody?"

Personally, I thought she'd given a very good imitation of someone who could. Nan and I crawled out from behind the love seat, brushing off our clothes as we stood up.

"Really, Leonard—it would be so untidy," Edna said with a little laugh. The woman was talking about shooting someone as if it were equivalent to throwing wastepaper out of a car window.

"I am terribly sorry," Leonard said, coming over to us. Still carrying the gun, he began brushing us off. "Are you two all right? Nobody's hurt, I trust. I can't tell you how sorry I am that this happened."

"We're fine, and we're going," Nan said, grabbing my arm and heading for the door.

Leonard turned a little pale, but he rushed after us, his eyes pleading. "Wait, don't go yet. Please, let me explain," he said. "Can I get you some tea? Something stronger?"

"We're outta here—right now," Nan said, still dragging me after her. We'd made it into the hallway and were heading for the front door.

Leonard followed us. "I'm so sorry. Please, you must understand. My wife has had a terrible shock. It's all my fault. Not hers. Please don't hold this against her. I'm the one that's in the wrong here."

"I'll second that," Edna added, from behind him.

Leonard winced, but he went right on. "There was no real harm done, really," Leonard was saying. "No use bringing the police into this."

I just looked at him. During all the years we were married, I don't believe Jake would have ever taken the blame for my trying to shoot somebody. This guy must truly love his wife.

I looked back at Edna.

She was still frowning as she reached down to pick up the little Yorkie.

Man, Leonard had terrible taste.

Chapter 17

●

Nan

I would've pulled away from the nuthouse, otherwise known as the Welch residence, a whole lot faster except that as soon as we got in the car, Bert turned to me. "OK, I'm assuming the pictures those crazy people are talking about are the ones you saw at the Haggerty house, right? So what's so awful about a few pictures of Leonard Welch that he'd pay blackmail? Was he with another woman?"

I stared at her, wondering where to begin.

"Another MAN?" she prodded, her eyes huge.

Answering those questions took a little time. Mainly because Bert kept interrupting me, saying things like, "Oh my God, the woman in the pictures was *Leonard?* Was he really in a negligee? What on earth would he do a thing like that for?"

I mentioned words like *cross-dressing* and *fetish*, and still Bert interrupted. "You are not telling me that the guy got some kind of weirdo kick out of dressing up like a woman. You are *not* telling me that, are you?"

I just looked at her. Bert is the same age as I am, except for ten minutes—ten minutes which she spent in the world doing God knows what, and I didn't. One thing for sure, it wasn't watching cable TV. With her head start, though, why is it that I know all this stuff, and Bert always stares at me as if I'm making it up? Where the hell has she been all our life?

I know the answer to that one, of course. Most of her life she's been in the kitchen, making Jake and the kids dinner.

Coming up with the answer to the question of where Leonard's photos were just then was a bit more difficult. "I don't have the slightest idea who could have the photographs now," I told Bert, as I rubbed the back of my head. "Somebody with a mean right arm would be my guess."

Bert shrugged. "Do you really think somebody has stolen the photographs from Haggerty's house and is getting ready to take up the blackmail baton where Haggerty dropped it?"

I shrugged. "What do you get when you cross an elephant with a rhino?"

Bert nodded.

One nice thing about being a twin: You can talk in riddles, and the other one still understands you. The answer to the elephant-rhino riddle was one that had cracked us up when we were in the fifth grade: *eleph-ino;* or, phonetically, *hell-if-I-know.*

I started my Neon. As we drove away, I was beginning to wonder if we hadn't been on the right track, after all—way before we went to see Edna and Leonard, otherwise known as the squirrel and her keeper. Maybe Bert and I had been right, back when we were looking for that missing Mulholland will.

Next to me in the car, Bert was unusually silent. Thinking, probably. Sleeping, hopefully.

If Edna had not been the person who'd broken into the

Haggerty place on the day he died, it could very well have been Chris's foster sister, Kaitlin. Maybe the same thing had happened to her as Edna Welch. Maybe Kaitlin had accidentally sold something to Haggerty that had the missing will locked inside. Maybe Haggerty had found it and was blackmailing Kaitlin, just as he'd been blackmailing Leonard Welch. Maybe Kaitlin had not taken to the whole blackmail scheme as well as Leonard, and she'd let Haggerty know by killing him.

That was a whole lot of maybes. But maybes that needed looking into. I turned to Bert just as she looked over at me, and we said it in unison, "We need to talk to Kaitlin again."

Sometimes, twin minds really do function alike.

But first, I had to get to work before Charlie Belcher completed my on-air shift and lost every single listener I had.

I dropped Bert at home, with the promise that she'd take a nap while I was gone. Then I headed into work.

Unfortunately for me, Charlie was running a special oldies' day every week; and this happened to be the day. Ever since our ratings showed that we had a large demographic of eighteen- to thirty-four-year-old listeners with a sharp drop-off of the thirty-five-plus audience, Charlie had been determined to build up a loyal group of older listeners, the older the better (although I could point out to him that building that particular loyal audience was a certain loser, since eventually they all *died*).

Considering the fact that I myself was already within, and about to burrow even deeper into, the "older demographic," the last thing I wanted to do was listen for a few hours to old people's music. Nevertheless, I had to sit through the likes of Kitty Wells, Ray Price, and Faron

Young singing through their noses about love gone wrong. Bummer.

The only good times in the shift came with Hank Senior and Patsy Cline—both of whom I personally consider age-less—and when Johnny Cash sang "Don't Take Your Guns to Town," which I mentally dedicated to Edna Welch.

I headed back to the house to pick up Bert as soon as my shift was over.

Bert looked a little better than she had when I left her—at least, it appeared her eyes were focusing now. She'd changed into her usual outfit—a sure sign she was coming around—skirt, blouse, and vest, and low heels. Her hair was combed and makeup carefully applied. Things were looking up.

"I've called Kaitlin's house," Bert told me as we left the house, "and the answering machine picked up. So, this little visit might be a waste of time if she's not home. Or she could just be letting the machine screen her calls." We stepped out on her front porch, and Bert turned around to lean down and lock her front door.

That's when we heard a sound like a car backfiring, and something whizzed by, right between us, burying itself deep in the wood of the door—right where Bert had been stand-ing. Wood chips flew everywhere, and Bert yelped.

It took me a second to realize someone was actually shooting at us.

"Oh my God!" Bert's face had gone white, and wouldn't you know it, she began looking around. Standing up, I might add. Short of painting a bull's-eye on her chest, it was not her most brilliant maneuver.

OK, so maybe Bert wasn't as rested as I'd thought.

I, on the other hand, had dropped to my knees, diving

behind the shrubs that Bert kept so beautifully untrimmed in front of her door. I reached up to yank Bert down right before another bullet bit into the door. More wood splinters.

"Oh my God! Oh my God! Oh my God!" Bert was not yelping anymore. She was shrieking. "I am getting so tired of guns!"

"Are you hurt?" I asked her.

Bert didn't answer. She just kept right on oh-my-Godding as if I hadn't said a word.

"Bert! Yo, Bert!" I yelled at her, grabbing her shoulders and trying to look her over for spurting blood or ugly black holes. "Are you hurt? Hey! ARE YOU HURT?"

"Oh my God, oh my God, oh my God," Bert replied. She did, however, shake her head no.

Well, at least, she wasn't hurt. I tried to think what to do. Believe it or not, we have actually done this kind of thing before—not the oh-my-God thing but the hiding-behind-bushes-while-being-shot-at thing. In fact, these very bushes.

Now that I thought about it, ornamental shrubbery really wasn't the best kind of cover—seeing as how a hurtling bullet could tear right through the branches, and then right into you. The only good thing about shrubbery was that the shooter couldn't see where you were.

"We need to get back inside," I yelled at Bert over her oh-my-Gods. "Give me your keys!"

She stared at me, wide-eyed, and then pointed.

I looked in the direction she was pointing in. The keys to the door hung where she'd left them when I'd yanked her down—right in the lock.

I sincerely hoped that she hadn't actually been able to lock her front door before the shooting began.

I took a deep breath, bounced up and tried the door,

just as another bullet bounced off the doorframe. Unhurt, I dropped like a rock back to the ground.

Damn! It *was* locked! This was just great. Bert would've picked this particular time to get this one thing done correctly.

On the upside, I was very grateful that this psycho was such a bad shot.

I started to bounce up again, when Bert caught hold of my arm, holding me down.

"*My* turn," she said very deliberately. I looked at her. Darned if she didn't look fully awake now. The determined look on her face made me realize that arguing with her at this point would be kind of a waste of time. She looked like she did the day she told me she was going to marry Jake— that time, too, I'd known there was no point in trying to change her mind. It didn't help to recall how well that had turned out.

Just like I had done, Bert bounced up to grab the key and turn it to the left quickly, dropping again as another bullet whizzed past her. This time the shot went wild and didn't hit anything.

"The door's unlocked now," Bert said. "Your turn."

I looked at her, realizing that the next step was to open the door and dive inside. I realized that if I made it safe inside the house, I'd have to wait in there, to see if she were going to make it, too. I really didn't think I could stand that.

I shook my head. "You go."

The same reasoning must've gone through Bert's head, too, because she slowly shook her head no. "We go together," she said.

I believe this was pretty close to what Butch Cassidy

and the Sundance Kid had done. I really didn't like how that had turned out, either.

Without saying another word, we both bounced up, and in one fluid motion, I grabbed the doorknob, turned and pushed hard. Bert flung herself inside on her stomach, with me diving in just a little behind her. We heard a bullet whiz by over our heads, just as Bert kicked hard at the door, and then another bullet hit the door as it slammed shut.

We'd also heard something else before the door closed— the sound of a police siren in the background. Apparently, gunfire was something our neighbors really couldn't tolerate. One of them had finally called the cops. Thank God, I might add.

In the distance, we heard another car start up and burn rubber as it drove off—it appeared someone was in kind of a hurry. We knew it was probably the shooter leaving, but Bert and I still sat on the floor, grinning at each other like a pair of idiots, and examining our body parts for signs they were all still intact. Aside from a couple of skinned elbows and Bert's torn panty hose, we seemed to be all right.

When the doorbell sounded, we both jumped.

Bert gave me a shaky look, and then, taking a deep breath, she got up to answer it. I got up, and moved to stand right in back of her. Bert took one look through the peephole and gasped.

For a second, I thought the shooter had to be standing there, gun at the ready, but no, that wasn't it after all.

Bert opened the door.

I looked over her shoulder. It was only Hank Goetzmann.

Oh, and there was Jake, standing right behind him.

OK, this should be interesting.

Chapter 18

•

Bert

Personally, I would rather be shot at than be in the same room at the same time with Hank and Jake.

But, since I'd already actually opened my door, and they both had already seen me standing there, my running away screaming would probably be noticed.

"Bert," was all Hank said, with a little nod of his head. Very formal, very businesslike. "I was nearby and I caught the call and I just thought—" His voice sort of drifted away.

Of all people to show up to investigate the shooting, wouldn't you know, it would be Hank.

I just looked at him for a moment. OK, he'd seen Jake trying to kiss me the other night, and he knew I was angry about the way he'd handled the Ellie mess. Still, I didn't think that was any reason for him to look as if he were having bamboo shoots stuck under his fingernails.

Behind Hank, Jake gave me a quick little wave with one hand. Funniest thing: Jake didn't look the least bit unhappy to have arrived at the same time as Hank. If anything, he looked rather delighted.

I stepped aside; and Hank slipped past me, brushing lightly against me as he moved by.

My silly heart gave a sudden leap.

I'd glanced up at Hank as he moved by, but he didn't even look down at me. Probably that whole brushing-against-me thing was just an accident—he was a big man, after all, and it was a small door. Of course, he was already inside the door when he brushed against me, but then again—I forced myself to stop thinking about it. Mostly because, as the saying goes, that way lies madness.

Not to mention, I was beginning to wonder if I was in high school all over again, trying to decide if the handsome drummer in the pep band really was looking directly at me when he played up there on the stage, or was he just staring dreamily into space?

Behind me, I could hear Nan greeting Hank. I turned to look at Jake, who certainly hadn't seemed to notice whether Hank had brushed against me or not. Of course, Jake's attention was somewhat diverted. He was standing stock-still on my doorstep, staring at my front door.

"Coming in, Jake?" I asked.

"Have you noticed these holes?" he asked.

I just looked at him.

The bullet holes that riddled my door were at eye level and huge—pretty much impossible to miss.

In the nineteen years that Jake and I were married and in the years since, the man has never failed—in stressful situations—to come up with the dumbest questions you've ever heard. It is a talent that, when we were dating, I never realized that he had, but it's one I've come to appreciate, lo, these many years hence.

There was, for example, the time I was bitten by some vicious insect and my whole hand swelled up so big, it looked like I had hot dogs superglued to my palm. Jake had taken one look and asked, "Is something wrong with your hand?"

Or the time my water broke when I went into labor with
Brian. Unfortunately, we were standing in line at the Winn
Dixie grocery at the time, waiting to check out. Jake had
taken one look at the puddle forming at my feet, and
demanded, *"What* do you think you're doing?"

Now I mentally counted to ten before I spoke. "Jake,"
I said, my voice infinitely calm, "of course, I've noticed the
holes in my door. Nan and I were just shot at. Why do you
think Hank is here?"

Jake, as usual, went all defensive. "I was just asking a
simple question, that's all. I came by to talk to you for a
minute, OK? And *please*, don't get me started as to why
that man could be here."

I decided that last comment wasn't something that even
deserved a reply. It did occur to me, however, that Jake
had a lot of gall, acting as if Hank dropping by my place
could possibly be inappropriate. The last time I checked, we
were divorced. Not to mention, I couldn't help but recall
that Jake had not thought it at all inappropriate to drop by
his secretary's apartment quite a few times while he was
still my husband. And now, he was making cracks about
Hank?

All this went through my mind in a rush, but I stepped
aside, most politely, I thought, so that Jake could follow
Hank inside. Jake did not brush against me at all, by the
way. In fact, he went past me, frowning. A few steps inside
the door, though, he came to a dead stop. Apparently, on
his way inside, he'd been mentally replaying what I'd just
said. Turning to face me, he asked, "What did you mean
exactly when you said, *shot at?"*

I stared at him again.

God give me strength.

Fortunately, I didn't have to answer Jake. Nan jumped in and started telling the story. "It happened just as we were going out," she began. As she went on, we all moved into the living room. There was an uncomfortable moment then, while everybody seemed to be making up their minds where to sit. Nan once again helped me out, though. She interrupted her tale, headed straight for the sofa, and patted the seat next to her. "Here, Bert," she said. I responded only a little more quickly than a trained spaniel would have, sitting down next to Nan and suppressing a sigh of relief.

Hank and Jake claimed Queen Anne chairs on either side of the couch. Hank moved his chair a little so that he could be facing us as Nan talked. Hank also whipped out a small, dog-eared notebook as soon as Nan began talking, and he started making little notes in it every few minutes. He didn't even glance at me or Jake as he wrote.

Luckily for me, Nan left out a lot of the oh-my-Gods I'd started babbling right after the bullets started flying. She actually made me sound, instead, like a rational human being. The woman has real fiction-telling talent.

About halfway into the story, though, Jake jumped up and sat down right next to me, close enough for me to smell his cologne. This time, it was, oh my yes, English Leather, my absolute favorite. I know it's not a scent that's particularly in vogue anymore, but I guess I learned to love it back in the sixties when it seemed as if every guy I knew was wearing it. English Leather is a scent that, under certain circumstances, has actually made me feel dizzy. I'd always bought Jake a bottle of the cologne or the aftershave whenever there was a gift-giving occasion. Of course, that had been years ago. Now I wondered, was this from a bottle I'd bought for him? Or had his girlfriend also liked Jake's

English Leather so much, she'd bought him a bottle of the stuff herself?

The thought made me tense up. That and Jake reaching over and grabbing my hand like he'd never let go. "Are you hurt?" he said, lowering his voice to a whisper and leaning even closer. "Are you all right?"

For a second, I'd actually thought it had to be another one of his stupid questions—I was still breathing and not bleeding anywhere, wasn't I?—but before I started staring at him and mentally counting again, I realized that Jake was only trying to be nice. He was simply expressing his concern—that's all. As Ellie and Nan so eloquently put it: no biggie.

"I'm fine," I said, patting his hand with my free one. "Really."

When I turned back to listen to Nan, I caught Hank's glance. His eyes met mine for just a moment, and then, abruptly, they dropped to stare pointedly at Jake's hand holding mine.

When Hank looked back up at me, his eyes looked pained.

My stomach constricted. Oh God, this was actually hurting him. Seeing Jake holding my hand. I was hurting Hank; and I'd never really meant to.

For an instant, my heart ached for him.

I repeat, *for an instant.* The very next instant, I thought, well, he'd certainly hurt me, too, hadn't he? Hank had hurt me in one of the worst possible ways—by hurting Ellie. I mean, what was the use of having a cop for a boyfriend if he couldn't keep your daughter from being charged with murder? I realized that it wasn't exactly like fixing a parking ticket, but Hank had to know that Ellie couldn't really murder anyone.

He had to.

And if he knew that, he should be able to do something about it. He was a homicide detective, wasn't he? So, for God's sake, man, DETECT!

I held Hank's eyes for just a moment longer, and then I deliberately looked away.

He'd let me down. That was all there was to it.

When I looked back, Hank's eyes were back on Nan, his mouth was a hard, tight line, and he was busy scribbling away.

And Jake, of course, was still holding on to my hand.

I drew a shaky breath. If, two months ago, anyone had told me that this scene would ever happen, I'd have thought they were crazy.

Now?

I just thought I was.

Chapter 19

•

Nan

I guess it's every woman's fantasy to have two men fighting over her, but watching Bert with Jake and Goetzmann in the same room together made me feel something I hadn't felt for quite a while.

I know it sounds rotten to say; but, at this very moment, I was so glad I was not Bert.

Watching her caught between the two of them made *my* stomach hurt. I couldn't even begin to imagine what her insides felt like.

Of course, when all this mess was over and she got back together with Goetzmann, I'd probably be back to envying her over having two men who were gaga about her—so I figured I should relish the moment.

When I'd finished answering Goetzmann's questions about the shooting outside—the gist of which was pretty much: *Bang! Bang! Bang! Bang! Bang! Bang!* since I really hadn't heard or seen anything to help identify the shooter—Goetzmann took a deep breath and turned to Bert.

I'd noticed that, except for only once, he'd avoided looking directly at Bert during my whole recital. "So," Goetzmann said, "do you have anything to add to what Nan just said?"

I almost smiled. Goetzmann looked as if perhaps, at the same time he was asking this, he was also suffering from severe gastrointestinal distress. Or, perhaps, hemorrhoids. He shifted around in that Queen Anne chair, as if trying to find a more comfortable position—and failing miserably.

Speaking of which, Bert looked pretty close to miserable herself. "Nope," she said. "I've nothing to add."

His question answered, Goetzmann started crossing his last *t* and dotting his last *i*. Finally, he snapped his notebook closed and shifted position again before he asked his next question. "I know that you two have been just sitting around the house, twiddling your thumbs, ever since Ellie was arrested, so I don't suppose that you've got any idea who might be trying to shoot you, do you?"

Sarcasm really did not look good on him.

I glanced sideways at Bert, and she gave a tiny nod. "You mean, as of today?" I asked.

Goetzmann frowned. "Something happened today? You mean, *before* the shooting incident?"

I nodded.

Bert nodded.

Jake looked a little more alert.

Goetzmann looked pained.

So, naturally, with that kind of encouragement, I launched into the sad saga of Edna and Leonard and their most recent reenactment of an episode of a television Western—with Edna playing the part of Matt Dillon, gun drawn, and Leonard playing the part of Miss Kitty, appropriately attired. I did point out, however, that since there'd been no actual gunsmoke and no need for a special appearance by someone playing Doc, Edna had probably been doing just what she'd said she was doing—trying to frighten us into not telling anyone about her husband's hobby.

"Oh, yeah, *that* worked," Jake muttered.

I ignored him.

"Besides," Bert added, "if Edna had really wanted to shoot us, she could have done so right then and there, in her house. Where she probably would've been able to cover the crime a lot easier." She looked over at me for confirmation of what she was about to say. "I honestly don't think the shooter could've been Edna."

I nodded.

Goetzmann nodded, too. He was still not looking directly at Bert. Instead, he studied the floor as if it held the answer to the meaning of life. I wasn't about to say anything— Goetzmann was a cop, and I never like to get anybody angry who regularly carries a gun—but, *puhleeze*, give me a break. Was this childish or what? Bert had made him mad, and now he was refusing to look at her? Why didn't he just throw a tantrum and be done with it?

The not-looking-at-me thing would not have worked on me. His not looking my way would probably have just encouraged me to start making faces at him, knowing that I could do pretty much anything—stick my tongue out at him, cross my eyes, wiggle my nose—and he wouldn't even know I was doing it.

Bert, however, looked as if it really was getting to her. She looked pained. Which, of course, made me want to stick my tongue out at idiot Goetzmann whether he could see me or not.

Hey, if he got to act like a big baby, why couldn't I?

Goetzmann finally hauled himself to his feet and went out on Bert's doorstep. Jake, Bert, and I all followed him, as if whatever he was going to do out there really would be worth seeing. It wasn't. After he dug a couple of bullets out of the front door with his pocketknife, dropping them into a plastic baggie he pulled out of his back pocket, he promptly left, mumbling something about needing to go see some people. By the name of Welch, maybe? Again, Goetzmann didn't so much as glance in Bert's direction when he said good-bye.

Jake, on the other hand, looked first at Bert, smiling, and then he turned to say good-bye to Goetzmann with such gusto, I thought I might have to grab him to keep him from jumping up and down with glee. "Thanks for dropping by, Officer," Jake said. Jake's voice seemed unnaturally loud.

Goetzmann mumbled something in reply, but thank God, we couldn't hear whatever it was. It was said very low, but it sounded as if it were just two words, and the second word, I believe, was *you*. I had a pretty good guess as to what the first word had been.

Once Goetzmann had pulled slowly out of Bert's driveway, and driven away without looking back, we all went back inside. We sat down where we'd been sitting before, as if maybe we were all attending a class with assigned seating. Sitting on the armrest next to Bert, Jake finally got around to telling us why he'd come over in the first place.

It wasn't good news.

Ellie's bail had indeed been denied.

Beside me, Bert actually winced, as if the words were a physical blow.

"I'm sorry, Bert," Jake hurried on. "I'm so sorry." Once again, he grabbed Bert's hand. "I tried to get the judge to do it—I really did." I didn't want to rain on Jake the Snake's parade, but I do believe that, technically, it was the attorney who tried.

According to Jake, the judge had held the scheduled hearing in his chambers, and had listened attentively to Ellie's attorney tell about Ellie recanting her confession. Then the judge had pretty much said, *Tell it to the jury.*

I do believe that Jake could've given all of this information to Bert over the phone, but, then again, he would not have gotten to hold her hand in a death grip, and she would've missed the smell of his yummy new cologne, Road Kill. Besides, as Jake was now saying, he'd wanted to "be there" for Bert when she got the bad news.

If he was any more "there," he'd have been in her lap.

Bert gave me The Look, about the time he said that. The Look is a lot like a twin whammy, but with more of a helpless "save me" quality to it.

So when Jake finished making soothing noises, I hustled him out of there, on the pretext that Bert really needed to get some rest after her strenuous day. I pretended not to watch as Jake bent to kiss her on the mouth right before he went out the door. I did, however, notice that Bert turned her head at the last moment so that old Jake ended up planting a big wet one on her cheek.

At least, Bert was showing she had some sense left. If she'd actually kissed the guy, I might've had to throw up.

"Look," Jake said, "I'm going to visit Ellie tonight. If you want to, I'll come by and pick you up."

I held my breath.

Bert, the idiot, said, "Sure, that'll be nice."

I blinked at that one. Nice? It was going to be nice to visit her daughter in the slammer with her ex-husband? Bert was obviously still very tired.

I decided the last thing Bert needed from me was a lecture on the dangers of hanging out with Jake the Snake. Oh, sure, I realize he is the father of her children—but that was just an accident of nature, right? Jo-Jo the Dog-Faced Boy could have been the father of Bert's children, if the time of the month had been right. And, of course, if Bert had decided to sleep with old Jo-Jo. Now that I think about it, though, after all the pain Jake has caused Bert, Jo-Jo might've been preferable. A couple of dog-faced children would've been a small price to pay never to have had Jake in her life.

After Jake finally shambled off, Bert and I decided to do what we were about to do before we became the targets in a shooting gallery: We headed over to Kaitlin Mulholland's house. I do have to admit we looked around several times before we dashed for my car, just in case bullets started to fly again. Probably, though, the visit by police would've scared away anybody out there with a gun.

On the way over, we talked about what we might say to the little bitch to get her to admit the existence of a will. We had a pretty good plan by the time we were walking up to front door of the house in Cherokee Park.

Kaitlin's pretty face puckered into an ugly frown the second she opened the door. "Oh," she said. "It's you two." Frowning, she added, "Whatta thrill."

Hey, sister, the feeling was mutual. This time, Kaitlin's fingernails and toenails were dry, but what do you know, she seemed to be every bit as gracious as she'd been the first time we'd talked to her. Kaitlin started to shut the door on us, but, true to form, Bert pushed right past her and hurried into her living room.

"Hey!" Kaitlin said, running after Bert. "Where the hell do you think you're going?"

Bert turned to face her. "Kaitlin, I know this is going to come as a shock to you. But we have reason to believe that Chris may have been responsible for your parents' car accident."

Instead of being shocked, grieved, or assorted other emotions that might have seemed far more appropriate—for a caring human being, that is—Kaitlin merely looked delighted. "Really? You do?" she asked, her eyes dancing. Santa Claus didn't look this merry.

I'd followed the two of them into the living room and spoke my part next. "We are very afraid that, if Chris killed once, he could certainly do it again. We think the police should be looking at him as a suspect for Franklin Haggerty's murder. That lets Bert's daughter, Ellie, off the hook, and that, of course, is why we're here."

"Well, I certainly think he did it," Kaitlin said, crossing her arms over her chest. "I think he killed Mom and Daddy and that Haggerty guy, too."

I stared at her. Why not throw in Jimmy Hoffa, while she was at it? "We actually have what we think is proof in your parents' case," I said. "Someone who claims to have helped Chris fix the brakes on your parents' vehicle has come forward. Chris had originally told Ellie all about what he'd done; and now this other young man is willing to testify against Chris."

"He is?" She was actually grinning from ear to ear by then. Lord, I really did not like this girl. "Have you told the police?"

"Not yet," Bert answered. "The problem is there's no

motive. Since your parents died without a will, Chris would not have profited by their deaths."

I shrugged. "If there's no will, there's no reason for Chris to have killed your folks."

Kaitlin stared at us for a second, tossing a long lock of blond hair over her shoulder. Then her big blue eyes turned crafty right before our eyes. "Well, there really was no will," Kaitlin said slowly.

Bert's face fell.

I didn't think we should just take this horrible young woman at her word. "Chris told us there was," I said. "He said he saw it with his own eyes."

Kaitlin gave a little dismissive grunt. "Chris would say he saw Christ on his refrigerator if he thought it would get him part of the estate. Or get his ass out of trouble." She eyed us. "Were you mad at him about something when he said he saw the will?"

Come to think of it, Bert had been a little miffed with him—in fact, she'd been miffed at him about the head and shoulders.

Kaitlin read the answer on our faces. "Pooh! Chris would lie through his teeth if he thought it would get him out of trouble. You ought to hear the tall tales he came up with to explain why he cut school or why he failed algebra or why—"

"We got it," I told her.

"Still," Kaitlin went on, her tone thoughtful now, "Chris really did have a motive to kill my parents. And he would've inherited half of the estate if he knew. Although, of course, Chris can't now, since you can prove he killed them." She said it like she were talking about the weather. Kaitlin went on. "I personally think Mom told him, too—it would be just like her. She always liked him better than me."

Bert and I stared at Kaitlin. The old sibling rivalry refrain aside, what was she talking about? "Excuse me?" we both said in unison.

Kaitlin walked over to one of her giant throw pillows and flopped down on one on her tummy. When she spoke again, her voice had taken on a petulant tone. "I was Daddy's favorite and Chris was Mom's. That's the way it always was. I never understood why Daddy always seemed to dislike Chris, because he'd let Chris come live with us, hadn't he? Chris was just this little crappy baby, and Mom was always making a fuss over him and everything. When we got older, it got even worse."

Bert and I looked at each other and then back at Kaitlin. This story had a point, right? "What got worse?" I asked.

"Everything," Kaitlin said. That pretty much narrowed it down.

"Anyway, Daddy never adopted Chris, either." Kaitlin hugged the pillow she was lying on as if she would strangle it. "Although I can remember Mom asking Daddy to do it— lots of times. At least, that's what I thought she was asking. She'd say, let him be *your* son, make him *your* son. Well, I certainly didn't want Daddy to adopt him—Chris was just this little annoying brat—but I kind of wondered why not."

Bert sat down on one of the pillows and I took one nearby. "And did you find out why not?" she asked gently. I glanced at her. She seemed to know what Kaitlin was getting at, but I didn't have a clue. So Daddy liked the little girl best and Mommy liked the little boy best—if that were really true—so what? Of course, the Mulhollands seemed to have taken it a little farther than most parents, but it did happen.

Kaitlin gave a big sigh and hugged her pillow again. "When they died, I was executrix of the estate and every- thing, and there was no will. So I had to write Frankfort— you know, the state offices—and get birth certificates and stuff."

It was beginning to come clear for me. "And?" I asked.

Kaitlin shrugged. "While I was at it, I wrote for Chris's birth certificate, too—I thought I'd get him out of my life forever and point him toward his real birth parents, so he'd forget mine."

Even after her parents' death, Kaitlin still didn't want to share. No surprise, there.

"That's when I found out," Kaitlin said. "Chris's birth certificate named my mother as his natural mother. *My* mother. Can you imagine how I felt?"

Happy to have a half brother, since the rest of your family was gone? I thought; but I figured hers was one of those rhetorical questions again.

"It was just so awful," Kaitlin said. "Chris's father's name was listed as *Unknown*, which is really kind of a gross thing to put on a public record like that, don't you think?" She looked up at us. "Anyway, I guess Chris was like some kind of love child of Mom's—she must've played around on my dad. That's why Daddy hated Chris so much—Chris always reminded him of Mom's affair."

I just looked at her. "You don't remember your mother being pregnant when you were small?"

Kaitlin sat up and crossed her arms over her chest. "I kind of remember being told that my mother had gotten very sick and had to go away for a while. My grandmother on my dad's side took care of me while she was gone. I think all the relatives were told by Daddy that Mom was, like, mental over not being able to have any more kids, so she got Chris given to her as a foster kid, and then she got OK again. I figure now what really happened is: She left Dad, had a baby from somebody else, and then came back to Daddy. With the baby. Nobody asked any more about it, and neither Daddy nor Mom ever said anything else. Daddy would've probably died rather than tell people that Mom had run around on him—especially since he took her back. And Mom always acted as if she were doing Daddy a big favor just being there."

I thought about it, trying to imagine what it had been like to grow up in a household with that kind of secret— the mother with her two children, the father with just his one. Playing out their resentments of each other through their kids. The Mulhollands might've been one of those couples to whom a marriage therapist would've screamed, "For God's sake, get a divorce already!" Rude and heartless as Kaitlin seemed to be, I actually felt sorry for this young woman for the kind of life she must have had as a child growing up.

For about two seconds.

Kaitlin had been looking pretty gloomy while she told about these beloved childhood memories, but all at once she brightened. "Actually, this is great. This whole murder thing really makes everything OK. When I got Chris's birth certificate, I asked around and everything. And because Mom hung in there for a while after the accident—you know, after Daddy had died—all their stuff would have gone to her. In the estate, I mean."

I stared at her. *Hung in there?* She was talking about her own mother, for goodness' sakes.

Kaitlin went blithely on. "Then when Mom died, all the

stuff would have to be divided between her birth kids—
that would have been me, but it would have been *Chris*, too.
Like, ugh! I always thought that sooner or later Chris would
find out and come around, trying to get his share. That's
why I've been selling everything so fast. Take the money
and run—that's what I'm going to do.

"But now, like I said," Kaitlin said, "everything's cool.
Now Chris won't be able to inherit. I still get it all. Because
the law says you can't profit from a death that you actually
cause, right? And since you've got proof he killed Mom and
Daddy, he can't get a thin dime." She smiled happily. But
just as fast, her expression changed again. Her eyebrows
knitted together as she thought. "I just wonder—" Her
voice trailed off.

You had to hand it to her. This young woman was actually
very bright—it was a shame she put so much of her thought
into such matters as cheating her half brother out of his
inheritance. I looked at the blond hair and thought about
the blond woman seen talking with Haggerty in the parking
lot the day he died. I wondered if Kaitlin might have spent
some of that quick intelligence on getting away with murdering Haggerty, too.

Kaitlin looked at us. "You know, if Chris knew about
this, and killed Mom and Daddy, I wonder why he hasn't
made a claim on the estate yet."

Bert and I glanced at each other, and we didn't say
anything.

"Did you go to Franklin Haggerty's house looking for
Chris's birth certificate?" Bert asked, trying to change the
subject.

"Huh?" Kaitlin asked, looking over at her.

"Did you go to Haggerty's house the day he died," I

repeated, "to find the birth certificate you'd gotten about Chris? Maybe you left it in one of the pieces of furniture you sold Mr. Haggerty?"

Kaitlin was obviously still thinking about Chris. She looked over at me. "What are you talking about? Of course not." She got up from the pillow and went over to a fabric tote bag hanging from a peg on the fireplace mantel. For a second, I thought she was going to pull the birth certificate out of the tote bag. Instead, Kaitlin pointed at the fireplace. "I burned that stupid birth certificate right here," she said with satisfaction, "the day I got it."

"Did Mr. Haggerty know that your mother was Chris's mother, too?" Bert asked.

Kaitlin shrugged. "Hell if I know." But her eyes had taken on that crafty look again. "Why should he?"

Why indeed. "Maybe he wanted to know the provenance on the estate he was purchasing," I said. "Those birth records are available to anyone who wants to pay the fee for them." Maybe Haggerty found out and had been black-mailing Kaitlin. "Why did you sell the estate to him so cheap?"

Kaitlin glared at me. She stood there at the mantel and crossed her arms over her chest, frowning again. "I was in a hurry, OK? I just wonder why Chris hasn't made a claim on the estate," she repeated.

We didn't say a word.

She looked at Bert and then at me and then back at Bert. "So, what's the name of this witness you've got against Chris?"

We didn't answer her.

It really did seem to me that it was time to go. It's amazing how hard it is to get up from a very soft pillow on hardwood floors when you're in a hurry, though. I felt as if I were pushing off from a slippery marshmallow.

Bert evidently had had the same idea about exiting; and she struggled to her feet off her own marshmallow.

The truth was, of course, finally dawning on Kaitlin. "You two lied! There is no witness, is there?" Her eyes were getting wild. "You had better not tell Chris about that birth certificate!" Kaitlin shrieked. "I will kill you dead if you tell!"

We ran for the door, just as Kaitlin began what had to be a world-class tantrum—generally stomping and flailing her arms around and shrieking. Wow. In the Tantrum Olympics, she was going for the gold. "You lying bitches! You twin assholes! You damn—" Her colorful language pretty much deteriorated from there.

A large porcelain vase—apparently one of the things Kaitlin hadn't gotten around to selling quite yet—crashed against the wall next to us as we escaped through the front door.

Chapter 20

•

Bert

"Personally, I think that little bitch did it," said Nan, as we drove back to my apartment.

"Oh, I don't know," I said. Even I could hear the weariness in my voice. I was really tired and really depressed. It was beginning to look as if Ellie were actually going to have to stand trial for murder. The thought made me want to sit and cry for hours. Goodness, if I thought it would help, I'd cry for days. Weeks even.

If only I could think. I mean, really *think*. Something had been playing at the back of my mind for a while. Probably, if I could just get a little sleep, I could figure out what it was. I shook my head. "I just don't think Kaitlin could have done it."

"Are you kidding?" Nan asked, glancing at me. We were pulling on to the Watterson Expressway as a general multitude of cars and eighteen-wheelers whizzed by, bent on destruction. Oh, yes, the Watterson Expressway continues to be Louisville's answer to the Indianapolis 500—a kind of do-it-yourself car-racing track. Only you don't get to drink milk when you're done. You just get to drink in a huge sigh of relief. I really wished Nan wouldn't even so much as glance my way when she was driving on this thing.

"Come on, Bert," she was going on. "Did you hear what Kaitlin said about killing us if we told about the birth certificate? You don't think she'd have killed Haggerty if he threatened to tell?"

I turned to look at her. "Nan, she's just a kid. Kids say they're going to kill each other all the time. It's just a figure of speech."

Nan shot me a quick look. "Bert," she said quietly, "sometimes, kids mean it. Remember the shootings that happened in those high schools?"

She had a point. One of the shootings had been right here in Kentucky. Just being a kid didn't mean you couldn't kill somebody.

"Think about it," Nan went on. "Kaitlin is a tall blonde, just like Ellie. She could easily have been the woman seen in the parking lot with Haggerty just before he was shot."

I shook my head. "I just don't think Kaitlin would kill to keep her brother from inheriting. Cheat, lie and steal, maybe. But, kill? I don't think so."

"OK, who else? One of those people who've complained to Grainger about Haggerty?" Nan asked. She honked at someone in front of her, then yanked the Neon into the fast lane, whipping around a minivan going about forty. The driver in the van showed Nan the finger he was most proud of. Nan only grinned at him.

I tried to concentrate on who those complaining people were—and not on how close on our bumper the car behind us was. Apparently, many drivers in Louisville believe that we're all playing train, and the idea is to see how close we can get to locking our cars together without actually doing so. Sudden death by automobile didn't even seem to faze Nan, as she whipped back into the right-hand lane.

While she drove, Nan continued going over other people that we'd talked to who pretty much hated Haggerty's guts. Even Sheila Haggerty was discussed and discarded. She was not blond, but she *was* tall, and the fact that she'd lived with Haggerty, as far as Nan was concerned, gave her motive enough to kill him. "Or how about Edna Welch?" Nan asked. "She's certainly nasty enough."

I shook my head. "The witness said a tall blonde, not a short one. Although *short* is pretty subjective term. Short to me is about five feet. Short to Michael Jordan is probably about six feet."

Nan nodded, avoiding certain death beneath the bumper of a semi by speeding up as she turned on to the exit for Bardstown Road.

I shut my eyes. "I'm starting to think that we might've been a little hasty about Edna," I went on. "She's the only person we've met who has demonstrated a clear tendency toward violence. If she were desperate enough actually to hit us both over the head the other night so she could search Haggerty's house, she was more than just a little put out about her husband's hobby."

I opened my eyes. What do you know? Nan was now driving down our street. "You've got a point. But, if it was Edna, how did she manage that, do you think? She must've been dragging a stepladder around with her. Don't you think she's a little short for hitting people as tall as we are over the head?"

I turned to stare at her. "Oh my goodness. That's it. You're right. Edna *is* short."

Nan gave me a look that was, unfortunately, getting all too familiar. The look said, "Your elevator is no longer going all the way to the top." She had pulled into my driveway, and I hurried to open the car door. I almost ran up the sidewalk, as Nan slammed and locked the doors and then nearly ran to keep up with me. "What's going on?" she asked.

"Oh, Nan, I have to call Hank right away."

I had my front door almost unlocked, when the tall figure came up behind us. Nan felt the person's presence almost the second I did. As one, we both turned toward the motion, and gaped.

At first, I actually thought it was a woman.

Dressed in Gibson-girl style, complete with blond wig, its piled-up curls offsetting the angular jaw, and wearing a light blue cotton summery dress with long, puffed sleeves and a billowing skirt just below the knees, our visitor—in all honesty—looked lovely.

It's a testimony again to my diminished state of mind that I took one look and thought that what the women's magazines were saying was really true—we women really can wear any skirt length these days and still look completely in fashion. Low-heel white slippers and hose and a matching white summer bag hung from Leonard Welch's arm.

Nan stared. "Leonard? Is that you?"

He really did look quite stylish. What ruined the whole ensemble was the black revolver he held in his right hand.

Chapter 21

●

Nan

When I first spotted Leonard in his Shirley Temple getup, the first thing I thought was, *You shaved your legs for this?*

I might even have said it to him, too, but right away I also noticed the gun he was holding. Giving him a fashion critique at that particular moment was probably not in Bert's or my best interest.

"Leonard," Bert said, her voice very calm for someone talking to a gunman wearing a dress, "what on earth are you doing?"

Personally, I thought that question might be up there with one of Jake's stupid ones, since it was transparently obvious what Leonard was doing. Then it occurred to me that Bert was just trying to encourage Ms. Leonard to think this whole gunpoint thing over.

Leonard flushed. "I'm really sorry about this," he began, pushing a stray lock of blond hair back behind one ear. He motioned with the gun to his car, a sleek black Lincoln Continental parked two cars down at the curb. I hadn't even noticed it when I pulled in.

"Please, both of you," Leonard said, his tone still apologetic. "I really hope you don't make this any harder than it already is. Just walk down there, nice and slow, and please get into my car."

I stared at him. *Don't make this any harder?* Didn't he mean, don't make *killing us* any harder? Hell, I planned to make it as hard as possible. I planned to make this the hardest thing he ever thought of in his sorry misbegotten life.

I opened my mouth to let go a earsplitting scream, when he gently took Bert's arm and tucked the gun under her elbow, pointing it at her heart. Bert's eyes went wide. "Don't," he said to me. "Please don't." Very quietly, very reasonably.

I got the message right away. If I screamed, he'd kill Bert immediately right there. Right in front of me. I closed my mouth.

Leonard turned to Bert, speaking just as quietly, just as reasonably. "Now. If you scream, I'll have to shoot you, and then your sister, too. Here—on your front porch."

He made it sound like shooting someone on a porch was the poorest of taste—like letting your dog doo-doo on it without cleaning the mess up afterward. Hey, I agreed. Only I carried it a bit further. I pretty much thought that shooting anyone anywhere was really tacky.

"I want you to know I'm truly sorry," Leonard went on, "but I really don't have a choice."

I couldn't believe this was happening. We were in broad daylight, and this very polite nutcase was going to make us both get into his car, and then he was going to quietly kidnap us, and then—probably very nicely—kill us.

As if she hadn't figured that out, Bert asked, "What will you do if we get into your car?" Her voice was no longer quite so calm.

Leonard shrugged. "We just have to go somewhere else less public. That's all." His tone was so reašonable. The part that he was leaving out was the important part. He was going to take us somewhere that was nice and quiet and out of the way, and then he was going to put some really ugly holes in both of us.

I met Bert's eyes. She looked at me, and then started talking very fast. "But, Leonard, *why?* Why do you have to do this?"

He sighed. "Edna is really, really upset."

"And?" I asked, trying to think what to do next. My heart was beginning to sound like thunder, as I looked around—at the ground, the porch, the bushes. Was there something heavy lying around that I could throw at him? A grenade, maybe?

"You may not have picked up on what Edna kept saying during your visit," Leonard went on. "When she kept saying to me, 'You know what will happen,' what she meant was that if my hobby ever becomes public knowledge, she's going to divorce me. There's never been a divorce in her family, but she doesn't care about that. She'll divorce me—she really will." He sighed again.

I tried to look sympathetic. Don't you hate it when all you want to do is try on some new duds and your spouse gets in a snit about it? Whatta bitch.

Leonard was gesturing toward his car again. "You know, we really do need to go."

"Leonard," I said, "people get divorced all the time." I could hardly believe what was happening. We were actually standing out on Bert's front porch, trying to keep this man from kidnapping and murdering us. Discussing it with him, as if it were a problem that could be simply talked out.

"But you don't understand," Leonard said. "Edna is the monied partner, you see. She'd divorce me with nothing to show for all the grief from her that I've put up with."

"This is about money?" I blurted.

"Well, I know that sounds kind of selfish," Leonard said, a little peevishly. "But I don't know how I would possibly live if I didn't have Edna. I don't have any training—I couldn't get a job, at least not a good one. I'm fighting for my life, don't you see?"

No, I thought, *you're* killing *for your life.*

"Then you were the tall blond woman seen talking with Haggerty that morning?" Bert asked.

Leonard ducked his head and actually smiled a little. "That was me, all right." I couldn't believe it. He was obviously pleased to have been taken as a woman.

I had no idea having people think you were a woman was such a big deal. Hell, it happened to me all the time.

"And it was you," Bert went on, "who knocked us over the head at Haggerty's house? When you were looking for your photographs?"

Keep him talking, Bert, I thought. That's what we have to do: stall for time until we think of some way to get out of this.

Leonard nodded, but looked over at his car again. "Yes, that was me at the house. I'm sorry about having to do that."

Yeah, right, your heart is breaking.

"Please," he said. "We have to go now. Move toward the car," he said, more firmly this time.

"If you wanted to shoot us," I asked, "why didn't you let Edna do it then?"

Leonard raised his eyebrows. "Really." He gave me a

look that said I should know better. "That would have been in our home," he said. "The neighbors would have heard the shot." He poked Bert in the side with his gun. "Let's go to the car. Right now."

"But, Leonard," Bert said, "you don't have to do this— the police already know about your hobby. We called them after you shot at us—that was you, too, wasn't it?"

Leonard shrugged again. "I realized during that unfortunate incident that I'm really not very good with firearms at a distance," he said, as if apologizing to us for being a bad shot. "And, yes, I surmised that you, no doubt, would've told the officers about me. But it's not the same as having it talked about on the radio," he said. "Edna said if you got on the radio and talked about my dressing up, she was calling her attorney."

I stared at him. This was because I was on the radio? He actually thought I'd get on the radio, and talk about his cross-dressing? Who did he think I was? *Jerry Springer?* I tried something else. "Look, Leonard, you're still not in much trouble. You didn't kill Haggerty on purpose. The police know it was Haggerty's gun. You could probably even convince them that it was self-defense—"

Leonard was already shaking his head. "I'm sorry, but Edna would still divorce me if I get charged with murder." He shrugged again. "Besides, it wasn't self-defense. Oh my yes, Mr. Haggerty did pull his gun on me and he waved it around and all that sort of thing. But I took it away from him very easily—he wasn't in very good physical shape, you know. Anyone could see that."

He was right. Haggerty had not had a cane for nothing.

Leonard went on, doing yet another apologetic shrug— a gesture which was getting more annoying by the moment.

"When I had his gun, I could've walked away from him," he said. "But that man made me do something I almost never do." Leonard's cheeks were flushed much pinker than any rouge would have made them. "That awful man started calling me names and brandishing that cane. And he made me do it. I never do that sort of thing, and he made me."

I just looked at him. What was he talking about? Haggerty had made him shoot him. I should hope it was something Leonard did not make a practice of doing.

Leonard drew a long breath, his eyes like slivers of gray ice. "That man made me lose my temper."

"Oh," I said. How dared Haggerty do such a thing?

"So I shot him. Dead." Leonard smiled. *Most politely*, I thought. Even as he gave Bert a little shove. "Now, we really have to go."

The words were no sooner out of his mouth than a car came around the corner, put on a turn signal and pulled into our driveway, right behind my car.

It was a silver Lexus.

On the driver's side, through the windshield, Jake smiled and waved at Bert. We were so surprised that the three of us, standing on Bert's little porch, just stared at him as Jake got out and sauntered up the sidewalk toward us. He was wearing his Sunday best this time—navy blue designer suit, white dress shirt, and his black shoes so shiny they seemed to glow. From where I was standing, he looked exactly as if he were dressed for a date. Also, from where I was standing, I could smell his cologne.

Standing next to Leonard, I could almost feel his confusion. I could practically hear him thinking, *What am I going to do now?*

I held my breath, trying to think the same thing—what

should *I* do now? Yell for help? Warn Jake? If I did such a thing, Leonard would shoot Bert. Maybe one of us would live, but Bert would be dead for certain. I couldn't take the chance. I just kept my mouth shut, watching Jake jauntily walk toward us.

Jake briefly nodded at me and then at the person he evidently took as just some other woman in a blue dress. In fact, Jake hardly even looked at Leonard, concentrating instead on Bert. "I tried to phone, but nobody answered. So I thought I'd take a chance and just drop on over. Are you ready to go see Ellie, Bert?" Jake asked. His smile was so wide you could see his back teeth.

Bert's mouth opened, but nothing came out. Leonard moved closer to Bert, making sure that Jake's view of the gun was totally blocked.

"Jake," I said, trying to make my voice sound normal, "this really isn't a good time."

That woke up Bert. She said, "Jake, why don't you come back a little later? I—uh, we—have to go somewhere right now."

Jake frowned. "Bert, you agreed you'd go with me to see Ellie tonight. Visiting hours at the jail have already started. I really think our daughter should see us together— like we're a family. She needs a united front right now."

Leonard took this touching moment to move a little closer to Bert, no doubt jamming the gun into Bert's side. Her face looked pained. Leonard's sudden motion made Jake finally look over at him. Jake's eyes widened as he took a good look at the man in the dress, wig, and heels. For a long couple of silent seconds, Jake stared at Leonard. Leonard stared right back. "Good God, buddy," Jake finally asked, "have you looked at yourself?"

I'd been right about Leonard not being receptive to a fashion critique. Or maybe he'd just finally decided that he was not going to be able to make the three of us get in his car. Leonard yanked the gun out, pointed it straight at Jake, and fired.

What happened next is a kind of blur.

As Leonard pulled the gun out from behind Bert, I tried to bump hard against Jake, trying to push him out of the way; but Leonard was standing right there. That damn gun was so close. I felt Jake jump a little as the bullet hit him; and he went down, with me falling to the ground almost on top of him.

I heard Bert let out a horrified scream; and, with the gun no longer trained on her, she kind of body-slammed into Leonard with more strength than I would've thought Bert had.

Lying on the ground next to Jake, I grabbed Leonard's slender ankles in his stylish white shoes, and I yanked his feet right out from under him. It was a maneuver, mind you, that Bert and I had perfected in the second grade out on the playground when the bully in the fourth grade had shoved us both to the ground. Leonard fell backward, banging into the concrete with his butt first, and then smacking his head against the sidewalk.

His arms flung out and his purse went flying, scattering its contents into the yard. The gun he was holding discharged, but since he really wasn't aiming at anything in particular, the bullet went wild. I grabbed his gun hand, while Bert stomped down hard on his wrist. Together, we wrestled the gun away from him.

As it turned out, wrestling the gun away wasn't all that difficult—mostly because, when Leonard had fallen, he'd cracked his head a lot harder on the sidewalk than we at first had thought. He was out like a light even before we jumped him.

I held the gun on him, in case he happened to wake up, while Bert ran inside and dialed 911. Next to me, on the ground, Jake moaned.

"Jake, are you all right?" I asked. A question even stupider than those Jake was known for, since a red stain was spreading across the front of Jake's white dress shirt. He clutched at his chest, his eyelids fluttering.

The cops arrived seconds before the ambulance. Which was really good, as far as I was concerned, because old Leonard was beginning to stir. I really didn't want to have to shoot the guy in the leg or something. Although I would, if I had to. He'd shot Jake and threatened Bert. Oh yeah, I'd shoot him in a heartbeat.

When the ambulance drove up, Bert had come back outside, and was cradling Jake's head in her lap, his blood soaking into her skirt. It looked to me as if he'd been hit in his left side. Bert had brought out a towel when she returned, and she held it tight against the wound, trying to stop the bleeding. "You're going to be all right, Jake," she whispered, her eyes filling with tears. "You will be all right—you hear me, Jake?"

Jake tried to smile, winced, and then held tight to her hand, his face very, very white. "Of course, I am," he said, his voice weak. "Because you and I have to try again."

I had to hand it to the guy. Jake could definitely pick his moment. Of course, this was the guy who'd proposed to her in front of the entire family.

The ambulance guys came up to them just then and got Jake on a stretcher. They took his vital signs, then hooked him up to an IV and a heart monitor. Or, at least, from what I've seen on that television program *ER*, that's what I thought they were doing. As they prepared to hoist Jake into the ambulance, he grabbed Bert's hand again, and she walked alongside him as they wheeled the stretcher to the ambulance.

"Bert, we can try again, can't we?" Jake asked. He was sounding a lot stronger, even now.

Bert stared at him, holding his hand.

At that moment, another police car screeched to the curb. The driver's door opened, and Hank Goetzmann got out. He took one look at the scene, and took off running toward us.

Bert glanced up and saw him, then looked quickly back down at Jake.

"Tell me that we can, Bert," Jake said, squeezing her hand so hard, her fingers were white. "Please. Say yes, darling. I love you so much. I've never stopped loving you."

I was standing just a little way from them. The police officers were still talking to me, but I strained to hear. OK, this was a tough moment, sure—with Jake hurt and everything, but Bert would have to simply tell him the truth. After all, there was Goetzmann—I'd seen the way she'd just looked when he got out of the police car. She was nuts about the guy. So Bert would just have to tell Jake she was truly sorry; but she really didn't think they could ever reconcile.

"Jake," Bert said.

I stopped talking for a moment, and turned to look.

"We can try again, Jake," Bert finished. "We can."

It was an effort to keep my mouth from dropping open.

Hell, it could only mean one thing. The strain of being held at gunpoint had driven Bert right out of her cotton-picking mind.

Chapter 22

●

Bert

I was not out of my mind.

I'd told Jake that we could start over again, as soon as he was well, because it was the right thing to do. He had taken a bullet for me. Not to mention that it would make our children incredibly happy. Ellie, especially, would be so pleased when Jake and I told her that we were going to try to work things out. We were going to try to become a whole family again.

Actually, it was amazing how really good everything can become in such a short time, once things start going well.

Just a few days after Leonard Welch was taken into custody, Nan and I found ourselves seated at my dining room table, looking at a huge white cardboard box that had just been delivered from the bakery. Sitting there, in that familiar room, it was hard to believe that less than a week ago, a man had held us at gunpoint on my doorstep and had actually shot Jake.

Jake, poor baby, was still in the hospital; but, according to the various nurses he had trotting in and out, doing God knows what, he was healing nicely. The bullet had cracked a rib, and done some pretty painful damage; but, luckily, it had not hurt any vital organs.

Jake had told me privately, "Hey, there's really only one organ I worried about, and that one old Leonard missed by a mile." Jake always was the one to put things into perspective. The doctors said he should have a complete recovery and would probably be released in a couple of days to spend some recuperative time at home.

I was planning to go over to the hospital—just like I'd done every single night since he was shot—and bring him a slice of cake. I looked at the huge thing, as Nan lifted it out of its white cardboard box.

It was rectangular, decorated in black-and-white icing, of course—with "Over the Hill" written in script at the top. Under that, there was a large tombstone that read: "Happy 40th Birthday, Bert and Nan."

Nan and I looked at each other and laughed—not for the sweet sentiment, of course, but because Mom and Dad had sent it. True to form, they'd gotten one birthday cake for their two daughters, just like they'd always done since we were babies. When we were little girls, we'd resented the fact that neither of us had ever had a cake of her own: now, so many years later, it just seemed nostalgic and sweet, a reminder of how pleased our parents must've been, and still were, to have had twins.

"So probably we should wait for dinner?" Nan asked, touching a fingertip to the icing and taking a taste.

I looked at her and headed for the kitchen for a couple of saucers and forks and a knife, while Nan followed me to fill two glasses with milk. Let's face it—there are some things that really do go better with milk and not Coca-Cola. Cake was one of them. We were carrying everything back into the dining room when the doorbell rang.

When I opened the door, bobbing black balloons filled

the doorway. The words "Happy 40th Birthday" crisscrossed the balloons, along with "Over the Hill" and "Kiss Another Year Good-bye." Then the singing started. Nan joined me at the door for the final verse to "Happy Birthday."

When the balloons finally came in, they were followed by songbirds Brian, carrying a grocery bag, and then Ellie, her arms laden with gifts for Nan and me. Naturally, the predominant color for the ribbons and the wrapping paper was black, also.

"I'll get more plates and milk," Nan said, heading for the kitchen, while I hugged my kids. Standing at the table, watching them laugh at the cake and tease each other, I almost lost it and burst into tears right in front of them. When I thought about the fact that I'd almost spent my birthday visiting Ellie in jail, I could pretty much dissolve into sobs any minute.

In fact, I don't believe, if I live to be a hundred, I will ever forget the first time I saw Ellie after she was released. I'd gone to the hospital with Nan, following the ambulance that had taken Jake there. We were waiting outside Surgery, after talking for just a moment to one of his doctors. He'd assured us that Jake was doing fine, but that he was now in surgery.

In the corner, Nan was pretending she could actually listen to the television that was on. I was so exhausted, I sat there with my eyes closed, my head in my hands. Brian had joined us at the hospital, and he sat beside me, flipping through the waiting room's most recent *Sports Illustrated* magazine—June, 1995.

I'd felt a light tap on my shoulder.

"Mom?"

When I looked up, Ellie was standing right there. I had

to blink my eyes several times to make sure that I wasn't dreaming.

After we'd cried and hugged and cried some more, and I'd assured Ellie that her father was going to be fine, I finally got around to asking Ellie how she got to the hospital.

"Hank brought me," Ellie said. "He said he knew where you were. Oh, Mom, he got me released on his own recognizance, because he didn't want me to have to wait for all the paperwork to go through. And, Mom, he *apologized* to me. Said he'd felt so helpless about everything. He's really an OK guy, Mom—you know?"

My mouth had gone dry.

"Where is he?" I could barely get the question out.

She shrugged. "He left."

The OK guy had not waited around to speak to me, the not-so-OK former girlfriend.

"You guys want to open your gifts first?" Brian asked, bringing me back to reality.

"Hell, no, they don't," Ellie answered for both Nan and me, and she was right. "Cake first. We also brought ice cream—Rocky Road."

We'd finally all settled back at the table when the doorbell rang again. "Ellie, will you get that?" I asked, as I sliced a piece of cake and passed it to Nan. Nan added a small mountain of ice cream and passed it to Brian.

"Look who it is," Ellie said after a moment. Her voice sounded a little strange.

I turned, half-expecting it to be Hank.

But it was Chris Mulholland who followed her in, looking a little sheepish. He had better look sheepish. And apologetic. And groveling. Sackcloth and ashes would be good for starters, but he was wearing what looked like a brand-new knit golf shirt and khakis, very collegiate.

I stared at him. Now that I thought about it, what he looked like was a guy who'd just come into a lot of money.

"Oh, you're having a party," he said. "I don't want to interrupt."

I did not invite him to join us, nor did Nan. I just sat there and glared at him. I figured I should get points for not hitting him again.

Chris stood there, staring back at us, awkwardly shifting from one foot to another. "Well, I just came over here to thank you"—he nodded at Nan and then at me—"to thank both of you, for what you did for me. For getting my sister to finally tell me about my birth."

"She *told* you?" Nan asked.

"Well, once you told the police about it, I guess she decided she had to come clean." He turned toward Ellie. "Because of your mother and your aunt, I'm finally getting what's due me. I'm inheriting my share of my mother's estate. I can go back to school full-time and everything."

Ellie smiled at him. I stared at her, amazed. "I'm glad for you, Chris," Ellie said. "I really am."

"You are?" Chris asked. Even he looked a little surprised at Ellie's demeanor.

"Well, sure," Ellie said. She was still smiling.

Chris looked elated. Looking at his handsome face, I began to get a little worried. He probably was the best-looking guy that Ellie had ever dated. Surely, Ellie still didn't care for this little twerp, did she?

"Listen, Ellie, can I talk to you?" Chris asked.

Ellie gave him a look. "You are talking to me, Chris."

"No. I mean, in private."

"Whatever you've got to say to me, you can say in front of my family," Ellie said. Her smile had faded.

Chris sighed, then turned a little to the side, as if he could keep us from hearing him if we were out of his line of sight. Or maybe he was just trying to keep from being nervous, what with all of us staring at him, and pretty much hanging on his every syllable.

"I've been trying and trying and trying to phone you," Chris said. "I've left messages on your mother's machine."

"I know," Ellie said. "I got them."

"You did? Then you *are* trying to avoid me." Chris ran a hand through his hair. "I don't understand. I know things were difficult for a while there, but it's all turned out all right. The real killer is in jail, and I don't see any reason why we can't put it all this behind us. We were so good together," he said.

Ellie just stood there, looking at him.

"OK, I admit that I behaved badly, but I'm just not as— as, well, *strong* as you are." He sighed, and gave her a sheepish grin. "Sometimes, I guess I'm just very weak."

I believe that what he meant was that he was a frigging coward. I would've liked to have helped him out with the correct words, but I didn't think I ought to interrupt.

Chris went on, his hands extended toward Ellie, his voice pleading. "I just couldn't face spending any time in jail. But I'd known that you were really innocent, so there was never any real danger that you'd be convicted. I knew that it would be all right. Surely you can understand why I did what I did, can't you?"

I felt like I was holding my breath.

To my horror, Ellie nodded. "Sure, Chris," she said, "I can understand."

"And you can forgive me?"

Ellie nodded again. She was smiling again. "Sure."

Chris was grinning now, showing his perfect teeth in an all-American winning smile. Boy, he really did look a lot like Brad Pitt. I was pretty sure I'd never be able to watch another one of that actor's movies without feeling a little sick. Chris was still grinning. "Then we can start again? Forgive and forget?"

Ellie took a deep breath, and smiled even wider. "Actually, no," she said.

I let out my breath with a little gasp of relief.

"Because I can think of one reason why we can't put it all behind us, Chris," Ellie said.

Chris looked confused. "You can?"

Ellie nodded. "The reason is that I cannot for a second ever forget that I can't trust you."

Chris left in a hurry right after that. He didn't even wish me and Nan a happy birthday.

When Ellie sat back down at the table, Brian elbowed her. "Way to go, El," he said.

I gave her a quick smile. And then I watched her as we ate the cake and ice cream. What do you know? You really can learn from your children.

I guess I stared at Ellie too long, because she finally put down her fork and looked over at me. "OK, Mom, what?"

"Ellie, what you said to Chris—"

She shrugged, "I know what you're going to say. You know, Mom, the one thing I've gotten out of all this—other than don't ever, ever, EVER confess to a murder you didn't commit—is that now I understand why you can't go out with Dad again. You just can't trust him."

I nodded, my throat tightening.

Ellie picked up her fork and took another bite of birthday cake. "Trust is a fragile thing," she said. "I think it's like Humpty Dumpty. Once broken, all the king's horses and all the king's men can't put it back together again."

That one made me smile. Can life really be as simple as a nursery rhyme?

Ellie, of course, was right. I was sorry, but I really couldn't start dating Jake again. I was sorry he got shot because of me. Hey, I was sorry about everything. I was particularly sorry that he'd had an affair.

I felt bad about everything, but I knew now that Jake and I could never get back what we'd once had. Like Ellie said, I could forgive him for his infidelity. But I could never forget that I can't trust the guy. I've even had a few passing thoughts about the nurses going in and out of Jake's hospital room. Sure, they're probably there to change his bandages, or take his vital signs, or whatever. And yet, that old familiar, nagging worry has already been in my mind. Is he flirting a little too much with one or two of them? Is he asking for her phone number?

The bottom line is: Jake is Humpty Dumpty.

When he was feeling better, I'd have to tell him that we couldn't ever put our life back together again.

I glanced at Nan, and her face looked so happy and relieved that I almost laughed. Sometimes, I swear that woman can read my mind. "Happy mutual birthday!" Nan said, lifting her glass of milk in a toast. Then she handed me two gifts, both wrapped in hot pink paper with a matching bow. "You might want to open the littler one when you're alone—" she began, but I was already tearing off the paper.

I lifted the box top, reached into the tissue paper to pull out—oh my yes, leave it to Nan—she'd gotten me a bra.

Not just any bra, either—this thing had more stuffing than
my last Thanksgiving turkey. If a Wonderbra was supposed
to give you cleavage, this little number would give you cleavage—and maybe a double chin. It was also done in a very
classy leopard-skin fabric. Brian and Ellie, Lord love them,
immediately began to snicker.

Nan snickered, too. "Well, I told you to open it in private,"
she said. She patted my hand. "Hey, as you enter your
forties, I just wanted to show my support."

A tag fluttered from one strap. Written in Nan's distinc-
tive hand, it read: "For your hope chest."

OK, so I had to laugh a little at that. I guess I'm not cool
enough to discuss underwear in front of my son, though. I
hurriedly stuffed the bra back into its box and picked up
Nan's second gift. I was almost afraid to open it now. Given
Nan's sense of humor, it could turn out to be a giant box of
condoms.

Instead, however, it turned out to be something I hadn't
even realized I wanted: my most favorite doll of all time—
an Effanbee baby doll called "My Baby," from the early
sixties. It was dressed in its original zip-up pink bunting—
the same outfit our identical dolls had been wearing when
Mom had given them to us for our sixth birthday.

My eyes actually filled with tears as I looked at the doll.
She looked a little like Ellie had looked when she was a
baby. "Oh, Nan, how did you think of it? And where on earth
did you find it?"

Nan shrugged, grinning. "Salvation Army Thrift Store."

Brian and Ellie hooted.

After that little disclosure, there was nothing I could do
but go get Nan's gift. I went and got it from my bedroom,
putting the gift in a large paper bag, covering it lightly with

tissue paper. I came back and placed the bag on the floor next to Nan's feet. The bag was almost as large as a paper grocery bag, its outside covered with stars and ribbons and "Happy Birthday" spelled out in stickers. Very perky.

As Nan reached for it, she suddenly let out a little shriek. The bag had moved.

"What on earth?" Nan asked. Brian and Ellie got up from the table and moved closer to Nan.

"What is it, Mom?" Brian asked.

"If this is some kind of exploding trick bag, I'll—" Nan began. She reached into the tissue paper and pulled out the calico kitten I'd adopted for her from the Kentucky Humane Society. The animal's huge dark eyes blinked in the light.

"Ooooooh," crooned Ellie.

Nan's eyes widened as she held the kitten out from her, as if it were something truly distasteful, and looked back at me. "You shouldn't have," she said.

"Really," she added. "I mean it."

I ignored her. "Nan, you're always saying you're going to end up an old lady with a bunch of cats—well, I thought I'd get you started."

Nan frowned at me.

The little kitten meowed right then, and Nan pulled it closer to her face, looking into its eyes. "Come on, I can't have a cat," she said.

The kitten looked back at her and yawned.

"Sure you can," I said. "You're the landlady—you can have anything you want."

"Well, I certainly don't want a—" As Nan spoke, the kitten patted her on the nose. A tiny, tentative little pat. And it meowed again.

Nan sighed, and cuddled the kitten into her arms.

"What's the matter, babycakes?" she said. "You little cutie. Are you OK, sweetums?" She scratched the kitten behind the ears, and it began to purr. A loud rumble that filled the room.

Nan turned to me and grinned.

I'd known it would take Nan about two seconds to fall in love with this kitten—because that's how long it would've taken me.

As we finished the cake and Nan's new kitten played at our feet with the ribbons from our gifts, I couldn't help but start thinking about what I was going to say to Jake. Come to think of it, I had a lot to explain to Hank, too. He might be mad at me. He might not understand why I did what I did, but I could at least apologize to him.

The doorbell rang again right after Nan suggested that we start on second helpings. "When in doubt—" she said, cutting another slice.

"Add more sugar," I finished, looking back at her as I opened the door. It was something we used to say in high school, when we'd failed an algebra test, or the guy that we liked hadn't asked us out. We would bury our sadness in sweets. It was a wonder we didn't weigh four hundred pounds.

When I turned around to the open doorway, Hank was standing there.

His shoulders were so broad, he filled the doorway. Hank held out a brightly wrapped package. It was in pink and white with roses on the paper and a large white bow. No black in sight. "Happy fortieth birthday, Bert," he said.

Speechless, I took the gift.

Hank looked past me to the group seated at the dining-room table. "I don't want to intrude. I just knew it was your day, and I wanted to drop this by," he said, turning to go.

I reached out and touched his arm. When he turned back to me, I said, lowering my voice, "Hank, I am so very sorry." I was very aware that everything had gone silent behind me, and I could practically feel three sets of ears tuning in on what Hank and I were about to say next. "I don't expect you to forgive me, but I was beside myself with worry about Ellie, and I acted—"

He cut me off. He didn't seem at all willing to listen to what I had to say.

He was, however, very willing to suddenly pull me close and kiss me.

Chapter 23

•

Nan

Watching Bert at the door with Goetzmann, I have to admit to having a pang of envy. Oh, yeah, I was back to that again. Ain't love grand?

Not to mention, if Bert had actually gotten back together with that two-timing, albeit bullet-ridden, Jake, I would've had to puke. I don't want to sound unsympathetic, but if she'd said one more time that Jake had taken a bullet for her, I would have had to slap her to snap her out of it. She'd been making it sound as if Jake had thrown himself in front of a firing squad to save her. I mean, it wasn't as if Jake had been given a choice. Jake, would you like to get shot? Or would you rather not? I was pretty sure, had he been asked, he would've elected to skip it, regardless of how much he'd suddenly decided he cared about getting Bert back.

Seeing Bert with Goetzmann again was a first-class relief.

Still, it did remind me that forty was looking as bad for me on the dating front as thirty-nine had. And thirty-eight, thirty-seven, thirty-six, et cetera, et cetera, et cetera. Thanks to Bert, I really was well on my way to becoming one of those lonely, pitiful old ladies who live all by themselves, cooped up with a bunch of cats. I reached down and scratched the kitten behind the ears. Hell, now I was going to have to think of a name for the thing.

Of course, Goetzmann joined us all at the table for another round of sugar, just as the phone rang. Since he and Bert were still billing and cooing, I said I'd get it.

"Nan?"

I pulled the phone away from my ear and stared at it. Some bozo is calling Bert's number and asks for me?

"Yes?"

"Wow. I thought that was you," the bozo said. "It's Sam Grainger. I tried your number, but your machine picked up over there. So I thought maybe I might find you at your sister's."

I was still a little confused. "So how did you know it was me?"

I could hear the smile in his voice as he said, "Come on now. Give me some credit. Don't you think I can tell your voice from your sister's?"

I didn't until this moment. I couldn't help smiling myself.

"So how about dinner tomorrow night?" Sam named an expensive restaurant in Louisville, and added, "Wow, I know it's late notice, so, if you have other plans, I can make it some other time," he said. "However, I warn you: I don't give up easily."

I actually thought about lying to the guy and telling him I did have plans, just so he wouldn't think I was desperate for male company. That's one of the things they tell you to do in that bestseller on the rules for dating. Never accept a date for the weekend after Wednesday.

I took a breath, all ready to play by the rules. Then something occurred to me. Being forty means being able to stop playing hard to get. In fact, it means pretty much being able to stop playing any of those stupid dating games.

I was still smiling when I accepted his invitation. OK, sure, at forty, I may be an antique; but, listen, Sam Grainger actually *preferred* antiques. Maybe I could even get used to a guy who keeps saying, *"Wow,"* all the time.

All I'll say about that first date is that we had a lovely, *expensive* time. Apparently, Sam was under the impression that buying me a lavish meal complete with an aged bottle of wine would impress me, and, what do you know, it worked. When Sam walked me to my front door, he leaned close, tipped my face up to his, and kissed me for a very, very long time.

When he finally pulled away and just looked at me, his eyes dark in the moonlight, I could think of only one thing to say.

"Wow."